WILD MONTANA WINDS

A Montana Gallagher Novel

MK MCCLINTOCK

What happens when a mountain man tries to tame the heart of a Highland lass?

LARGE PRINT EDITION

Trappers Peak Publishing
Bigfork, Montana
www.mkmcclintock.com

Publisher's Note: This is a work of fiction. Names, characters, places, and incidents are a product of the author's imagination. Locales and public names are sometimes used for atmospheric purposes. Any resemblance to actual people, living or dead, or to businesses, companies, events, institutions, or locales is completely coincidental.

Wild Montana Winds; novel/MK McClintock
ISBN: 978-1733723275
LARGE PRINT EDITION

Cover Design by MK McClintock
Cover images from Shutterstock

PRINTED IN THE UNITED STATES OF AMERICA

PRAISE FOR
THE MONTANA GALLAGHERS

"The Montana Gallagher Collection is adventurous and romantic with scenes that transport you into the Wild West." —*InD'Tale Magazine*

"Any reader who loves Westerns, romances, historical fiction or just a great read would love this book, and I am pleased to be able to very highly recommend it. This is the first book I've read by this author, but it certainly won't be the last. Do yourself a favor and give it a chance!"
—*Reader's Favorite* on *Gallagher's Pride*

"*Journey to Hawk's Peak* by MK McClintock is one of the most gripping and thrilling western novels that anyone will ever read. This is probably the best novel that I have yet read as a reviewer. It clicks on all cylinders—grammar, punctuation, plot, characterization, everything. This novel is a serious page-turner, and for fans of western fiction, it is a must-read." —*Reader's Favorite*

To learn more about MK McClintock and her books,
please visit www.mkmcclintock.com.

For Prince and Lorraine.
The noble steed and the woman who loved
him. I'm honored to have immortalized him in
the series that brought us together.

And for Verna.
You and Lorraine are the best editing team an
author could have. Thank you for joining us on
another adventure.

AUTHOR'S NOTE

Dearest Reader,

Whether you have been with us from the beginning or are meeting us for the first time, it brings me great joy to have you here, for you are now a part of the Gallagher family. I do not know what I had once imagined would happen to this delightful group of people when I first met them, but with each story came new ideas and characters with whom I was not ready to part. *Wild Montana Winds* experienced many changes over the course of its writing. I always knew the story would be about Colton Dawson: ranch hand, tracker, mountain man, and of course a member of the Hawk's Peak family.

However, the woman meant for him changed a few times in my mind. All the others in this series had met their perfect match, and I could not rest until Colton found his. Ainslee McConnell proved to be that match—and then some. I love them together and I love them as individuals, proving once again that Hawk's Peak is one of my favorite places to spend time.

This book has been written to stand on its own. You will meet previous characters and read mention of events from the first five Montana Gallagher books.

They are here to enhance Colton and Ainslee's story, for neither would have his or her own tale without those who came before.

I hope you enjoy reading this romantic western adventure as much as I did writing it.

Be well, be kind, and stay bookish!

~MK McClintock

1

Briarwood, Montana Territory
August 5, 1884

COLTON DAWSON REACHED the ravine and looked over the edge into the river below. He'd ventured far enough from the ranch and town to make him wonder if the men he currently tracked knew something about the area he didn't.

Not likely.

There wasn't a copse of trees, a body of water, or a mountain peak within one hundred miles that Colton hadn't scouted, drunk from, or climbed since his arrival in Montana a decade earlier. The Gallaghers' ranch had spanned more than thirty-five square miles ever since they tore down the fence between Hawk's Peak and the former Double Bar Ranch. All of it had been explored at one time or another by a Gallagher and half the men who worked the land, cattle, and horses.

The cattle were a prize to any rustler and it was well known throughout the territory that the Gallaghers' horse breeding operation produced the most highly valued stock in the area. No one had yet been able to figure out whether the cattle or horses drew the raiders onto Gallagher land, but they intended to find out.

Colton gentled his horse until it stood as silent as its rider. He listened to the wind move through the trees and caught the scent of summer pine. The river below rushed over rocks and echoed through the gorge. He knew the land leveled and the river rose a few miles to the south, where it wound back again toward the ranch.

The tracks pressed into the soft ground

indicated the riders had shifted direction and now headed north, away from the river. Colton concluded the men didn't know where they were going, which gave him the advantage. The mountains and forests that stretched north is where Colton gained his education, where he'd learned how to trap, hunt, and track.

His horse scraped a hoof over the ground and sidestepped back from the ravine, but it wasn't the drop or the water below that bothered the gelding. Colton smelled the fire and the burning flesh, and he searched the sky on the other side of the river for signs of smoke.

Flames licked the damp air and the fire sizzled with each drop of rain. Sunshine quickly made way for dark, rolling clouds, and Colton doubted the two men in the makeshift camp had anticipated the sudden change of weather. He followed the smell of the fire and wasn't surprised when some of the rustlers' tracks crossed the same path.

He dismounted and crouched behind a boulder, his horse now six yards away. Colton watched the men scramble to keep the flames alive by tossing wet sticks onto the smoky pile. They were no longer on Gallagher land, but the meat roasting over their fire no doubt came from Gallagher stock. A carcass lay a dozen feet away from the camp, on the ground in the open for any animal to find.

Idiots, Colton thought. He despised fools and rustlers alike, and these men were both. If he moved closer, he knew he'd find the staggered HP brand of Hawk's Peak Ranch on the remains. He listened and waited. The tracks told him more than two men rode with the outfit currently making rounds of cattle ranches in the region. Hawk's Peak was bigger than most in the state, which made rustling the cattle tempting. More cattle meant more land to cover, and people of a mind to steal might figure a few head here and there would go unnoticed.

A good cattleman always noticed.

Ethan Gallagher, head of the family, had put a bullet in one two nights ago, and the culprit now sat in the Briarwood jailhouse awaiting transport or a judge, whichever came first. Three men who lived in or close to town were rotating the watch at the jail, but it had been a heavily spoken-about topic for some time. His younger brother, Gabriel, was able to catch another one, but the thief managed to ride away into the night.

They needed a sheriff, someone with experience they could trust. Ramsey Cameron, Eliza Gallagher's husband, was an obvious choice. He pinned on his marshal's badge when needed, though they knew he did not wish to make it a long-term profession. Ben Stuart, Hawk's Peak foreman and close friend of the family, had the necessary experience, yet he was more valuable at the ranch. Colton knew it was only a matter of time before more of these rustlers were brought to jail, the doctor, or the undertaker. He didn't care which one.

The rain fell hard from the sky, dropped from branches, sizzled on the dying fire, and slickened or muddied every surface. The men scrambled, shouting at each other. Colton could handle two of them without worry. He watched the direction where the other riders had gone and heard nothing.

He raised his rifle and stepped out from behind the boulder. He was close enough to the men, and he didn't have to shout over the weather. "Meal time's over."

They both turned. Colton followed a low curse with, "What the hell have you gotten yourself into, Ike?"

Ike didn't answer. His partner raised a pistol to Colton, who fired, disarming the other man and putting a hole through his hand.

"What you go and do that for!"

"You're next, Ike, if you pull that shooter from its holster."

"I ain't goin' to jail." Ike's hand hovered over the butt of his gun. "We didn't harm no one."

"You're rustling. You've worked the land. Hell, you've worked one of the ranches that have lost stock."

Ike spit on the ground. "Not no more."

Colton knew Ike had a reputation for spending too much time at the saloon. It was why when he first inquired about work at Hawk's Peak, they had turned him away. "It's your drinking that keeps you out of work, not the ranchers."

"Them Gallaghers never gave me a

chance."

Colton kept Ike's partner in the edge of his sight while he spoke with Ike. He preferred taking both in alive. "The Gallaghers offered you a train ticket out of Bozeman to a place where no one knows you. You could have a new start, Ike."

"Money is what I need."

"Stay sober and you might keep a job. But not this time."

Colton recognized the panic in the other man's eyes. He looked like someone who believed he didn't have options. Ike's hand returned to the butt of his pistol.

"Don't do it." Colton aimed, his finger on the trigger of the Winchester rifle that had seen him through a decade of life in these mountains. "There's still a way out of this."

"To jail?" Ike's hand gripped his gun handle. "It wasn't my drinkin' this time, I swear it. Couldn't do it no more, scrapin' and beggin' from these ranchers. They don't deserve any of it more'n I do!"

Colton had heard it before, from drifters and out-of-work cowboys who detested wealthy cattle ranchers because they'd been in the right place at the right time and worked hard to build their empires. He knew some came by their spreads through less than honorable means, but most fought to carve out a life in a land where most folks found it tough to survive.

"You're going to jail. Nothing you can do about it."

Ike's eyes softened around the edges. His shoulders relaxed. Colton saw defeat and expected Ike to make the second worst decision of his life. The first had been to join up with the rustlers. Ike drew, but before he pulled the trigger, a bullet from Colton's rifle sliced through Ike's upper thigh. The pistol dropped from Ike's limp fingers and his companion became bold, reaching for the fallen gun.

"It would be a shame to lose the use of both hands."

The rustler pulled his uninjured hand away from the gun. "Who the damnation are you, mister?"

Somewhere Outside of Briarwood, Montana Territory August 5, 1884

HER HANDS SLIPPED for the second time. She struggled to remove her gloves and remain on the wagon bench. A few more minutes and she would lose the battle with speed and gravity. She reached for the reins and prayed for a miracle.

The driver was slung over the bench, lying between Ainslee and the brake. Not far ahead, she saw a turn in the well-traveled dirt road. Beyond the bend was a thick copse of pines.

"I'm so sorry, Mr. Sykes." Ainslee heaved

with all her strength and rolled the body off the bench.

The pair of geldings pranced at the sudden shift of weight. Ainslee fought to maintain her balance while keeping the reins in her grasp. She failed. One of the leather straps flew forward, snapping against the right horse's rump before flailing to the side of the speeding animal. She glanced up. The turn was no more than a few hundred yards, and the horses would cover the distance faster than she could regain control—a doubtful prospect. Her untamed riding over the hills in her beloved homeland did not prepare her for a runaway team of horses and a wagon more suited to the firebox.

With one strap in hand and a silent prayer, Ainslee pulled, much to the annoyance of the animals. They tugged and she pulled again. "Please! Dinna dae this to me now, laddies!"

Gunfire. Ainslee had spent enough time in the company of hunters, primarily her father and his brothers, to know the sound of gunfire. Not rifles or shotguns. Her father boasted an impressive collection that included an original Thomas Guide creation from 1646. What she heard now was newer and too close. She wondered what kind of bullet had put an end to her driver.

The horses jerked and shifted course, away from the turn and off the road. The wagon slowed as the team pulled it over rough terrain in an open meadow, heading toward a forest so heavy with pine trees, she saw no light beyond the first branches. Ainslee looked over the side at the ground. It appeared to be moving but she knew that couldn't be right. A rush of dizziness overcame her, and she fought it back before she contemplated jumping.

The rumbling of riders, horses' hooves

pounding over earth, drew closer. A stranger rode up alongside one of the animals, reached for a loose rein, and pulled back on the harness. Ainslee didn't know how he managed to get so close or why the team pulling her wagon—Mr. Sykes's wagon—chose to listen to the man rather than to her.

Ainslee righted herself and continued to hold tightly to the back of the seat in case the animals got the idea for another run. The pair of horses breathed heavily, and Ainslee imagined they needed water. She faced the man.

Filthy. No other word in any language was more apt. With his hair matted in tangles and dirt, she couldn't tell the color. Light brown, perhaps? From his torn clothes and muddy boots, to the thick beard and yellow teeth, Ainslee nearly gagged. It was one thing to see such a man described in the pages of a novel and another to be so close that even the breeze didn't mask his putrid scent. Her parents had guarded her from such men back home, and for the first time since she reached adulthood, she silently thanked them.

Ainslee considered her options and thought of the dirk in her valise. The worthy weapon had been used by Highlanders in battle. Surely it could get her out of this mess, if she could reach it. A gun would be beneficial, but it fell from Mr. Sykes' hand when the bullet hit.

"Lucky we came along, missy."

We?

Ainslee shifted when she felt the wagon move from extra weight in the back. Another man, not quite as disgusting yet still in need of a good bar of soap, had dismounted and now stood in the wagon bed. Caught between the two, Ainslee wished she had not decided to make her visit a surprise. The train didn't go to Briarwood, the stationmaster had informed her, and wasn't that Ainslee's bad luck.

Instead, she was now at the mercy of two ruffians who were bound to carry her into the forest, commit a heinous act too horrific even for words, and leave her to die. Her vivid imagination played out every possible scenario, one of which she was the heroine with a broadsword and the men stood no chance against her unmatched skills.

Think, Ainslee. The words remained a whisper, or so she thought, until the men started laughing. She was raised in a land of heroes and barbarians. Without doubt, she could handle these two. Maybe. The thought fleeted as the man in the wagon moved forward.

"What do you think, Virgil? She pretty enough for ya?"

The man still on his horse laughed louder and smacked his lips. "She sure is, Lee. Why don't you make her comfy and I'll—"

A bullet pierced the side of the wagon. A single shot landing an inch away from Lee, who stopped moving.

"Where'd that come from, Virgil?"

He quickly scanned the area. "I don't see nothing!"

Ainslee took advantage of their distracted state and reached for her valise beneath the wagon seat. She had the bag open before Lee yanked her back against him and lifted her from the seat into the wagon bed. Another shot, this time into Lee's leg. His scream rent the air, and as they say in the dime novels Ainslee read too many of, "All hell broke loose."

Virgil fired wildly toward the trees. Ainslee slipped away from Lee who held his bleeding leg against his body while he writhed. Ainslee fought with her skirts before she climbed back over the seat, reached for her bag, and pulled out the dirk. Her arm was raised, but she didn't move. Virgil's pistol now pointed at her as he moved his horse closer.

"You out there!" Virgil held his gun pointed at her, but his eyes shifted to the trees. "I'll kill 'er!"

He reached for her and Ainslee slapped his hand away. A bold move under the circumstances. A dirk in a skilled hand was useful but rarely against a bullet. "Ye might live if ye leave now," Ainslee said. Her confidence rested entirely on the hope that whoever came to her rescue was on her side and not someone eager to take these men's place.

COLTON FOLLOWED THE other rustlers' tracks on the most convoluted path he'd ever seen man or horse take. They wound around where he'd found Ike and the other one, a Jesse Pitts who had paper on him. The doctor assured him both of the men would live and then kindly asked Colton to stop bringing him any more business.

An outbreak of desperate, out-of-work cowboys plagued the area, and all the men at Hawk's Peak and the surrounding farms and small ranches pulled together to do their part. Most folks in Briarwood and the neighboring area looked to the Gallaghers and their men when trouble broke out.

Colton accepted the responsibility of tracking while the other hands ran the ranch. Ethan, Gabriel, and Ramsey rotated the duties of tracking and overseeing the cattle and horse operations. They considered anything that happened on their land their responsibility and never shirked their duties.

Colton was the best tracker in the area, possibly the entire territory. He'd heard men speak of his reputation; more still sought him out to find what was lost. He didn't pay them much mind unless it was a child or missing person in danger. He preferred to remain anonymous, but even in a territory where a man could lose himself for days or weeks at a time, anonymity wasn't easy. He worked for the Gallagher family of Hawk's Peak, which meant at some point someone would hear of him.

He used those tracking skills to guide him through a thick forest along a deer trail almost too narrow for a horse. The riders went over a hill, backtracked, and returned to another trail more well-used than the last. They'd obviously been lost, which told Colton they were just as stupid as the last two. By the time he followed the tracks to where they met with the main road between Bozeman and Briarwood, he was a day and night's ride from town.

The men tried to cover their tracks on the road, but even the fresh wheel imprints of a wagon didn't cover the hoof indents made by their horses. Colton turned and made his way back toward Briarwood. Rain earlier, followed by sun, had turned the road into caked mud, and the wheel impressions revealed a heavy load, more than one person or a driver with a lot of cargo. The tracks were fresh after the rain, which meant they weren't too far ahead.

He urged his gelding into a gallop. Two miles up the road he saw the wagon and pulled his horse to a stop. Colton stood far enough away to not be noticed but close enough to see a woman and two men. He'd bet his Winchester the men were his elusive rustlers.

He slid the barrel of his rifle from the leather scabbard. In a smooth and natural move, he raised the gun, aimed, and fired. The bullet flew past one of the men, close enough for him to know the next shot would hit flesh.

The men scrambled, one of them reaching for the woman again. She raised her arm, holding something Colton couldn't identify, and brought her hand down onto one of her attacker's arms. A loud shriek followed. The woman lifted her skirts and jumped from the buckboard.

Colton swore and rushed toward them, firing another two shots at the fleeing man, who caught a bullet in the shoulder. The woman ran away from the wagon— away from him. Impressive considering her skirts. Knowing what awaited her if left to her own defenses, Colton abandoned the bleeding culprits in favor of going after her.

She spun around and threw a knife, narrowly missing him.

"Damn it, I'm not going to hurt you!" Colton brought his horse up alongside her and cut her off. Sliding off the animal's back, he held up his hands, one still holding the rifle. "I'm not going to hurt you," he repeated.

"Och, I'm to believe ye?"

Colton turned his back on her, a sure sign of trust, and slid the rifle into its scabbard. When he faced her again, she'd backed away another half a dozen feet.

She raised a neat brow and pointed to his hip. "Ye'r still armed."

"And you almost killed me with your knife."

"'Tis a dirk."

He studied her with both curiosity and interest. Her thick curls of dark hickory hair fell loose and free around her shoulders, tangled from the wind and her struggles with her attackers. He moved his eyes over her, from the brown leather boots peeking beneath her full skirts, over her bodice and face, stopping at her eyes. They were almost the same shade of grayish-blue as her dress.

Colton knew the voice, or one similar, and he hadn't heard the likes of it since Brenna Cameron, now Brenna Gallagher, arrived at Hawk's Peak less than three years earlier. "Your *dirk* almost hit me. Either you have good aim or you got lucky."

She smirked as though daring him to guess which.

"I'd like to go back and tie those men up before they hightail it." Colton looked beyond her shoulder. "Then again, it appears to be too late for that."

"Then ye should have gone after them instead of me."

"I don't care if they live or die."

Her features softened, giving Colton a chance to study the delicate lines of her face. Freckles, a shade lighter than her hair, dusted her fair skin.

"Ye'r really not here to hurt me?"

"I'm really not." Colton grabbed the reins of his horse. "My name is Colton Dawson. You have no reason to trust me. I can understand how it looked, me riding after you." He saw no injury beyond a few scrapes on her bare hand, but he had to ask. "Did they hurt you?"

She shook her head and wiped her hands together. "Ye stopped them. I am grateful, Mr. Dawson. Ah'm Ainslee McConnell, and not in the habit of trusting men I dinna ken. If ye'll point me toward Briarwood, Ah'm sure to find my way."

Colton glanced at her hand and saw no ring. No sane husband would allow a woman like her to travel alone. "I'll guide you there, Miss McConnell."

"I didna ask for help."

"Do you have family back in Scotland?"

Surprised, she stared up at him. She had a fair way to look up, standing no taller than Brenna. "How did ye know?"

He smiled. "You'll have to be in America a long time before you lose the accent."

"Ye get many from Scotland here?"

"We get all kinds, but no, not too many in Briarwood, though some in the territory. Happens that I know a woman from your country. You sound just like she did, when she first came. Her accent wasn't as strong. I like it." Colton didn't know why he added the last part. "Listen, I can wait out here all day and night with you until you come to your senses, or we can start back. We're only a day and bed away from town."

"A day and . . . ye'r no thinking quaht ah think ye'r saying, ur ye?"

Colton had to stumble through the words. Her brogue thickened when she spoke quickly.

"I'm thinking you'll have to sleep in the back of the wagon. I need to go back and bury your driver, then we can head out."

"Ye saw him?"

Colton nodded. "What happened?"

"A bullet. He was slowing down the wagon and I had to push him out. I pray his soul forgives me."

"His soul will understand. Why didn't you take the stage? There's a private coach that still runs from Bozeman to Briarwood every seven days."

"Aye, the railroad man told me, but it dinna come around for four mair days."

Colton did not comment, for they both knew her lack of patience almost got her killed.

"You do that nicely, moving from your words to ours."

"I prefer mine." She surprised him by grinning. "I attended college in England. I find people treat me differently when they hear me speak like I have just climbed down the highest peak in the Highlands."

"It's a pretty way of speaking. Even with your fancier talk, you can't hide the Scottish."

"Ah dinna want tae."

He smiled again at her and started walking. "I'd offer you my horse, but we're not far from the wagon, and I'm not certain you wouldn't ride off and leave me."

"'Tis possible." She fell into step beside him, keeping more than a few feet between them. She stopped to pick up her dirk, kept it palmed.

Not a fool, Colton thought.

"This woman you met from Scotland," she said. "What was her name?"

"I know her still. Brenna Gallagher."

Ainslee halted, and Colton suspected he only needed one guess as to why.

"Ye ken her?"

"How about you tell me first how *you* know Brenna."

"She is my cousin."

"Your cousin?"

"'Tis clear you do not believe me."

Colton gave her a sardonic smile. "You have the accent down, and you look Scottish enough, though seeing as how Brenna is the only Scot I know intimately—"

"Intimately?"

Colton held up a hand. "Wrong choice of words. Brenna is a friend. I knew her husband, Ethan Gallagher, long before they met."

"I apologize."

"Temper isn't too far off, either. Could be you're related."

"Mr. Dawson."

"Colton."

"Mr. Dawson, you have saved my life and 'tis grateful I am for your service. I will be going now."

"Sorry, Miss McConnell, but whether you come with me or I follow you, you're not going alone."

2

"YOU ARE NOT invited, Mr. Dawson." When they reached the wagon, Ainslee went immediately to find her valise beneath the bench. "My bag is missing."

Colton tied his horse to the back of the buckboard. She caught his raised eyebrow and his cursory glance of the large steamer trunk and smaller, leather suitcase. "Not those. My valise. I need to retrieve it."

"The men won't get far with their injuries. When I get you back to town, I'll head out again. If they still have it with them—"

"Nae, Mr. Dawson. Ye dinna ken. Ah'm

needin'—"

"Slow down, Miss McConnell. You need to find it. Is there anything in there that can't be replaced?"

Ainslee ignored him and searched around the wagon. When she didn't find the leather bag, she started to walk down the road.

"Miss McConnell." Colton caught up to her, his hand brushing over her arm. "I'm sorry, but you can't just go walking off around here alone."

She took a deep breath and steadied her gaze on him. "I have walked the breadth of Hadrian's Wall, explored the Caringorms with my father, and crossed an ocean by myself to get here." She swept her hand over the dirt beneath her feet. "I suspect I have it in me to walk along this road."

Colton held up his hands and backed away, making Ainslee realize her temper had been unleashed without plan. "It is my turn now to apologize, Mr. Dawson. I need to find my valise."

"I thought I wasn't invited to join you."

Her cheeks reddened. Colton never did like to see a woman in distress.

Ainslee glanced back at the wagon and dropped her shoulders in defeat. "It was under the bench when the wagon stopped. I pulled my dirk out and . . . they must have taken it. I had hoped . . . never mind." She looked up at Colton. "I will pay you handsomely for its safe return."

"There's no need for that. If the men took it, and still have it, then you'll get it back. You have my word." He moved around the two horses hitched to the wagon. "This shaft isn't strong, but it's still intact. We'll have to move slow and walk part of the way. We'll bed down tonight and head out at first light."

Ainslee moved to stand next to him, forcing his attention. "I did not think you were serious about sleeping out here." She believed he smiled but couldn't be sure.

"We won't make it to town before nightfall, Miss McConnell. There's no other place to sleep and I won't risk the injury to the horses, or us, by traveling in the dark. A lot of animals come out when it's dark and we don't want to be caught unawares. We'll stick by a fire."

Ainslee had slept beneath the stars a few times in her adult life, though never with a stranger. She'd traversed the Caringorms, yes, but only with her father and people she knew. Horses, tents, and a few servants to attend the camp had accompanied them. Not to fret, Ainslee thought. "'Tis only for the one night. I suppose if it is not spoken of, there should be no harm."

"No harm will come to you while I'm here, from me or anyone else, but you ought to be more cautious. These mountains are full of dangers for men and women."

Ainslee studied Colton, growing increasingly fascinated with him the more he spoke. She'd come across a real western cowboy. The few dime novels she'd managed to have shipped to her while in England had long since been worn through from reading. She had become fascinated with the short works of sensational adventure fiction when the friend of well-traveled parents to America introduced her to the wild tales of mountain men, soldiers, and explorers. Colton was right. Her own expedition to America could become a penny dreadful if she was not careful.

"I have no choice but to trust you, Mr. Dawson. For the moment, my life is in your hands."

He grinned, though she couldn't imagine why. She followed his gaze to her hand. "Except, Miss McConnell, you still have your dirk."

AINSLEE ENJOYED SEEING the landscape from a new vantage point. The expensive, yet sensible boots she had purchased in Chicago provided protection from the rocks and twigs and lent comfort as she soaked in her surroundings while on foot.

She snatched glimpses of Colton as he walked ahead, next to the pair of horses still attached to the wagon. Her interest in him escalated while she watched him move or listened to him speak with the animals. She couldn't hear his words most of the time, but his soothing voice appealed to the creatures.

Colton stood over a head taller than she with a strong bearing, almost military. Strong cheekbones sat prominent on an intriguing face, half covered in a beard the color of coffee before the beans have had a chance to fully roast. Thick hair of the same color brushed against his shoulders. His sage-colored eyes saw more than they revealed. He dressed as she imagined men would in the great open American West— black pants, a dark shirt covered in dust up the front, and a long, light-colored duster. None of the men she'd met thus far possessed his physical demeanor.

Ainslee saw him easily as a hero in an adventure novel, though not a single hero in her imagination was his equal. She'd have to think on it, and as they walked along, while the sun descended in the vast sky, she wondered just how well he knew her cousin.

"How is Brenna and her family?"

Colton slowed his walk. "They're happy. Brenna once mentioned family still living in Scotland, but she doesn't talk about it much."

"We're not close, exactly. Distant cousins through her father and my mother. I haven't seen her in ages, though we have written over the years. I was traveling a few months ago to London and visited Cameron Manor on my return. Iain and Maggie, who helped raise Brenna, still look after her home. Has Brenna mentioned them?"

Colton nodded and Ainslee continued. "They told me about Brenna coming to America to Montana Territory and finding her brother. I never knew she had a twin brother, Ramsey, or I another cousin."

"And no one tried to stop you from coming here alone?"

"My mother and father are understanding, and I'm quite old enough to make my own decisions."

Ainslee saw Colton smile, though he said nothing. She felt like she'd been talking for hours while he contributed only a few nods and words when asked a direct question. "Maggie told me that Ramsey lives close to Brenna's family."

"He and Eliza—that's Ethan and Gabriel's younger sister—live on Hawk's Peak."

"And do you live nearby?"

He kept his eyes forward when he answered. "I live on the ranch. Have for a long time."

Colton responded with few words. Ainslee found most people eager to speak of themselves. He held out an arm to stop her.

"What's wrong?" She studied their surroundings, finding no sign of human or creature. Darkness cloaked the edges of the sky, and soon it would envelop them fully.

"We'll make camp ahead. There's a creek for the horses and for washing up."

"Can we not travel more before the sun sets?"

Colton shook his head without sparing her a glance. "We need to prepare camp while it's still light out."

She marched alongside him now, unwilling to let him outpace her. "And if you were out here alone, would you continue on?"

He smirked and this time he did look at her. No, not a mere look, Ainslee thought. When his eyes met hers or perused her face, a shudder rushed through her body and caught her breath in mid-exhale.

"Miss McConnell, if I was out here alone, I'd be hauling two disgruntled and bleeding men back to town. Under the circumstances, your company is an improvement."

Ainslee narrowed her eyes even though he'd looked away. "Under what circumstances, Mr. Dawson?"

"Do you hear the creek? That's where we'll stop for the night."

He'd changed the subject without a hitch in speech, as though her previous question had been unasked. She opted to ignore her traveling companion. When they walked into a clearing, Colton stopped the horses next to a few trees with the creek nearby. Ainslee soaked up the loveliness of her surroundings and decided to forgive Colton his high-handedness in making them stop for the evening.

When her weary feet found purchase in one spot, exhaustion pushed at her from all directions. She touched the back of one hand to her brow to wipe away a sheen of moisture and realized her hands felt colder than they should. Perhaps Colton had been right to stop. Her long journey had been an adventure, and she'd enjoyed the new experiences, but today's escapade might have been more taxing than she originally credited. She only needed a few minutes for her body to rest, and with that thought, she walked to the creek.

Ainslee's sensible boots were her new nemesis. They'd rubbed blisters into the backs of her feet. When she pulled her boots off to wash her feet in the cool water near their campsite, she gritted her teeth and scrunched her eyes against the pain and eventual relief. After she removed her stockings, she braced her feet on one of the smooth rocks beneath the creek's surface, and sighed as the water flowed over and around.

She listened to Colton moving around not far from where she sat on the grassy edge. She kept her back to him and attempted to maintain some modesty while holding her skirts high enough on her legs to remain dry.

The horses nickered and stomped, relieved to be free from the wagon harness. He tightened a rope between two trees and after he watered the animals, he secured the individual horse leads to the main line. He gave the horses space between each other and was generous with the rope, allowing them to graze. He'd yet to see to himself, and guilt weighed on Ainslee for she'd gone straight to relieving her own pain.

She rose from her place by the creek, slipped on the smooth rocks, and landed back first in the water. She grappled for the edge and found her hand grasped by another. Her sodden dress weighed heavy when strong arms pulled her from the water and onto the bank.

"Are you all right?"

Ainslee wiped water from her eyes and leaned her head back a little so she could see his face. He smiled but thankfully hadn't laughed. "I'm clumsy, and yes, I'm all right. Thank you."

"It's easier to take a bath without all those skirts on."

"I hadn't intended on bathing." She lifted an arm and pointed to the camp. "I wanted to help. I was here resting while you worked, and it was wrong of me to expect you to take care of everything."

"I appreciate the thought. It's warm now but it gets cold at night up here. You'll want to change into dry clothes."

He'd already turned away and walked back to the horses before she could respond. Ainslee looked around to find a place that offered enough privacy for her to change. When she returned to the wagon and opened one of her trunks to locate a dry skirt and blouse, she saw Colton shake out a blanket from his bedroll and string it up using some of the rope securing the horses.

He shrugged when she looked pointedly at the blanket. "It's the best I can offer you in way of privacy. I don't recommend going into the trees with night near upon us. There are some bushes—" Colton indicated a grouping of dogwood shrubs a dozen yards to the left "—for you to . . . well, anyway."

Warm heat rose to Ainslee's face. Colton didn't appear embarrassed, except perhaps in deference to her, and why would he? Living in this wilderness as he did, a lack of amenities was commonplace. Even when she traveled through the Highlands, the camp resembled a small village with everything Ainslee could possibly need.

"I'm going to gather firewood and then I'll make camp. It'll be rough, only a couple of bedrolls. Your driver had an extra one in the wagon. You can sleep in the wagon, but it will be warmer by the fire."

Ainslee stepped forward, her dry clothes

momentarily forgotten. "I would rather be warm than off the ground. I'll gather the wood for a fire."

"That's not—"

"Please, I'd like to help."

He nodded and indicated the ground around them. "You should be able to find enough twigs and branches close by. Stay clear of anything green."

Ainslee mustered energy stores she'd thought depleted and set about her task.

COLTON WATCHED HER put aside the dry clothes and walk a short distance away. She picked up twigs and fallen branches in a variety of sizes. Most would burn too quickly, but Colton planned to search the nearby woods for larger pieces. Her movements were unhurried and she labored to bend over, but when she raised a delicate brow and stared at him as though he'd interrupted, he left her alone.

Colton tended to keep to himself. Outside of the long days at the ranch or visits to town, he rarely ventured too far unless necessary. He'd heard about the rise of new cities and the birth of new laws, rail systems, and roads throughout the country. Some folks in Briarwood liked to keep abreast of whatever news they could get from Bozeman, Denver, and as far as San Francisco, Chicago, and New York. Most, though, felt as he did. They lived among the mountains and open valleys, where wildlife, cattle, and horses outnumbered the people, and they lived here on purpose—with purpose.

He'd met enough city people in his life to know they didn't belong in the West, at least outside the more established areas. Ainslee surprised and confused him. She spoke of life in the Highlands and mentioned time spent in London like they were of equal challenge and joy. With her impeccable manners and fine clothes, he immediately judged her for a woman who should turn around and return home. He remembered thinking the same thing about Brenna when she first arrived, and she'd proven him and everyone else wrong.

Since Ainslee hid a dirk in her valise and didn't want him thinking she was a simple-minded lady who needed to be waited on, he'd let her help. Tomorrow morning, he might even suggest she learn how to harness the horses.

He watched her closely while he searched for and found a few larger, fallen branches on the forest floor. When he saw her return to camp and find him gone, she hastily picked up her dry clothes and moved behind the blanket he'd fashioned into a changing area.

Colton turned his back and breathed

deeply. Not liking city women didn't mean he wasn't attracted to this one. He just wished he knew what it was about her. He heard his name and turned back to face the camp. He saw the top of Ainslee's head above the blanket. She hadn't moved when he heard her call his name again.

Colton dropped the wood he'd gathered and ran toward camp, stopping on the other side of the changing area. "What's wrong?"

When she spoke, Ainslee's voice held strength and vulnerability in equal measure. "Ordinarily I would never allow a man, especially a stranger, to do what I'm about to ask you to do, but you're the only one here, and I'd rather not die from blood loss tonight."

Colton didn't wait for permission to walk around to her side of the blanket. She was still dressed in her layers of skirt and a camisole, her corset loosened. She held her blouse pressed to the front of her body. "A pain struck when I pulled my clothes. I canna see it or reach it myself. I didna feel anything earlier, but now. . ."

"It's all right." Colton stepped closer, trying to calm her. She slowly turned her back to him, and he saw that she had managed to extract some of the laces, but it was the dark red blood stain near the center that drew his attention.

In their short acquaintance, he'd figured out that in instances other than when she was in the mood, her accent became stronger. "If it was serious, you wouldn't be standing up, talking to me. It's a wonder this didn't pain you earlier." He reached out, then pulled his hand back. "I'll need to loosen the rest of the laces to see the injury."

Ainslee's breath shuddered when she exhaled. Colton caught her imperceptible nod but asked again to ease his mind. This time she nodded and vocalized her consent. He heard the strain in her voice and was careful to touch only the laces. He'd never removed a woman's corset with such care before, as a lover or husband would. He cleared his throat and finished the task.

He turned away briefly while Ainslee unhooked the garment in the front. Colton heard it drop to the ground and faced her again. The red blood offered a stark contrast to the white camisole. "It's torn. I need to pull the fabric open a little more, and away from you so I can look at the wound."

"Ainslee."

Colton did not look up. "What?"

"This will all feel less . . . improper . . . if you use my name."

This time Colton paused long enough to smile and ask, "May I get a closer look at the wound, Ainslee?"

It took a few seconds, but she nodded. "Call me Colton."

"Colton." He barely caught the whisper of his name on her exhaled breath. She tensed when he made the first tear to the delicate fabric. Colton watched his hands even though he was aware of every sound and movement she made. "How'd you manage getting in and out of that thing on the journey?"

"What?"

He shrugged, though she couldn't see him. "Seems like it would take more than one person to make it work."

"Are you really curious about how a woman dresses or are you trying to distract me?"

Colton smiled. "Is sass a Scottish trait or restricted to the McConnells and Camerons?"

"You're saying my cousin is sassy?"

"More or less, but I'll deny it if you say I

said so."

"Maids at the hotels assisted me."

Lucky maids, he thought. Colton pressed the flesh around her wound. Her breathing became louder. "Ainslee, it's all right. It's more of a scratch."

"How did I get scratched beneath my corset, and why is it bleeding so much?"

"It's not bleeding much anymore." Colton leaned down to pick up her corset and found a bullet lodged in the center of the back. "A bullet, or what's left of one, grazed you and was stopped by . . . what is this?"

Ainslee turned and stared at him holding the feminine garment. Her skin warmed from embarrassment. "'Tis whalebone. A bullet? How, I wasna . . . they didna . . ."

"A pistol isn't always accurate, especially in the hands of someone who doesn't know how to use it. Looks like it punctured the corset enough to break the skin beneath. You're very lucky. It bled, but this contraption applied enough pressure to keep it from bleeding too much."

"Lucky? I was shot! I should have felt—"

"Stress keeps the body from feeling a lot of things." Colton handed the corset back to her. "If you'll allow me, I'll see to the wound. Make sure it's clean."

Ainslee's gray eyes narrowed as she studied him. Colton remained still as he met her scrutiny. He'd asked a lot of her, trusting him not to harm her and escort her safely to town. He knew the moment when she realized his intentions were honorable because she nodded again and presented her back to him. "Should I remain standing?"

Since she no longer faced him, Colton said, "If you sit on the log over there, I'll get water and start a fire." He thought to remove his coat and cover her with it, but he'd been on the trail a few days with a lot of riding and walking in between. His clothes needed cleaning. "Do you have anything in your trunks to wear that is loose, to keep you warm while I gather what I need?"

Ainslee nodded, moved to stand, then sat back down. "I was fine before I knew I'd been shot. Now I feel stiff all over. There's a shawl in the first trunk, on the top."

Colton retrieved a shawl of soft wool plaid and closed her trunk. He also rummaged through the driver's wooden box secured against the back of the wagon seat. Colton removed a tin cooking pot, noticing the rest of the items were meant for the horses and wagon.

He paused when he returned to Ainslee's side, unfolded the shawl, and draped the fine material over her shoulders. He heard her murmured thanks when he turned away to fetch water. Colton placed his knife beneath the flames, and when he returned, Ainslee had pulled it from the fire.

"Ye dinna mean to use this on my back, do ye?"

Colton set the pot of cold water behind her where he could easily reach it to tend her back. "I don't have any medicine or needle to stitch the wound closed. It needs to be washed out and cauterized."

Ainslee shook her head and started to rise. Colton placed a hand on her shoulder. "Please, sit, before the wound bleeds again."

Ainslee lowered herself to the log once more but continued to shake her head. "Do you have salt?"

"Yes. I'll use some in the water, but unless you want to part with one of your petticoats to use as—"

"I want to part with one! Take a trunk of

clothes if it means not pressing that scorching blade to my skin. I have heard the screams of a man subjected to such torture. I canna bear it, Colton."

Colton knew from experience that the pain was fierce yet fleeting. The wound wasn't deep, but blood began once again to trail down her back now that the pressure from her corset no longer applied to it. He returned to the wagon and rifled through the larger of the two trunks until he found one of her petticoats near the bottom. Using the still-warm blade, he sliced it into long strips. Using the largest of the remnants, he wet the cloth and pressed it against her back to stem the blood flow.

He moved away long enough to set the pot of water onto the fire and add more twigs to increase the flame and heat. He replaced the bloodied cloth with another until the bleeding stopped again. "The bandages aren't going to keep the wound closed. There's a doctor in Briarwood, but we have a bit of traveling tomorrow. Even riding my horse, you risk it starting up again."

"You'd rather burn me?"

Colton added salt to the water and using a third of the petticoat strips, drizzled water over the wound, pressed the cloth against the opening, and repeated the process. "There might be a slight scar, but you'll have that anyway. The salt water will only help to clean around the wound, it won't stop the bleeding. The knife doesn't have to be too hot. I'll only warm it, and just maybe it will be enough until the doctor can stitch it."

Ainslee squirmed on the log and adjusted the clothing she held against her chest. "I have needle and thread in the smaller trunk. It's in a leather box at the top."

"You'll trust me putting a needle to your

skin? It will still hurt."

"But it won't burn."

Colton returned once more to the wagon. He'd never spent so much time going through a woman's belongings, thinking such things were sacred and no place for a man's mind or hands. He set the box on the log next to her, opened it, and saw that it was well stocked. Colton selected a needle that wasn't too small for his hands, and the finest thread he could find. He extracted a box of matches from his saddlebag and struck it while holding it away from his face. Ainslee coughed once against the sulphur from the match. "I have to heat the needle. I'll let it cool before I use it, though." He held the needle over the flame until it flickered out.

The smooth skin of Ainslee's back held Colton's attention. He breathed deeply, steadied his hand, and pressed the tip of the needle to the frayed skin around the wound. It was a scratch, as he had told her, compared to what it could have been had the bullet traveled another path. The depth of the wound was not great, but the lead still managed to do some damage.

Ainslee stiffened when he made the first pass through with the needle, and he wished he had something to give her to ease the pain. He handed her a clean strip of petticoat. "Roll this and bite down, it will help. Try not to stiffen up or move."

She said nothing but accepted the cloth and did as instructed. Colton took his time, making the stitches as small as possible. He'd sutured wounds before, but never on a woman. She would carry a scar as a reminder of this day.

Colton tied off the final stitch and cleaned the area once more with salted water to remove excess blood. Ainslee remained silent while he took the remainder of her torn-up petticoat and wrapped it around her middle. She held her blouse away far enough for him to cross over the sutures three times.

When he finished, Colton moved to kneel in front of her. Silent tears glistened in her eyes, and he removed the rolled cloth from between her lips. "You're a brave one."

She met his studied gaze. "How many?"

He knew what she meant and said, "Twelve. I made them as small as I could, but I'm no doctor. He'll want to take a look when we get into town tomorrow. Cauterizing might have been less painful."

"No, I don't believe it would have been. You have a gentle touch." Ainslee covered herself with the shawl, tugging the edges over her chest until they lay under her arms. "Thank you."

Colton remained kneeling in front of her for a few more seconds before he stood. "Do you need help dressing?"

Her expression conveyed her shock at his offer, before the lines of her faces softened again. "I suppose that was a fair question, considering your administrations thus far. Thank you, but no. I can manage."

"Stay here then, I won't be long." Colton heard the abruptness in his own voice and offered Ainslee more of an explanation. "I'll bring back dinner. If you need anything, call out. I'll be close enough to hear you."

3

AINSLEE FELT THE tug of her skin against the thread Colton used to close her flesh. For a fleeting moment she wished she could examine the damage and then thought better of it. She had held onto her courage for as long as possible, and only now when she believed Colton far enough away not to hear her, she let loose the tears to roll down her cheeks.

The pain had pierced through the veil of armor her mother called pride, but she had not allowed him to see her cry. She took for granted the ease of her journey across the sea and the eastern portion of America. When she reached the territories, Ainslee doubted the wisdom in venturing to this land alone. Yet, she continued. Brenna had traveled alone and survived. Surely she was as capable. She had not expected to miss the train and well-appointed hotels so much, however.

Ainslee exchanged the dress she had taken from her trunk earlier with another that did not require a corset and buttoned up the front. She dressed more simply when at home in the Highlands, often wearing looser dresses over her chemise and petticoats, the McConnell plaid, and foregoing a corset entirely. When she left her family's estate, or when they entertained, she subjected herself to the latest fashions, most of which she found uncomfortable.

Ainslee cast a detestable look toward her ruined corset and without hesitation, picked it up and dropped it on the fire. The flames rose in a wild dance as they quickly engulfed the fine material around the whalebone stays.

She managed to dress without disturbing Colton's bandage. She left her boots off, for she did not believe herself yet able to bend over far enough to fasten them. However, Ainslee still intended to make herself useful.

When Colton returned a short while later, it was with wood in one arm and a rabbit hanging from twine in the other hand.

She smoothed her skirts when he approached and gathered her shawl more tightly over her bodice. He dropped the wood on the ground next to the fire and raised a brow in question. "You've been busy. Are you sure—"

"I was careful." Ainslee was pleased with herself. She had managed to keep the fire going and prepare a makeshift cooking stand. Immediately next to the fire, she dug a hole in the ground, smoothing the edges and removing rocks and twigs. She gathered stones and wiped away the dirt before dropping them into a cleared area at the edge of the fire. It took a little searching to procure two strong sticks to be used to lift the hot rocks. She reached for them now, but Colton's gentle voice stopped her.

"Let's not risk ruining my great stitchwork anymore."

Ainslee sat back on the log and blinked. "My father's gamekeeper taught me to prepare and cook game when I was young. I haven't tested my skills in many years, but I remembered some. I was careful."

"I wasn't criticizing, and I'm sorry if it came out that way." He nodded to the cooking hole she prepared. "I'll move the rocks after I prepare this by the creek and bring it back for cooking."

"I can help."

When his eyes rested on her and held her gaze, Ainslee hovered deeper beneath the shawl to ward off an involuntary shiver. Colton's lips turned up at the edges in a barely perceptible smile. He said, "I won't be long." He took a few steps, stopped, and turned. "It could be my initial impression of you was wrong. You're a . . . very strong woman."

Ainslee held off on asking what else he'd thought her incapable of. Instead, she smiled and set a piece of wood on the flames. She followed his movements and watched unabashedly as he worked by the stream.

COLTON STARED AT her for a few seconds while he moved his eyes to take in her changed appearance. She still wore expensive clothes and sat with a back straight enough to make any finishing school proud, but something in her had already changed. Wisps of her vibrant red hair fluttered from the loose locks trailing over her shoulder, and she appeared more relaxed with her surroundings—and with him.

When he returned with the small game, Colton moved the hot rocks from the fire pit to the smaller hole prepared by Ainslee's capable hands. What he should have told her was how much she'd impressed him. Colton generally measured a person's abilities and trustworthiness soon after meeting them. He never once doubted he could trust her, but she'd surprised him more than once throughout the afternoon.

He'd witnessed stronger men unable to withstand the pain of flesh being sewn together by a needle, at least not without the help of a dose of alcohol in their system first. Colton convinced her to let him check the stitches before they ate. She'd pulled them a little with her exertions, though not enough to open the wound.

He wasn't the type of man to put his hands on a lady in such a personal way, the exception being in the case of helping said lady. Although they both knew his intentions were honorable, Colton had not expected Ainslee to be comfortable and relaxed with his ministrations.

He considered the likelihood of Brenna's cousin being raised in a less-than-proper household. He discounted the possibility almost immediately. Then again, the way she spoke of her childhood, it sounded as though she had more freedoms growing up than Brenna had enjoyed. Everything about Ainslee interested him, more so with each new piece of information he learned about her. The only problem Colton could figure was this: He didn't want to be interested. Unfortunately, he noticed all things about her, from the way she sat with her legs tucked close and covered to the subtle movements of her fingers and lips.

Colton watched her shift once, twice, and a third time. He suspected she found the log an uncomfortable place to sit, but when she closed her eyes, tilted her head back, and lifted her shoulders in a circular motion, Colton lowered himself to sit next to her. He preferred the log to the stone he'd been occupying.

"Is the wound bothering you?"

Ainslee blinked open her eyes. "You surprised me. I had not expected you to sound so close, and here you are."

"Smoke is drifting the other way." It wasn't but Colton didn't flinch at the obvious lie.

"No, the wound isn't too much of a bother. I suppose it is the sitting with my back straight that is a little uncomfortable.

I will be quite sore in the morning."

Colton fetched the top blanket off his bedroll and smoothed it over the ground next to the log. "If you sit there, you can rest your back."

"Thank you." Her words were soft, putting him in mind of the skin on her back, skin his fingers still remembered touching.

She lowered herself to the ground without assistance. Colton sensed she needed to do that much on her own. If the hour was not still too early, he would have suggested she sleep. Ainslee didn't appear ready for bed, evidenced by the hint of a smile as she once more closed her eyes and faced the sky. Her chest rose and fell gently with each breath. "The air is different here, lighter somehow. It fills the lungs quickly."

"Why did you come here?" Colton had not intended to ask the question. She spoke of visiting her cousins, yet he suspected there was another reason. Perhaps it was the urgency with which she came or her willingness to travel alone when both parents still lived.

Ainslee did not answer right away. She lowered her head to stare at the flickering fire. Crackles accompanied the tiny flecks of light that rose above the flames to mingle with the smoke. "I'm not entirely certain you would understand."

He credited her with not lying. It wasn't his business what she did with her time or how she chose to travel, but he wanted to know just the same. "Perhaps not. If you'd rather not say . . ."

She asked a question of her own. "Why do you live here, in the mountains with hardly anyone around, rather than in a city?"

Whether or not her question was to delay her own response, Colton was not sure, but it left him more curious. "I'd suffocate."

Ainslee nodded as though she understood perfectly. "I enjoyed my time in England and the rarified education my parents gifted to me. I wanted to learn and knew I could not stay in the Highlands to garner all the knowledge I desired. What I discovered, though, was no matter how much I studied, or how far away from home I traveled, I wanted to know more." She shifted slightly in order to look up at him. "I am here to see my cousins, that is true. I ache for home every day, and yet, I also had to leave for *me*. My parents plan to spend the winter months in Edinburgh moving forward rather than at our home on the island. I could not tolerate the endless onslaught of grand dinners and social calls year after year. I would have *suffocated*."

"And here you are." Colton leaned

forward to move off the log. He sat on his boot heels while he added a few smaller pieces of wood on the fire. Her confession did not require further response, though he wondered if she expected one. "Would you have gone anywhere or was Montana convenient because your cousins live here?"

"Both," she said without hesitation. "I wanted to see this country, to travel the open prairies and to see for myself the mountains, so grand they cannot be imagined."

"I've heard of mountains as big, maybe bigger, in places like Switzerland and Asia."

"You know about the world then, beyond this territory?"

Colton stared into the fire. His unconventional upbringing and the way he chose to live gave the impression he was little more than what he seemed: a horseman, a tracker, even a mountain man. People were rarely only what they revealed. "I know some. Nothing like what you had in your fancy school."

"Anyone can learn. Not everyone chooses to learn more than what they need to get by."

Placing more wood on the fire occupied Colton's hands for a minute, even though the flames needed no more encouragement. Despite the chill in the evening air, their camp remained warm. "I don't understand you."

Ainslee's subtle smile came and went quickly. "I do not always understand myself, Mr. Dawson."

Sensing the need to speak of other things, Colton asked, "What is in the bag you lost that is so important?"

"Another reason I am here."

She offered no additional explanation and Colton did not ask. When she wanted to stand, he stood first, grasped both her forearms, and lifted her with gentle ease. "Didn't want you pulling the stitches."

"Thank you."

She held onto him for a few more seconds and Colton allowed himself to imagine it was disappointment that crossed her face when they parted. She released him, smoothed her skirts, and looked all around. When her complexion blossomed to a hue that even the darkness could not mask, he realized her predicament. "I'm going to check on the horses and wash up. I won't wander too far, so shout if you need anything."

By the time Colton finished checking the horses and cleaned off as much of the trail dust as he could at the stream, Ainslee was sitting on her bedroll, her legs tucked beneath the folds of her skirt. Without the extra trappings women were inclined to wear, she looked more accessible. She finished braiding her hair when he knelt on the other bedroll. He'd been careful to put them on opposite sides of the fire, as much for her comfort as his.

"It is a pity to waste such a beautiful night with sleep."

Colton gave careful thought to her words before responding. She had not meant what his brain automatically heard. "You'll see the same sky tomorrow night."

"But it is not the same sky, not really."

He considered her, admired her insight. "No, it's not, and it is. There's comfort in knowing I'll look up at the same sky every night. It's the stars and light that change. They make it interesting. I always know where I am by those stars, but some nights you can see more than others and some nights, none at all."

"The constant and the new."

Colton nodded. "Exactly."

"I would say you are like the sky,

constant and changing."

He left her comment between them without a response.

"I make a study of people, in part, because I find them fascinating."

"People are people, no matter where you go. They might talk and dress different, but not much else changes."

When she inclined her head, her braid slipped over her shoulder. She'd used a blue ribbon to tie it off. Colton looked away and listened when she said, "I suspect you would rather see as few people as possible."

"I'm not opposed to conversation."

"You are quite good at it, in a taciturn way."

Now he looked up at her again, this time waiting until their eyes met and held. "Why do you think you know me so well after a few hours together?"

"I did not mean to presume, but . . ."

She kept him waiting for a full minute. He counted the seconds.

"You are as simple as you are complicated. You live in this wilderness, yet sometimes the way you speak, if not the words, leads me to believe you are more educated than you wish people to know."

"I never went to a fancy university."

"Education is delivered in a variety of forms, and I would venture a guess that yours has been extensive."

Colton no longer wanted to talk. He was happy to listen to the lyrical words she spoke—he could listen for hours—but he didn't want someone reading him like she'd deciphered every year of his life. He preferred to watch her.

There was no mistaking the fine quality of her clothes, but seeing her more relaxed and at ease with how the day ended with them camping, made him believe the stories she told about exploring the Highlands. She'd left the top buttons of her blouse open so the fabric didn't cover her neck. Dust covered her fine leather boots that sat at the bottom of the bedroll. Whenever she moved, even a little, Colton noticed her wince. Instead of complaining about the pain, she hummed softly and watched the flames while the silence between them grew.

"How do you do it?"

Ainslee responded as though she had expected him to speak all along. "Do what?"

She knew what he meant, but Colton was patient enough to indulge her. "Know me."

"It is a matter of watching and translating what I see, what I hear. I have almost always been able to meet a person and know within a few minutes if they can be trusted. I take after my father in that regard. My mother believed the special insight to be a hindrance."

"Hindrance to what?"

"Matrimony."

Colton chose not to explore that line of discourse. "You surprise me. Again." When she raised a brow and said nothing, he added, "This afternoon when we first met, you threw a knife at me. Now you speak as though we are old friends."

"To be exact, 'twas a dirk."

Colton chuckled and nodded to her in defeat. "A dirk."

Ainslee appeared to give careful thought to her next words. "I haven't known many friends. I preferred remaining at home more than I did attending parties. I went to please my mother, to keep peace with her. It is at these gatherings I learned people were far more interesting to watch than to converse with. I . . ." She tucked her skirts beneath her legs. "I believe should we part tomorrow, never to see each other in all our days hence, I could still call you friend."

She did not wait for comment. Colton watched her slide beneath the blanket and lie down with her back to him. The crackle of embers and flickering of flames were all that accompanied the night silence.

4

SLEEP TEASED AND evaded her through the long hours of the night. Colton opened his eyes for the third time to a sky, still bright with stars. A faint blue light hovered behind the mountains. It would not be long before the sun arrived, though their departure was still a few hours away. He rolled from his uncomfortable bed on the opposite side of the fire from where Ainslee slumbered.

With movements so quiet as to not startle deer or birds, should they be nesting nearby, Colton added wood to the fire and stoked the embers. He watched her while she slept. He could not help but follow the dance of flames over her face, the way the fire illuminated her fair skin and deepened the red hues in her hair. Colton had been mistaken in calling her hair a simple red. In the firelight, the strands shifted from deeper rusty hues to golden copper. The spray of freckles across her face was more subdued in the dimmer light.

His stomach tightened the more he studied her, and to assure himself that he was indeed a gentleman, Colton looked away and up to stare at the stars instead of Ainslee.

"'Tis beautiful."

He shifted his gaze back to her. The heavy-lidded eyes attested to her recent awakening, and yet he could not help but wonder if her night had been as restless as his. "Out here, there is nothing to take away from their brightness, except the sun."

"It is the same in the Highlands. There are more stars than a person could count in a million lifetimes."

Colton watched her move enough to rest her head on her arm. She remained lying beneath the extra blanket he'd given her but did not raise it when it fell from around her shoulders. If the cold penetrated her clothes, she gave no indication. The hair he admired tumbled down her side and back, unbound and untamed from the braid. He made himself more comfortable, keeping his attention on her. "You and Brenna amaze me. I could not imagine traveling an ocean and continent away from home."

"Sometimes we must go far to find ourselves, even if the distance is painful."

He wanted to erase the pain, to make sure her choice to come here was not a mistake. Colton wanted to give her everything she searched for, longed for, and the wanting caused his chest to tighten. "Why painful?"

Ainslee shook her head to ward off answering the question. "I do not suppose anyone with sense enjoys a sea voyage."

What, he wondered, caused the brief shudder in voice? "How long do you intend to stay in Montana?"

"The answer is the same one I gave my parents—I dinna ken. Perhaps when I have found what I am seeking. Perhaps I will seek more. There is much to see in this world."

Colton moved to lean against the large log. "What do you seek other than family and adventure? You wouldn't say before when I asked what you'd lost in the bag."

She shook her head, and he could not tell if he imagined the slight upturn of her lips or it was shadow cast from the fire. Ainslee said, "It is my secret."

Amused now, Colton stared at her.

"Secrets can get a person into trouble out here."

"This one will not, at least I do not believe it will. It is nothing nefarious."

"Have you shared your secret with anyone?"

Now, there was no mistaking her own amusement and the smile that followed. "My parents, and one other who in turn keeps my confidence. The world is rarely kind to women with secrets, and so I keep it close. Will you continue to ask, prod until I confess?"

Colton shrugged, though it cost him to feign indifference. "Not if you'd rather I didn't. People are entitled to secrets."

"You are an—"

"Quiet." He rolled over onto his knees, his back to Ainslee. He moved his eyes over the dark landscape, examining the areas beyond the light cast from their fire. Colton listened and hushed her again when she would have spoken. Whatever he heard was not animal. Whoever he heard moved through the woods, the steps heavy. Their attempt at stealth had failed.

Colton reached for his gun belt, secured it around his hips. "Don't move too quickly, but you need to get up and sit on the log while I break camp."

"Ye'r frightening me. Ye'r certain tis not an animal?"

He helped Ainslee stand and move to the log. Her eyes closed for a second and a quick exhale left her lips, but she made no sound. "I have nothing for the pain, but when I've readied the horses, I'll check your wound."

When he let go of her arms, her hands still gripped his. "Colton?"

"I'm certain it's not an animal, but you already knew I suspected it was a person out there."

Her accent shifted back to English,

telling him she had calmed down again. "Your hard, determined expression when you faced me gave you away. An animal would require caution but not as much worry."

"You'd think differently if you saw a bear or wolf, but the horses would sense those." He smoothed his hands over her shoulders, and this time she loosened her hold on him. "I will not move outside the reach of the fire's light, and I won't be long."

"Are we leaving in the dark?"

Colton shook his head. "Not unless necessary. When the horses are ready and the wagon hitched, I'll put out the fire." He glanced toward the lighter hues rising over the mountain. "We'll have enough light soon."

It did not take Colton long to saddle his horse and hitch the other two to the wagon, but they had to be watered first, their hooves and legs checked, and that required extra time. His gelding raised its head, ears forward, and glanced beyond to the trees. He nickered before lowering his head once more to the water. If another animal had been nearby, the horses would know it. No, it was a person, but whether they intended to approach the camp was another matter. Friendly folk tended to call out to announce themselves rather than skulk in the shadows.

What surprised him was how close Ainslee managed to get before he heard her behind him. "Did your father's gamekeeper teach you how to approach without making noise?"

"'Twas useful when hunting. I thought it would be more suspect for me to sit while you did all of the work."

"Not when you're injured." Colton went through the motions of fastening the cinch, running the latigo strap through the ring on the saddle, and tying it off. He lowered the stirrup and smoothed a hand over his horse's neck. "You can't lift or carry anything without opening your wound. The stitches will hold, but only if you're careful."

Ainslee walked away as soundlessly as she approached. Not two minutes later, Colton heard the hiss of the fire being extinguished. He turned to see her holding the tin pot by her side as she returned to the stream. She bent down, scooped up more water, and upended the pot once more over the fire. It was not enough to extinguish all the flames, but it was a good start.

"You're a stubborn one." Colton took the pot from her and handed her his horse's reins. Without explanation, he doused the remaining fire and then scooped up cold dirt to sprinkle over the wood. He separated the leftover wood pieces and repeated the process until he was certain no hot embers remained.

"You're going to ride my horse."

"But you said—"

"I know what I said. Now I'm saying you're going to ride." Ainslee crossed her arms and planted her feet. To Colton, she looked like a general ready to advance.

"Ye dinna need to be rude."

"You're maddening."

"So my mother says."

They were at a standoff and Colton had no idea how they got there. "I'm sorry. Will you let me help you on the horse?"

"You are worried I may have to ride if something goes wrong."

"That instinct you have about knowing what a person is thinking, it's annoying." He held out his hand, waited for her to accept it. When she did, he pulled her close and guided her left hand to the saddle horn. "I don't want you to pull up.

I'm going to lift you onto the saddle. Have you ever ridden astride?"

"Many times. What are you not saying?"

He lowered his voice, conscious of the rising breeze blowing toward the trees. "The men who attacked the wagon yesterday are rustlers. I found who I believe are their partners earlier and took them into Briarwood before heading back out. That's how I came upon you. I was looking for the others. If they get a chance, they'll shoot first."

"We have done nothing to them. They could have ridden free when chance presented itself. They *did* run away. Why do you think they'll return?"

"Revenge, to steal whatever else you might have in the trunks, anything. Men like that don't need good reason." He held her gaze steady. "They'll aim to shoot me. They have reason to keep you alive."

Ainslee opened her mouth to speak but

it remained open without words forming.

Colton sighed and lifted her into the saddle, careful to hold onto her until she was settled. Her skirts covered her legs but left her boots and a strip of petticoat exposed. "We'll take it slow and easy. Keep the horse walking alongside the wagon."

"Do you really believe those men have returned?"

"One of them was injured, but it only takes one."

"Have you ever lost a gun battle?"

Colton did not know how she managed to draw a half smile from him. "We don't have gun battles."

"Never?"

"Not around here."

"You've never had to kill a man?"

Flashes of hard-won and short-lived fights against old enemies went as quickly as they entered his mind. When the Gallaghers had fought to protect their ranch and their family from Nathan Hunter, a man who, by regrets, had been grandfather to Brenna and Ramsey, lives had been lost, and a few more since. Brenna's letter writing to Ian and Maggie was well known at the ranch, for she often shared tales from Scotland. Colton wondered how much of the history Ainslee had been told when visiting Cameron Manor, Brenna's ancestral home.

"Killing a person isn't a badge of honor."

"Colton, it's sorry I am for asking. I did not mean . . . I get curious and do not always . . . I am sorry."

"I'm not angry with you." He wasn't and needed to remember that. People from cities or foreign lands thrived on the stories of death and adventure. Colton had met too many who arrived with expectations of entertainment. Ainslee was not one of them. "Most of the folks out here are like everyone else. They want to build something tangible, take care of their families, and survive. Sometimes surviving means pulling a trigger. It's as simple as that."

5

IT WAS NOT simple, Ainslee thought. Nothing about this man or territory was simple. She remained quiet for the next hour of their journey. Colton moved from one side of the wagon to the other, walking alongside the horses, saying only once or twice how much farther they had to travel before reaching Briarwood.

She did not ask again about the rustler he believed sneaked around back at their camp. Ainslee neither heard nor saw anyone. She did her best to relax and enjoy the scenery. The mountains jutted above the fog that had rolled in to mingle with the trees and hover over the valley. The mist lent a romantic and mysterious ambience to the landscape, and soon a narrative formed in Ainslee's imagination, carrying her away from present circumstances to another world of adventure.

The story began in the middle with a mountain man, tall and strong with kind eyes. The heroine found herself in trouble, running from danger. She tripped, the dirk flying from her grasp. She heard the sound of hoofbeats not far behind. Her legs became tangled in her skirts and she fought against them to stand. She screamed to herself to move, to run. It wasn't the villain who found her—no—it was her mountain man. He'd saved her once before, but she believed him gone forever. He swung down from his horse to land beside her. Those wonderful eyes . . . what color . . . she could almost see them . . .

"Ainslee?"

"Gracious!" Ainslee grabbed the saddle horn to prevent herself from falling.

"What are you doing?" Colton helped keep her upright with one hand at her waist and the other on her leg. "Are you trying to kill yourself?"

She shook her head to give herself a moment to dislodge the breath stuck in her chest. "My mind wandered. Your voice brought me back—abruptly." Ainslee saw they'd moved beyond the fog. Ahead the forest would close them in on both sides of the road.

"We're about to lose our advantage when the trees take over the valley. There's a mile of forest before it opens up again." Ainslee returned his scrutiny, met his eyes. She held them steady when he continued speaking. "Are you sure you're all right?"

It was his eyes, she thought. Colton's

eyes were the same as the mountain man in her story. "We have been traveling for more than an hour. If who was at the camp planned to attack—"

"They would wait until I might not be able to see them coming."

"Is there another road?"

Ainslee gave him credit for not vocalizing his exasperation. "None that will accommodate the wagon."

"Leave the trunks." Ainslee had her center of gravity back, as well as her sharpened senses, and raised her body enough to drag her right leg over the horse to dismount. Two strong hands stopped her from reaching the ground.

"If you're of a mind to pull those stitches and bleed to death, tell me now and I'll leave you to it."

The awkward position prevented Ainslee from looking directly at Colton. "You are obsessed with the wound. It no longer hurts." A lie—a small one—but she was comfortable with the falsehood. "I promise that before I bleed out, I will write a letter swearing it was by my hand and own folly."

She waited a few seconds and cut off a squeal when Colton lifted her and lowered her to the ground. For a few heartbeats, he held her close, her back to his front, before releasing her.

"You get real prim and proper when you're riled."

The amused tone in his voice had her turning to face him. His lips did not form a smile, but the subtle sparkle in his eyes revealed a touch of mirth. Sparkling eyes? Ainslee removed the silly thought from her head, and yet she could come up with no other word for what she saw. "I said to leave the trunks."

"You'll never see anything in them again if we do."

"They're things. Certainly nothing worth dying over."

"Then why all the nonsense about losing your bag yesterday?"

Ainslee tried to imagine any scenario in which she was strong enough—or at least clever enough—to throttle him. "I need what's in *that* bag. I'm not trying to be noble. Replacing my clothes and shoes will be difficult but they can be replaced."

Colton considered her words while he ran his hands over the sides, necks, and legs of the horses. He checked the harness, wheels, and axles before coming back to stand in front of her. "The shaft is holding. For now, your trunks go with us."

"We could arrive much sooner if only on horseback." Ainslee stepped back a few inches, then a full two feet when Colton closed the space between them. His once sparkling eyes now glinted with something between humor and exasperation. She imagined now he was thinking of ways to throttle *her*. "Never mind. You know what you are doing."

He nodded by way of an acknowledgment. "Can you handle a short distance in those shoes?"

"They're sturdy." He raised a brow at her response, and Ainslee realized she hadn't exactly answered the question. "Yes, I can walk all the way to Briarwood if necessary."

"That won't be necessary."

Twenty minutes later, Ainslee rethought her bravado. The shoes she wore, while sturdy, were not meant for long walks. She suspected by the time they did reach town, she'd have a few more blisters. She was saved from the indignity when Colton stopped abruptly and faced her.

"Stay here."

"Why?"

His narrowed eyes looked heavenward

before settling on her. "Do you smell anything out of the ordinary?"

She gave her attention over to the air and was met with the pine-rich fragrance of the forest. "No."

"That's why you're staying here." He softened his order with a request. "Please."

Ainslee nodded and remained within the same two-foot cube while she waited for Colton to return. She heard him enter the trees and then silence. Not even the wind and forest creatures broke through the stillness, as though Nature herself waited for the unknown outcome. Fifteen minutes passed, followed by another ten, before Colton's footsteps alerted her to his presence.

He stepped from the forest onto the hard-packed dirt road. He was carrying her bag.

"Colton?" She held out her hand, but he

bypassed handing it to her. Instead, he carried it to the back of the wagon where he placed it within her reach.

"The bag is dirty and torn some, too. Anything you need from it should fit in the trunks."

She didn't care about the bag, not right now. "What did you find?"

"One of the men who attacked you yesterday. Looks like he's been dead a few hours, maybe more."

"Which one?"

"Not the one I managed to shoot, but a bullet finished him." He shook his head and pointed to her valise. "I haven't looked inside."

"Colton?" When he raised his eyes to meet hers, Ainslee held back her shock at the unadulterated anger. It wasn't directed at her, but she felt its energy. She grasped his hand, lifting it toward her. "You truly hate death, even for your enemies."

"It's not about hating it. Life deserves respect. It doesn't always matter how a person lived, they came into the world as more than nothing. Someone cut him up and left him."

Ainslee wondered if he realized his hand squeezed hers a bit tighter.

"I've killed men. When I took their last breath, I harbored no doubt they deserved it. They were buried or burned, but not left like that."

Ainslee had once seen the remnants of a stag torn apart by predators. It had been on her first hunting trip with her father. She remembered crying well into the night, and the next day she had refused to leave the camp. Before they returned home, her father had explained about the natural order of death and life and how they always circled around to each other. She learned how hunting the animals was for the good of the herd, but they were noble creatures who demanded respect. Death did not always carry a negative connotation. Sometimes it simply was the price paid for living.

She had never seen a human suffer the same fate. "Do you want to bury him?"

"I do, but it's not a sight you should see." He dropped her hand and moved toward the front of the wagon.

COLTON RETRIEVED A small shovel from the wooden box with rusty hinges. She remained at the back of the wagon. He sensed her watching him and it twisted him inside. He stood by every word he told her, and yet death had never tangled his conscience before. Death had always been a part of life's circle. The gun he carried was a useful tool. He'd used it many times before and would do so again.

Somehow, death's impact was heightened because of her presence. Colton didn't want her to see how cruel men could be to each other. She should see her family and then go home.

He swore and walked back to her. "It's not a sight you'll ever be able to erase."

"Nor will you."

"I've seen worse. I don't want that for you."

Ainslee's misty gray eyes held sympathy and understanding, perhaps even gratitude. He refused to let any of it affect him. "I am staying here with the wagon."

"No. There's a spot not too far, but where I can still see you."

"You enjoy saying 'no.' I prefer to stay here with the horses."

He handed her a pistol. "You know how to use one of these?"

"Aim and pull the trigger."

Colton had to remind himself again that

his anger was not her doing.

"Wait here."

To Colton's relief, she did not argue. She covered her nose with the back of her hand and nodded. She stood close enough for him to see and hear her, far enough so she couldn't see what she shouldn't.

When he reached the body, he studied it for a few seconds before pushing the tip of the shovel into the soft earth. The animals would smell it, come looking, and unearth it eventually.

They would have raped her, Colton thought, as he continued to dig. Toyed with her, raped her, and stolen everything they could carry. He'd seen them from afar when they attacked the wagon, but whether a few dozen yards or a few feet, he did not have to see into their eyes to know their intentions. They enjoyed scaring her. Whoever had done this enjoyed death.

Colton hurried through the motions,

ignoring the twinge in his back from hunching over. When the hole was deep enough, he rolled the body into the shallow grave and covered it with earth. What the animals left behind, the ground would swallow until all that remained were bones. He'd accidentally uncovered a few unmarked graves in his time. The skeletons always told a tale of either violent death or peaceful leaving, but they remained as they were, at rest in their burial place.

Justice would be served if Colton left the man for the animals to feed on, when he had so little respect for life. Life deserves respect. He meant what he had said to Ainslee, and yet this man was different. For what he might—no, would have—done to Ainslee had she been left to his mercy. Colton would not have harbored regret for leaving him to lie in wait of scavengers. Except, it mattered to him what Ainslee thought. Colton had yet to figure out why her good opinion of him weighed heavily, but it did.

"Colton?"

"Almost done."

He finished and looked to where he left her, quickening his steps when she was not where she should have been. He caught a glimpse of her in between tree trunks and branches. Sunlight had peeked through the mist and her face captured the rays. She was brushing her hand over the thick mane of one of the horses, speaking to it softly. The animals conveyed their impatience, yet it was another sound that drew Colton's attention. Each step over the underbrush was carefully calculated for maximum silence. Ainslee remained oblivious to his closeness.

Each breath released in silence as he spotted his quarry. If he left the cover of trees too soon, Ainslee could end up in the crossfire. He'd left his rifle in the saddle scabbard, his Colt with Ainslee.

He moved, listened. Ainslee turned and faced the man who now stood ten feet from her. Colton kept his eyes on the target, all the while hoping she would see him approach. She said nothing. The man Colton should have put a bullet in spoke first.

"Where's the cowboy?"

"I don't know." She inched farther from the horse.

"Saw you go into the forest with him."

"To bury the man you killed."

Colton noticed the makeshift bandage on the man's arm, an injury caused by Ainslee's dirk, which made this man Virgil. He watched Virgil smirk and run his tongue over dry-crusted lips.

"Dumb cuss got himself killed. Besides, I don't like to share."

"You are no wiser than him."

"Huh?"

Virgil took two steps forward. It was the force of being slammed against a solid chest that caused him to shriek. His cry was silenced by a firm hand over his mouth and a knife at his back.

"Drop the gun."

In response, Virgil raised his pistol. The hammer was already pulled back, had been before Colton approached from behind. Colton heard Ainslee's quiet gasp but kept his focus on the gun. If he tried to disarm him, the gun could go off. He glanced up at Ainslee—couldn't help himself—and found her staring at him, not at Virgil. Colton did not see fear in her eyes. Worry, yes, but not fear.

Colton tried one more time, removed his hand from Virgil's mouth. "Jail is better than dead."

"You stick me with that blade and she's dead, mountain man." Virgil's voice had grown edgy.

"You're not going to kill her."

"I ain't going back to jail." Virgil raised the pistol higher, his finger hovering over the trigger. A sickening laugh escaped on a half-cry. Colton understood what Virgil was doing and willingly played the other man's game. The laugh ended on a cough when a smooth blade drove into his back, puncturing his right lung.

His body dropped to the ground in a heap. Colton stepped over Virgil to shield Ainslee from seeing the last breaths. Two sputtering coughs later and Virgil fell silent forever. When Colton's eyes met Ainslee's once again, he noted the shock gazing back at him, the stiff body that remained still even as she glanced once more at the dead man.

"You killed him."

He wished he hadn't in front of her. "Hate the act, but I—"

"Nae. Dinna say it." She held her palm flat to her chest and stepped back, putting a little more distance between her and the body. "I have never seen a person die, not like this. I saw the truth of him in his eyes. Never have I known such contempt. He wanted you to kill him."

Colton had seen men take the coward's way out. "Some people choose death over prison."

"'Twas my fault. I heard the horses and thought to soothe them. You were not far. I didna think." Ainslee looked directly at him. "Thank you."

Colton did not want her thanks. "Not for killing. Don't—"

"No, not for his death. For my life."

6

THEY ARRIVED IN Briarwood in the early evening before the sun tucked behind the highest peaks. It was exactly what Ainslee imagined a frontier mountain town to be, with its rows of wood and stone buildings and dirt roads. She fancied her arrival to be accompanied by a gunfight in the saloon that drifted into the street. A sheriff wearing a shiny badge would step in right before two gunfighters drew their guns.

Colton had warned her about stereotypes, and she found herself grateful the silly novels had been proven wrong, at least in the case of Briarwood. Setting her imagination free allowed her, for a few minutes, to forget the scene on the trail.

He said nothing to her from the moment he killed Virgil. He buried the body, dragging him into the trees where she could not see. When he returned, his coat lay over his arm. He tossed it in the wagon and without warning, lifted her onto his horse. He walked while she rode, stopping only to give her water and dried meat. Still, Colton remained quiet.

They captured the attention of anyone standing outside. Most nodded or waved, obviously recognizing Colton, who returned their greetings. She wished she could see his face, but he stood with his back to her. He stopped the wagon in front of a livery, and the horse she rode followed suit.

A brawny man of average height wearing a wool cap called out a hello. He set what appeared to be a chisel on a worn table and removed a thick, leather apron before approaching Colton with an outstretched hand.

"You look like you've had a spot of trouble, Colton."

He acknowledged the comment with a brief nod but no explanation. "How are you, Otis? I have someone to deliver to the ranch. I'll need to borrow a wagon if you have one available. This one won't hold up much longer and the horses need looking after."

"I've got a buckboard you can use. I'll hitch up a pair of horses and help you move these trunks."

It was then the man called Otis looked up at Ainslee. She saw his eyes widen a fraction before shifting his gaze back to Colton.

"Does she need Doc?"

Colton nodded. "Our next stop. Ran into some trouble on the road from Bozeman."

Until this moment, Ainslee wondered if

he would ever acknowledge her again. He moved to stand beside the horse and with great gentleness, lifted her down, using his chest to brace her descent. Despite his care, he quickly put an arm's length distance between them. Otis had followed Colton and now stood nearby.

"Miss Ainslee McConnell, this is Otis Lincoln. Otis owns the livery."

Otis removed his cap to reveal his bald head and offered her a friendly smile. "Pleasure to meet you, Miss McConnell. Sorry for your troubles."

Ainslee liked the man immediately. "Thank you, Mr. Lincoln." They both smiled at the same time.

"Folks just call me Otis."

"And I give you leave to call me Ainslee, in gratitude for the warm welcome."

He studied her with a puzzled expression and his grin widened. "We don't get too many folks with that accent.

It was real gentle-like when you first spoke, but I hear it all right now. Colton said you're going to Hawk's Peak. You friend or kin to Mrs. Gallagher?"

"If you mean Brenna Gallagher, then yes. I am her cousin."

"Well don't that beat all." He secured his cap back on his head and said to Colton, "You take her on over to Doc's. The wagon'll be ready when you come back. You sure you want to head out tonight? It'll be dark in an hour."

Colton nodded. "I'm sure."

When they were alone, walking where Colton guided her, Ainslee said, "I am content to wait until tomorrow. Perhaps there is someone I can hire—"

"No."

When they reached the boardwalk, he helped her up the three steps. "I am grateful, but—"

"No."

Ainslee stopped, forcing Colton to either stop as well or drag her. He opted for the former. "Thank you. Now stop telling me no. I will never be able to repay what you have done for me, but it is quite obvious you no longer wish to be in my company."

"What gave you that idea?"

"Exasperating, infuriating man!" She ground out the words so as not to be overheard.

"I've been called worse. How about we get the Doc to check your wound. If he says it's all right, we'll drive out to the ranch tonight to save your indignation. If Brenna hears you arrived today and waited until tomorrow, it'll be my hide."

"You make my cousin sound like a harridan."

"There's no women I respect more than the Gallaghers. Harridan, no. Bossy, yes."

Ainslee smiled at the ridiculousness of the conversation. She sobered before speaking again. "I thought . . . you have not spoken to me since . . ."

"Circumstances required we be on more intimate terms than was proper. You're here now, though, and I'll see you safely to the ranch."

"Where I will no longer be your concern?"

He did not answer. With a gentle nudge he directed her to a tidy wood building with a sign next to the door that read: Doctor Brody. "Is he a real doctor?"

"Medical School of Harvard."

"All the way out here?"

Colton shook his head in exasperation. "The American West is still rough and a lot of it still wild, but more and more settlers come every year. Doctors, miners, immigrants, wealthy businessmen looking to profit off the land—we see them all. Whatever you've heard or read about the western territories—"

"I've insulted you."

"No, you haven't. Don't assume you know what it's really like out here. There's good and bad, like any other place. People like Doc Brody, educated and trained in skills desperately needed on the frontier, do a lot of good out here."

Ainslee didn't have a chance to reply. They were inside of the office that, although rustic, appeared spotless. She allowed herself a moment of surprise and shame for her assumptions. Shelves lined two of the walls. One of them was filled with books, the other with glass jars holding what she guessed were medicines, along with some she recognized as herbs. Footsteps sounded behind one of the closed doors.

The man who stepped through stood taller than Colton and was wide across the chest and arms. If ever there was a man to wrestle a bear and win, it would be this one. Ainslee guessed him to be at least fifteen years her senior. His thick head of dark hair lent him a youthful appearance, but upon closer inspection, his eyes said they had seen a great deal of life.

He offered a big warm smile. "Colton, I told you not to bring me more wounded." The doctor paused and moved his eyes to look them both over. Ainslee accepted it for what it was—a physician studying a potential patient. "But if this young lass is the wounded, then you've taken defending the ranch and town a mite far."

Ainslee decided she liked Doc Brody. His accent was unmistakable, and instantly she longed for home.

Colton placed a hand on the small of Ainslee's back. "Wasn't me this time, Doc, but she did get caught in the middle. Miss Ainslee McConnell, this is Doc Brody."

"It is a pleasure to meet ye, doctor."

"Ah, a fair Highland lass. We're after

being neighbors."

Ainslee accepted the doctor's hand as he helped her toward a table covered in thick padding and a clean, white sheet. She smiled up at the man. "I have walked the lovely streets of Dublin and stood on the Cliffs of Moher. It is a beautiful country, your Ireland."

"Not so lovely as your Scotland. I studied for a year in Edinburgh before coming to America." Before he could help her onto the examining table, Colton beat him to it. "Thank you, Colton. Now, lass, you have a clever way of going from Scots to English."

"I attended school in England."

"A lucky one you were. Not many fathers in our verdant shores would see fit to do the same for their daughters. Now, tell me what our Colton has gone and done to you."

Colton explained before she could. "Bullet skimmed her, broke the skin, bled a lot. I stitched it but I want to make sure it won't get infected."

Ainslee focused her eyes on Colton until he looked at her. She wanted him to see her annoyance at speaking on her behalf. He glanced her way, almost daring her to say something. Instead, she confirmed what Colton had told the doctor. "It stings a bit, but the pain is not so great."

"Where did it get you?"

"In the back. My . . ." Ainslee pointed to her back. "My corset stopped the bullet from doing too much damage."

"A small blessing. Colton, why don't you wait outside. I'll call you back in when we're done."

Ainslee watched Colton, and his hesitation was the first time since they'd left the scene of Virgil's death that he showed any outward emotion toward her. She would have to give his behavior more thought. Perhaps she mistook his quiet for disinterest.

COLTON SAT ON the narrow bench outside the medical office for thirty minutes. Twice he considered going back in to see what was taking so long when he heard nothing from within. Darkness arrived while he waited. Homes and businesses either lit lamps or closed up for the night. He liked dawn and dusk best, when the shift from day to night and night to day gave people enough pause to remain silent for a few seconds before they went about their business again.

He knew the café would be busy for the evening meal. Tilly's cooking was popular among the locals, and few ever missed a chance to enjoy her pies. The usual sounds from the saloon were missing from the night air. Colton stood and walked to the end of the boardwalk. He saw a few men standing outside of the double-swinging doors in quiet conversation.

He heard the doctor's office door open and walked back to where Brody stood. "You did a fine job on those stitches, Colton. I cleaned it again and sewed the wound back up. I gave her a wee dose of valerian root in brandy. Part for the pain and part to help her rest."

Colton couldn't see around the doctor into the room. "I hoped to get her out to the ranch tonight."

Brody nodded. "She said she was kin to Brenna and Ramsey. She's well enough to travel out there. It's not too far, but fair warning, she may be asleep before you get there. A night's rest without riding or bumping around in a wagon will do her good."

Colton stepped around the doctor and into the office, grateful that Brody remained outside. Ainslee was dressed and wrapping her shawl around her shoulders.

"The doctor said you would have made a fine healer."

"I'll leave the healing to him. You're all right?"

She nodded. "He gave me an herb mixed with brandy. Not what I would have expected from a Harvard doctor."

"Doc Brody uses the strong stuff when called for. Medicines aren't always easy to come by out here, what with no train into Briarwood, and Doc has learned to use what's available."

"My grandmother was a healer of sorts and swore by herbs. I admire your doctor's open mind."

They stood staring at each other, neither sure what to say or do next. Colton wanted to leave and get her to the ranch before too much more time passed. He watched her labored movements when she walked toward the door and changed his mind. "The family has a cottage here in town, near the meadow past the schoolhouse. It's probably best if you stay there tonight after all, and we'll ride out first thing tomorrow."

"You aren't worried about Brenna's wrath?"

Colton smiled because he knew she wanted him to. "She'll understand when she learns what you've been through."

Colton informed Otis they wouldn't need the wagon until morning except to transport the trunks. When Otis asked about the two mares who came in with the wagon, Colton told him to keep them. "If you don't mind boarding my horse overnight, I'd appreciate it."

Otis grinned. "Already have him in the corral and gave him some oats. Your saddle and tack are inside the barn."

Colton thanked the man, shook his

hand, and turned back to Ainslee. "Do you mind walking? It's not far, and the wagon is going to be less comfortable."

"I prefer to walk."

They remained silent until they reached the cottage ten minutes later. Colton extracted a key from his pocket and unlocked the front door. "It's cleaned weekly. Only the family and occasional guest use the place. Ben—he's foreman at Hawk's Peak—and I keep a key for emergencies since we're in town more often than the rest."

He waited for her to enter before him. Colton stopped to look around, to try and see the place from a stranger's point of view. It was a simple, one-level cottage made of stone. Every room was tidy and well-organized. "Brenna fixed the place up last year and brought in some new furnishings and linens. Ordered everything from the big cities. Maggie sent a couple crates of things from Scotland, but most of those are at the ranch or in Ramsey and Eliza's new place."

Colton waited for her to say something—anything—but all she did was walk from room to room. She had talked about hunting and trekking with her father, and she'd done well enough sleeping outdoors with him. But he couldn't forget the expensive and stylish clothes she wore when they first met, or the cultured tones of her speech, no matter what language she spoke. Would the simplicity of Briarwood be enough for her?

She turned to him and smiled. "'Tis perfect."

7

THE COTTAGE REMINDED Ainslee of home in many ways. It resembled the gardener's cottage near her mother's prized and vast gardens. She saw a woman's touch throughout and recognized the fine wool tartans of Scotland. She imagined someone sitting by the cozy fireplace, wrapped in one of them while the quiet world beyond the windows and walls passed by. A shelf of books was within easy reach, and all around there were touches blending old and new.

If she were to write the perfect home for a heroine in a small, Montana territorial town, this would be it. The cottage had no need for embellishment or grandeur.

"It has been a long time since I have seen Brenna." Ainslee returned to the front door, where Colton had remained, content to wait. "Has she changed, being here? Has this place, the people, so far from home, changed her?"

"Doesn't everyone change?"

"Not everyone."

"Sometimes change is good for a person." He set her satchel down—she had refused to part with it, claiming it could be cleaned and mended—and leaned against the doorframe.

The cool night air drifted in, bringing with it the scents of nearby pines and the flowers that lined the front of the house. It was warmer tonight than it had been the night before when they made camp under a blanket of stars. Ainslee expected to sleep well. Colton had been right to have her stay in town.

"What I am asking—"

"She'll be happy to see you, Ainslee. They all will."

He so easily read her worry.

"I should have written first."

He wondered about her sudden trepidation and sought to ease her concern. Colton stepped onto the compact front porch and motioned her to follow. "Do you hear the creek beyond the trees?"

"It sounds close."

"It flows all year round but never in the same pattern. Spring runoff after winter carries debris that diverts water, and sometimes it finds new paths on its own. It changes all the time and still stays the same."

She enjoyed the comfortable rhythm she thought they had lost after he saved her from the rustler on the road. "You mean to say that Brenna is like the creek?"

He shrugged. "Something like that."

"You're no longer angry with me?"

"I was never angry with you."

Ainslee appreciated that he didn't try to feign ignorance. "What has changed?" His stance relaxed.

"The lack of . . . boundaries we've had were necessary. When get to the ranch tomorrow, we won't see each other much."

"Why not? You live there, yes?"

"I do, but I'll be back on the trail again soon if the rustling continues, and there's always a lot to do at the ranch."

"You have already handled—" The sharp look he gave her had her carefully choosing her next words. "That is to say, those men will no longer be a problem."

"Maybe." He stepped away from her, back to the ground, leaving her alone on the porch. "I'll bring your trunks over. You'll need to lock the door tonight."

"I was led to believe Briarwood was a

safe town."

"It is, but we still lock doors."

"Colton?" She walked to the edge and stood on the top step. "I don't need all of my trunks. The smaller one will do." The satchel resting on the clean, wood floor inside did not need to be mentioned again. Ainslee regretted the fuss she had made over the bag. It was Colton who brought it up.

"You never did check to make sure everything was still inside. I was surprised it was left behind."

She studied him, trying to discern his mood. He was good at masking what he did not want to be seen. "If he had looked, he would have found only papers, nothing of value to him."

"But of value to you."

"I thought so, before." How did she apologize for being the reason he had to kill a man? "Colton, I am terribly sorry."

His eyes locked onto and held hers for the space of seconds, minutes maybe. Her own thoughts became flustered.

"I'm not."

Two quiet, yet firmly spoken words created a silence she did not know how to fill.

He broke the growing quiet. "Are you all right?"

"You know I am. Your Doctor Brody expected me to heal in quick time."

"I don't mean the wound on your back."

"I know." Ainslee longed to ease his guilt. She saw plainly he believed her injuries were his doing. For not finding her sooner? How could any one man accept such a burden? "My mind is not fragile. I expect the images will enter my dreams, turning them to nightmares, but not because of what you did. We both know what would have happened had I been alone. It is my own recklessness that

I must accept." She smiled for him. "I should have waited a few more days for the stagecoach."

"You're here now, and that's what's important. I'll be back soon."

She followed him with her eyes as he walked down the road and disappeared around the corner. Instead of returning inside, Ainslee sat on one of two hickory chairs gracing the porch, and looked toward the meadow. Enough time had passed for the moon to rise and spread a soft glow over the little red schoolhouse and green meadow. She listened to the water flow, to the leaves rustle from a gentle breeze, and she wondered what tomorrow would bring.

Colton returned with all of her belongings and lit the fires in both the kitchen stove and main hearth. He also brought her dinner. "From the café," he had said and she was left to wonder why his mood had once again shifted. He declined her invitation to join her and exited as efficiently as he'd entered. Not a half dozen words passed between them while he made sure she had everything she needed to pass the night.

Ainslee had returned to the porch until all sounds from town diminished. She moved inside and after a moment's debate, turned the key in the lock. Did Colton have true reason to worry, or did recent events make him overprotective? She readied herself for bed, grateful she had thought to pack her lighter-weight cotton nightgowns. During the evening ablutions, her thoughts turned to the enigmatic hero of her real-life adventure.

Thoughts of Colton moved her to sit at the square table between the kitchen and main living area, picking up her satchel, still by the front door. The fire Colton set earlier warmed the whole cottage, yet she wrapped one of the wool tartans over her shoulders. Not for the warmth, but for the comfort of knowing it came from home.

She withdrew a rumpled sheath of papers from the satchel and spread them over the table. The inkwell had spilled over the bottom of the bag, staining the heavy fabric and leather, and bleeding over many of the papers.

Perhaps it was for the best, she thought. Losing the words she had carefully penned did not bring her sadness as she had imagined. The heart of the story remained, yet the hero had evolved. He was now more complex in her mind, more honorable, more secretive, more . . . everything.

Her parents had indulged her the many hours she had spent writing. Only after she returned from university and had proven her work worthy of publication, did they understand she would not turn away from her dream. With her father's help, she had found a publisher willing to take a chance on an unknown author—so long as her name did not grace the cover.

A Highland adventure tale written from her heart and memories, yet no one would ever know it was Ainslee McConnell who created the story. "Adventures were told by men, not women," they had said. She wanted to prove them wrong. They suggested she pen a demure tale of romance, the kind women read written by women. The idea held no appeal for Ainslee, for what did she know of romance and reticence?

And so Finn Pickett was born. She grew to love Finn Pickett and the anonymity he provided. The first story sold and the public craved more. She wrote a dozen more, each one a grander adventure than the last. It was then the tales of the American West consumed her. Cowboys, natives, great herds of bison, and pioneers all fascinated her.

Her mother worried that her penchant for locking herself away for days to write would adversely impact her marriage prospects. Ainslee played the dutiful daughter and attended events she could not talk her way out of and allowed eligible men to call upon her after social functions. Most lost interest when they realized they could not capture hers, and those who did not were more interested in her inheritance. Those men she sent away with quick vigor.

The stories excited her. No man had ever been able to compete with the heroes of her imagination . . . until Colton. It was not a penny dreadful or dime novel she yearned to write but a true frontier adventure about the men and women who settled the land. She yearned to learn how they lived and survived so far from what many considered civilization. Colton's teasing proved that her research had obvious gaps.

Ainslee gathered all of the papers from the table and her bag and carried them to the fire. She dropped them into the flames a few pages at a time, watching them burn to ash.

THE LAST LAMP was extinguished and darkness engulfed the cottage. Colton stepped quietly onto the porch and sat in the chair Ainslee had occupied earlier. He crossed his legs at the ankles, intertwined his fingers over his stomach, and closed his eyes.

8

COLTON SAT ON the top porch step, relaxed against the railing, and listened to Ainslee move around inside the cottage. He had expected to leave an hour ago but figured she needed the sleep more than he wanted to return to the ranch.

He needed to speak with Ethan, Gabriel, Ramsey, and Ben about what had transpired. Two rustlers were in jail and two more dead. It wasn't the outcome Colton wanted, but given the circumstances, he'd rather they be dead than Ainslee.

Colton thought she would have been repulsed by what he'd done. He stayed quiet during the walk to Briarwood and tried to keep his distance last night, but there was never recrimination for his actions. He had killed a man in front of her, without thought to anything except her safety, if not her emotions.

Blood still stained the shirt he ended up tossing in the forge at Otis's livery. The blacksmith asked no questions, though he had raised his brows and shaken his head a couple of times last night, and again this morning when Colton returned for the wagon and his horse. Otis harnessed a fresh pair of mares, assuring Colton he could bring them back when he was next in town.

The horses and wagon now stood, content to wait, near a tall aspen tree. His own mount enjoyed a patch of grass nearby. Colton shifted on the stair when the door opened and stood when she stepped outside. Ainslee did not express surprise as his presence.

"You slept here last night."

"You knew? I didn't hear you wake up."

"I often wake in the middle of the night and have learned to move around quietly. I forgot to close the curtains before retiring and saw you on the porch, sleeping. There was enough moon to not require a lamp."

"Spent more of the night awake than asleep."

"Thank you. You must be exhausted."

He noted the formal way she spoke. "You learn to make do without much sleep on the trail."

"Would you like breakfast before we leave?"

Again, a formalness to her words, yet he grasped onto the bit of warmth he heard underneath. Apparently, she was going to accept what he'd said about boundaries. Colton tried to ignore the annoyance he suddenly felt for placing limitations on their acquaintance.

He heard her question yet did not respond immediately. She wore a stylish dress meant for life in the city but without a bustle or a corset—he'd swear she wasn't wearing a corset. Ainslee's demeanor suggested she was more relaxed than the evening before. The deep blue in her gown was picked up by the black-and-blue plaid ribbon on her hatband. The hat was unlike anything he'd seen before. It was practical, like the hats seen every day on most men in the western plains and mountains, except this one boasted a flat crown and wide brim, all made of some kind of hide in black, and definitely made for a woman.

"Where did you get that?"

Her eyes drifted up. "My hat? I had it made for this journey. I went to a great deal of trouble trying to explain to the milliner in Edinburgh what I required."

She tapped the edge. "Is it wrong for here?"

Colton shook his head and grinned. "It's just right. As to breakfast, we can stop at the café. You must be eager to see your family." He watched the flash of doubt and nervousness cross her features. Fine. If she needed to delay or move slower, he would accommodate her. He knew when they arrived at Hawk's Peak, there would be no reason to speak with her again, except in passing.

She jumbled his thoughts and twisted his insides until he didn't know if he wanted to stay away or never leave her side. The feelings were unfamiliar and unwelcome. "How are you feeling this morning?"

"Rested, thank you. Your Doctor Brody's herbs worked well. I thought, perhaps, we could stop in so I may procure more before heading out."

Colton nodded as they walked toward the café. "We can do that."

"I know I am delaying our departure."

He continued to walk deciding to let her talk it out with herself.

"I do want to see Brenna and Ramsey and meet their families."

Colton was inclined to agree with her, though whether she would be unexpected in a good or bad way he was still figuring out.

"It is bad form to arrive without notice, even if my intention to surprise them is good."

Again, he silently agreed.

"You're not going to say anything?"

He ushered her to a table under a constructed shelter that allowed for sitting outdoors during the warmer months. "The pie here is excellent."

"Very well, do not say anything. And pie is not breakfast."

"It is when Tilly bakes it."

A young woman wearing an apron, a bright smile, and an unruly crop of blond curls approached. "Good morning, Mr. Dawson."

"Good morning, Alice." Colton quickly made the introductions. "Miss Ainslee McConnell, this is Tilly's granddaughter, Alice."

"Right nice to meet you, Miss McConnell."

"And you, Alice."

"What'll you all have this morning?"

Ainslee smiled first at Colton and then at the girl. "Do you have cherry pie?"

The girl's smile widened. "Sure do. Fresh from the oven not twenty minutes ago. It's my favorite."

"Wonderful. I will have a slice and some tea. Mint, if you have it."

Colton held his grin in check when he placed an order for cherry pie and black coffee. "Pie isn't breakfast?"

"I did not say I do not like pie."

"Wise."

"I too often think so."

She said the last with a smirk. He liked the way she raised one of her brows whenever she was amused by someone, even herself. Colton thanked Alice when she brought their orders.

"Where did you attend school?"

He shrugged again and drank from the coffee mug. The hot liquid scalded his tongue and heated his throat on the way down. Colton followed it quickly with a bite of pie. As he hoped, Ainslee let the subject go while she ate her pie and sipped her tea. When they had both finished—he long before she—she squared her shoulders and declared herself ready to leave for Hawk's Peak.

"We'll stop off at the Doc's first to get more of the herb he gave you. There'll be brandy or whiskey at the ranch, if it goes down better that way."

The doctor did more than give her the herb. He checked the stitches and redressed the wound while Colton waited outside. When the door opened again, Ainslee held a cloth-wrapped parcel. Doc Brody bid them good day and went back inside.

"Fresh dressings?"

Ainslee nodded.

"Any of the women will be able to help with those. Elizabeth, Brenna and Ramsey's grandmother, has tended the most wounds, other than Eliza, but she's not always at the big house."

"Eliza is Ethan's sister and Ramsey's wife, which would make her a sister-in-law twice over, once through Ramsey and again through Brenna?"

"That's right."

"Tidy."

When they reached the cottage, he helped her into the wagon before going inside for her trunks. One at a time, he hauled them out and hefted them into the back of the wagon. He was somewhat winded by the time he joined her on the wagon bench. "How much of the history—about the family—were you told?"

"Maggie and Ian told me a little. They said it was not all pleasant. I know there is a story surrounding Brenna and Ramsey's grandfather—their   American grandfather."

Colton set the horses in motion and turned them onto the road leading north of town toward the ranch. Hawk's Peak and wilderness were the only destinations this particular road led. The town liked it that way and it suited the Gallagher family, knowing anyone traveling this way was likely headed to their ranch. They liked to see what was coming—good or bad. The unexpected rarely brought good news.

He glanced at Ainslee and reconsidered. Unexpected sometimes brought nice surprises. Deciding to pass the time and appease Ainslee's curiosity, Colton told her the story of the Gallagher's former neighbor. It was a story meant for the family to tell, yet it had become a part of them all. Every family member and ranch hand alike had bled, lost, and fought to keep each other safe.

AINSLEE LISTENED TO every word. It was like one of her stories, though far more tragic.

"Nathan Hunter lived on the ranch bordering Hawk's Peak. His ranch was almost as big as the Gallagher's spread. He's the reason Brenna came out this way."

"Maggie told me that Brenna hired a private detective to find her grandfather."

"That's right. Long before she arrived, Hunter and the Gallaghers were enemies. They lived side by side because the Gallaghers had no proof of misdeeds that could get him run off his land. Without proof, the law wouldn't touch Hunter, and the Gallaghers weren't going to risk their own necks by killing the man outright. Hunter was always very careful."

"Run him off?" Ainslee was familiar with the concept. Many she knew in Scotland had been run off their lands, though she doubted Nathan Hunter deserved similar sympathy.

"People around here take stealing land seriously. You want to run a person off their land, you need proof that will send them to jail or the grave."

"And what did he do?" Ainslee wanted every detail, but she realized then the story was going to be much shorter than she wanted. "You aren't going to tell me."

"Not everything. Some of it is better coming from Brenna or Ramsey. A lot of really bad things happened. We lost a few good men at the ranch and nearly lost Eliza toward the end. Their stories end happily, and that's what matters."

"How did Nathan Hunter die?"

Colton stopped in the middle of the road, climbed down, and rolled a large rock into the tall grass. When he joined her again, he went on as though there had not been an interruption. "Yes, Hunter died, but not by one of our hands."

Ainslee decided she did not want to hear more, at least now, and it was not a topic of conversation one broached under casual conversation. "You love them, don't you?"

He spared her a long glance. "Yes."

Ainslee needed time to think, and she

did her best thinking alone. What brought a man like Colton Dawson to a place like Briarwood? How did he become so engrained with the Gallagher family, to the point where he would lay down his life for them? She could assume it was her imagination that led to such a conclusion, but no, he loved them. He would do anything for them and said as much with his firm, "Yes." She wanted to know more about his journey. What brought him here? Why *this* family? She did not believe herself possessed of the persuasive ability to break through his reticence, but she would find a way.

It was not too much longer before structures took shape in the landscape. Both large and small buildings dotted her vision until they drew closer and those shapes became identifiable. "'Tis a village on its own!"

Colton chuckled beside her. "It

sometimes feels that way. Welcome to Hawk's Peak, Miss McConnell."

"Maggie suspected they were prosperous, but I do not believe she truly understood."

Colton guided the team beneath an impressive entrance arch made of heavy logs, surrounded by stone at the base. The long, sturdy sign beneath was etched with HAWK'S PEAK RANCH. "Prosperity out here usually means a lot of hard work."

"What about the cattle and copper barons I have read about, or are those stories embellished, as well?"

"Robber barons is what a lot of them are called. Some stories are true enough. Men making their fortunes off the hard work of other men. Some put a lot of money into the land only take a lot more out of it."

"You don't approve of mining?"

"I understand why people feel it's necessary, and I know what it can do for progress, but not enough miners respect the land."

"And the Gallaghers have never considered mining?"

"Never," Colton said in a definitive tone.

He grew quiet and they moved closer to the buildings. Ainslee was eager for the ride to end and just as eager for her time with Colton to be extended.

He spoke again, unexpectedly. "The Gallaghers have always worked as hard—sometimes more—than anyone who works for them. They've been a part of every stone that has been placed and every wood plank that has been nailed."

"Surely they can't always be there to—"

"They can, and have. If one is gone, there are two more, but always one of them is present. Ethan, Gabriel, and Eliza take very seriously what their parents envisioned when they first came up from Texas. They consider everything that happens on this land their responsibility."

"The good and bad?"

Colton nodded. "That's how it works."

"Admirable. If they are as you say, I understand why you are so loyal to them."

"It's not the same with your family?"

"My father works hard for he enjoys the challenge of good business. Like many of our acquaintances, our money, lands, and homes were inherited. There is no shame in it, but the fortune was built by others and passed down. The land is worked because it must be to support the estate, but not by us. This—" She swept her hand in front of her. "This is different."

As Colton eased the team and wagon to the front of the house, people appeared, a few from the paddocks, two more from the house. A new story formulated in her mind. She was given no time to adjust when Colton helped her down. Her thoughts remained with the tale she weaved, and it was a gentle nudge on the small of her back that returned her to the present.

She looked up first to the expansive porch on the house, impressive in both size and quality. On the porch stood a petite woman with thick hair the color of night fire draped over her shoulders. Vibrant eyes widened, and recognition was immediate for them both. Brenna's jaw slackened before her mouth spread into a surprised and genuine smile.

"Ainslee!"

She hurried down the steps and embraced her cousin. Ainslee was grateful for the support of Brenna's arms around her, for her cousin's enthusiasm almost knocked her backward against the wagon.

Brenna stepped back and grasped Ainslee's hands. "I never expected such a wonderful surprise. It has been ages, but I would recognize you anywhere. You have the hair of your grandmother's people and the eyes of your mother. How have you come to be here? Does your family know? Och, it has been so long! Goodness, you will want to meet Ramsey." Without slowing down, Brenna shifted Ainslee with ease so she could see Colton. "Did you find her in town?" To Ainslee she said, "We would have come to greet the stage had we known."

"I did not take the stage, cousin, and yes, Mr. Dawson found me. When he learned I was destined for Hawk's Peak, he offered his escort."

Brenna smiled at Colton, "Thank you for bringing her safely to us."

Ainslee met and held Colton's gaze, something they had done often and with ease during their short acquaintance. He would not reveal what happened on the trail, Ainslee thought, at least not yet. His eyes arrested her and without fail, suggested he could see through into the confusing depth of her thoughts. The connection this time was brief while she wanted it lengthened. Colton broke it first, said something about bringing her trunks inside, and turned away from her.

Another man, tall—a few inches over Colton—with thick, dark hair and startlingly deep-blue eyes, strode across the distance between a barn and where they stood. From the newly-formed smile on Brenna's lips, Ainslee guessed she was about to meet Ethan Gallagher.

"ETHAN, WE NEED to talk."

"Do I need to be worried?"

"Not right now."

Ethan dismounted and led his horse into the barn to remove the saddle and brush down the animal. Their new stable boy was still wary of Ethan's stallion, and the animal responded best to Ethan's ministrations. He nodded, unstrapped the saddle, and removed the rigging and blanket from the horse's back before giving his attention to Colton.

"Is it Ainslee?"

Colton should not have been surprised at Ethan's perception, for he was not the first to have remarked on the glances Colton gave Ainslee when they first arrived. The behavior had gone unnoticed by himself. In fact, he thought he had done well by guarding everything Ainslee churned in him. He'd been wrong.

The day had passed and evening arrived. No one had approached him about the events on the trail, which meant Ainslee had remained silent about her ordeal.

"Yes, in a way it is about her. It's about what happened on her travels from Bozeman."

Ethan nodded and brushed smooth

strokes over his horse's back. "She told us the man she hired had died and about you finding her. I'm glad you said something because I haven't had a chance to thank you yet, for bringing her safely to the ranch."

"What else did Ainslee tell you?"

Ethan stopped stroking. "From your tone, I'm guessing not everything."

Of course, knowing her already as he did, Colton suspected she would not be forthcoming about what happened on the trail.

It took only five minutes to relay the condensed version of events to Ethan. When Colton had finished, Ethan contemplated the report and guided his horse into his stall, removing the lead from around his neck. After checking the feed and water, Ethan closed the door and leaned against the stall. "I owe you a hell of a lot more than a thank you. We all do.

She hasn't told Brenna because my wife would have said something to me if she had."

"I figure she doesn't want anyone fussing over her. When Brenna didn't mention—"

Ethan held up a hand. "I get it. I've learned the Scottish are a stubborn breed, at least, the one under my roof. Ramsey has proven himself as obstinate as his sister at times. Must be in the blood."

"And here I always figured it was a Gallagher trait."

Ethan chuckled. "You're probably right. This is a hell of a thing, Colton. If anyone else would have come along to find her . . . No, I won't even think it. You're sure Brody said she was all right?"

In his abridged version of the retelling, Colton left out the part about him becoming intimate with parts of Ainslee's body in the course of treating the wound.

He hadn't said, but knew Ethan could hear what wasn't said.

"I'm sure. The wound wasn't too deep and it doesn't appear to have affected her movements, which is likely why no one noticed. But she isn't the only reason I'm telling you this."

"The man you killed?"

"I can't imagine a situation where a woman could see that and not come out the worse for it. She appears a mite too agreeable, considering. Then there's the other body."

"The one you found in the woods?"

Colton nodded. "I can't think of a reason why he would have been killed and butchered that way unless someone either wanted to make it hard to identify the body or they enjoyed it. Seeing as how Ainslee's bag was left behind, I'm thinking the latter."

"And you don't think it was this Virgil?"

"I don't. He in a roundabout way claimed it was him, but it's hard to believe him capable. The way the body was cut, there was precise method to it. Virgil was volatile, not orderly."

"Which means this is about a lot more than rustling."

Colton shrugged. "I'm not saying that."

Together he and Ethan walked to the barn doors, closing them when they stepped outside. A half-moon shined above them, the evening meal a few hours past. It was habit for Ethan to ride most nights before he retired. Colton had been unable to convince himself he was tired enough to sleep. Instead, he had waited for Ethan to return, content until then to listen to the other ranch hands play cards inside the bunkhouse.

"Could be rustlers and there's one among them who gives no hesitation to killing. I won't know until I ride out, try to find him."

"There's been no loss of cattle since you took those two men to jail."

"I can't explain it, Ethan, but I know it's not over."

Ethan moved his eyes to follow the outline of the landscape. "A lot of blood has been spilled on this land. Too much. I suppose I hoped we had seen the end of it. There's a lot more to lose now."

Colton understood he meant the people, not the roofs and walls that housed them. "There always is when people you love are involved. I'll be three, maybe four days. If I don't find anything, I'll come back and let it go."

Ethan leaned against one of the corrals, resting his arms on the top beam. "We're good at what we do. I'd be hard pressed to find a group of men and women better with cattle and horses than those on this ranch."

Colton agreed, though said nothing.

"But there is no one I have ever met who knows these mountains and valleys like you do. I've seen you track people into places that befuddles the mind, but you do it." Ethan turned to Colton. "If you say there's something we're not seeing, I trust you to do whatever you feel is needed."

"I'll leave day after next."

Ethan nodded. "Not alone this time." They remained standing near the corral in silence while the night sky darkened and the air shifted, grew heavier.

"There's been nothing I can't handle alone. The rest of the men are needed here."

"We don't often pull rank around here, Colton, but this is getting more dangerous. If this outfit is bigger than we thought, no one should be riding alone right now, at least not beyond where one of the houses can be seen."

"You're right. I'll take one of the men with me."

Ethan did not agree, just asked, "Are you going to tell Ainslee you've told me?"

"Maybe. Probably. Eventually."

Ethan said, "Usually takes a woman to twist up a man's thinking that much."

Colton refrained from comment, drawing a chuckle out of Ethan.

"I'll tell Ramsey about what happened, but I don't think Brenna needs to hear it yet. It would be a shame to spoil the reunion with worry. She'll give me hell for it when she does find out. Ainslee must have her reasons for not saying anything."

Colton believed Ainslee had reasons for doing a lot of things. "You know why I told you?"

Ethan exhaled, slow and deep. "I can guess."

9

"YOU'VE BUILT AN amazing life for yourself, Brenna, here in this wilderness." Ainslee stood next to her cousin on the porch at the back of the house, where the view opened up to pastureland that stretched for miles. Mountains, unlike any she had seen until coming west, jutted above the earth, their peaks glistening in the afternoon light.

"I never imagined myself staying in Montana." Brenna glanced her way with a smile on her lips, the kind of smile only women understood. "Until I met Ethan."

Ainslee had been impressed with Brenna's husband, and her brother-in-law, Gabriel, and his wife, Isabelle. She'd met Brenna and Ethan's son, Jacob, and the Gallaghers' adopted daughter, Catie, who they found last Christmas sleeping in one of their line shacks. Andrew, younger brother to Isabelle and now Gabriel, had swept in with young Jacob on his heels to say hello before they were scooted off with Amanda, Ben Stuart's new bride. She had yet to meet the foreman, for he was with Ramsey and Eliza in Helena, and not expected to return until the following day.

"You and Ethan certainly know how to make beautiful babies." Ainslee winked at her cousin. Jacob looked so much like Ethan, and their baby, little Rebecca Victoria, already mirrored her mother in appearance. Isabelle and Gabriel's first baby, August, bore the fair hair of his mother and the captivating blue eyes of the Gallaghers.

Her introduction to so many wonderful

new people had been idyllic. And with the exception of a few stretches of time when Ainslee was focused on remembering names and cooing at the babies, her thoughts often drifted to Colton. She wondered what had occupied his attention in the hours since their arrival.

"It is so wonderful to have you here."

Ainslee turned her focus back to Brenna when her cousin clasped her hand. "I did not imagine it would look like this." She closed her eyes and inhaled the sweet fragrance of grass and alfalfa with the woodsy scent of pine. "The air is so different here. Lighter." When she opened her eyes again, they settled on a patch of color to the east. "Is that heather?"

Brenna smiled and nodded. "Ethan went to a great deal of trouble to have it brought over. He surprised me on my last birthday with the cuttings, carefully cultivated by Maggie and Ian from Cameron Manor, and brought here. A few of the plants did not make it, but there were enough. We put them far enough away from the pastures so they can grow wild like they do at home."

Ainslee's heart fluttered at the thought of home. Already the internal conflict between returning or staying began a battle in her mind. "Do you miss Scotland?"

"Always." Brenna lifted herself enough to sit on the porch railing. One of the famed hawks, often seen soaring above or diving toward the land, flew and circled back around. "I accepted long ago that my heart belongs to two places—at Hawk's Peak and in the Highlands."

"Maggie said that you have only returned once."

Brenna nodded. "When I was carrying Jacob. Ethan and I had planned to return with Ramsey and Eliza, but then I learned

I was with child again. I want Jacob and Rebecca to know both worlds."

Ainslee had not imagined leaving Scotland forever and wondered if she would be as strong as Brenna, should she ever have to make the same choice. "And your grandmother?"

"Elizabeth has been staying with an expectant mother, Betty Wittier, on a farm south of town until Betty's sister returns, though I expect her back soon. Betty's husband is laid up with an injured shoulder right now. Elizabeth will be thrilled to meet you, and so will Ramsey and Eliza."

"You all come together and look after each other."

"Of course."

"Like home," they said in unison and mirrored their smiles.

"Where are your parents now? The island or on the borders?"

Ainslee jerked when she heard a horse bray the other side of the house. She gripped one of the posts and shook her head. "It's so quiet," and then suddenly . . . "you've a beautiful home." The last came out as a murmur before Ainslee answered Brenna's question. "Mama and Papa are in Innerleithen for another week or two, then they will return to the island." Since Ainslee was a child, their family had spent summers on the Scottish Borders visiting her father's family, and the rest of the year on the Isle of Lewis in the Outer Hebrides.

"I always wanted to see your island home. My mother spoke of it fondly, remembering the times she spent there in her youth."

Ainslee had always wondered why Brenna had not left home more often. Unlike her own parents, who had given her more freedom than most young women of their age, Brenna's parents had sheltered their daughter. "I was so sorry to hear of your parents, and even more that they were buried before news reached us."

A tear slipped down Brenna's cheek. "The burials were quiet, just as they would have preferred. 'Twas Maggie who sent word to family each time."

Regretful that she had brought a shroud of gloom to their conversation, she decided a distraction was needed. "What do you know of Colton?"

Brenna's evident surprise brought a rush of heat to Ainslee's face. It had worked, though, to draw Brenna out of the momentary melancholy. "In what way?"

"Well, he's educated, though he did not mention from where."

"What an odd question. I never asked him."

"You're not close to him?"

Brenna laughed, a full laugh that brightened everything about her visage.

"Oh yes, we're all quite close around here. I remember as a girl you liked stories. Well, I've amassed a number of stories since I arrived here, and Colton—all of them—play roles. Not all of the tales are good, but they have certainly colored my life. On an occasion when I was kidnapped—"

"Kidnapped!"

"Yes, by my grandfather's men," Brenna spoke with a calm voice, "Ethan, Gabriel, Colton, Ben, and the others set out to make sure I returned safely. There have been many similar instances."

"With you being kidnapped?"

"Well, no, but other events. As I said, not all of the stories are good, but each one brought us closer together. They are my family, as much as my own parents ever were. There is not a person on this ranch who would not give their life for one of us."

Ainslee expected there would be grand

adventures in America's great western plains and mountains, but this she had not anticipated. "Your grandfather was Nathan Hunter."

Brenna blew out a long breath. "Colton was uncharacteristically talkative with you."

"We had some time to pass." Not as much as I would have liked, Ainslee thought. "Do you mind?"

"Heavens, no. It is just unusual for Colton to share so much. He is not often one for conversation." Brenna once more grasped her hands, giving them a gentle squeeze. "You are bound to hear a great deal more about my grandfather and his unfortunate past while you are here. I am not ashamed of where I come from, but I am ashamed of him. Ramsey carries a greater burden, having known our grandfather longer, lived with him. Sometimes I think much of what Ramsey has done with his life has been to make up for Nathan Hunter's wrongdoings."

"He took the Cameron name."

"Yes, he did. Eliza did as well, though she and everyone else still call her Gallagher. It is a legacy, that name, and a proud one. Ramsey did not want her to lose it."

"Cameron is also a proud name."

Brenna grinned. "That is what Eliza says."

Ainslee wanted to ask more about everything, including Nathan Hunter and Ramsey's time with him but stopped herself because she wasn't entirely sure of her own motives. Did she want to know more because it gave her the kind of vibrancy she liked to include in her books? Or, did she want to know in order to better understand Brenna and Ramsey's life here? She wished it was exclusively the latter, and yet she did not believe herself so selfless and noble.

"I look forward to meeting Ramsey and Eliza." She grinned. "And Ben, and any others in your new family."

"Not a *new* family," Brenna corrected. "My existing family simply grew."

"Quite a lot!"

Brenna agreed. "What brought you here, really?"

Ainslee's moment of truth. The question she hoped would not be asked, even though she had already shared some of it with Colton. Somehow sharing with him had been easier than admitting her flight-of-fancy to Brenna. She opted for an abbreviated version She was talented at spinning partial truths. "I wanted an adventure, to escape the society parties my mother so enjoys. I longed to learn more about this untamed West I have read so much about, and since you were here in Montana, I knew it would be a chance to see you and meet Ramsey. It's odd to think of how I did not know about him, even stranger for you, being your twin brother. 'Twas a shock to hear of him from Maggie."

"He was a tremendous surprise. I was thrilled when he and Eliza married because I knew I could keep him close always. We had missed so many years together. I am only sorry he did not have a chance to meet our parents." Brenna added, "I should have been the one to tell you about Ramsey and about leaving Scotland. After Papa died, I lost focus on everything except finding the truth about my grandparents and my brother. I wrote to Maggie, but I should have written to you. We promised each other—"

"None of that, now. It does not matter when or how; I am here now." Ainslee feared the mood was turning melancholy again, and she refused to allow it. The afternoon was glorious and she had monopolized Brenna's time since her appearance only that morning. "I hope my unexpected arrival is not too inconvenient."

Brenna waved a hand in the air as though to ward off Ainslee's worry. "It is blessed, not inconvenient. I have selfishly stolen you away when I know the others would like more time to visit. The children especially love guests. Jacob, Catie, and Andrew will badger you endlessly for tales of home."

"I came with plenty to share." Ainslee moved her eyes to sweep over the landscape once more. "Already I have imprinted this spectacular beauty to memory."

"It is spectacular always, though I will admit the winters are harsher than we are used to in Scotland. Even your island winters with their dark skies and soft gales are pleasantly mild compared to the months of deep snow and frigid cold in these mountains."

Ainslee did not think she would mind at all. "Perhaps I will see it." After almost a minute of silence, Ainslee looked at Brenna, noticing her bemused expression. "What is it?"

"You are not telling me everything about why you have come. And now you may stay to see winter when it is only August, months from now." Brenna stepped closer. "Is all well at home?"

"Home is wonderful as it has always been." There was the problem. Always the same. No matter how glorious and privileged her life, Ainslee had needed more, which is what led her to Finn Pickett and his grand adventures. If her journey thus far had taught her anything, it was that *writing* the adventures was no longer enough. She wanted to *live* them.

"Brenna?"

They both turned at the call of Brenna's name through the open window next to the back door. Amanda stood in the threshold with baby Rebecca in her arms. "She's wanting her mama."

Brenna held out her arms and the burst of sparkle that shot through her eyes could only be described as love. In that second, Ainslee felt a brief, though powerful, flare of envy. Unaccustomed to the emotion, Ainslee merely nodded when Brenna excused herself to feed her daughter.

Amanda remained in the doorway, arms at her sides, her head swaying gently to one side like someone viewing the world from another angle. She crossed the wide porch to where Ainslee stood.

"We were introduced briefly before the young gentlemen had to be taken away to baths."

Ainslee remembered Andrew and Jacob,

covered to their knees in mud and who knows what else. "You all have your hands full. With those two, especially."

Amanda smiled in agreement. "Catie is a big help when she's here. She has been spending more and more time with Eliza and the horses. She loves those animals. It's hard to believe she's only been with us since last Christmas."

"Brenna tells me you have recently joined the family as well."

"I came here originally to help with the house. I needed a place to . . . find myself again. The Gallaghers gave me that. I met Ben Stuart and fought what I felt for him, until one day everything made sense. We married last month." Amanda's cheeks brightened to a deep rosy hue. "My goodness, I haven't said that aloud before, about fighting my feelings, at least never to someone—"

"You just met?" Ainslee winked at the

woman she now considered a friend. How quickly she opened herself to these people. "Your secret is safe, though I daresay your husband already knows."

"True enough." Amanda leaned against one of the posts and sighed. "I still cannot believe this is my home."

"Do you live in the house?"

Amanda shook her head and turned toward the door when voices drifted through. "Only when Ben is away. We have a cabin not far. We'll build onto it when . . . well, when we're ready to start a family of our own."

Another pang of envy speared through Ainslee's heart and every sensitive nerve in her mind shifted to think of Colton. "'Tis a beautiful place to call home."

"It is." Amanda murmured her agreement. A clatter sounded from the kitchen on the other side of the open door.

"I'd better go and see what's happened

in there. Catie is alone in the kitchen, and some of the heavier pots are too much for her to put away. Brenna won't be long, if you'd like to—"

A second clatter echoed beyond the walls. Amanda cast an apologetic glance toward Ainslee before hurrying inside.

"And life goes on," Ainslee murmured, though it brought a fresh smile to her face to be in the midst of such a warm, chaotic, and loving group of people. She heard a few quiet voices until they faded, and she opted not to follow Amanda into the house.

Ainslee longed to remain in the fresh air and to walk. Puffy white clouds dotted the vast blue sky, making an inviting canvas for the sun's rays to spread over the land. Hawk's Peak Ranch covered an impressive amount of land, and she doubted even a year would be enough time to fully explore every meadow, wood, and hidden place.

Used to answering to no one when the mood struck, Ainslee stepped off the porch and onto the grass. She did not bother returning to the comfortable guest room for her hat or plaid. The mountain nights cooled, as she had discovered when camping with Colton, but the day was vibrant with warmth. She wanted it to seep through her clothes into her skin.

The sun shined gloriously bright some days on her home island, glassy on the sea's surface, but this drier sun caressed her skin in a way she had never before experienced. Her legs carried her across the meadow to where Brenna's heather had caught root and flourished. What must it be like for a man to love a woman so much that he would find a way to bring Highland heather all the way to Montana.

She had never witnessed such a thing. Her parents certainly adored each other and were good friends, but nothing like the love as deep as she saw in Ethan and Brenna's eyes or what she saw flash between Gabriel and Isabelle when first introduced to them. It was as if they could not be within sight of each other and not let their feelings show.

A new story churned as she bent to pick a sprig of purple heather from the largest shrub. Ainslee held it between her fingers while she walked and with each step came closer to losing herself in the words brewing in her imagination. She had always been most comfortable in her own company, where the lives of her characters and stories burned bright and true.

She cast her glance to a far pasture dotted with cattle, no doubt taking advantage of good grass. Ainslee imagined the winter Brenna had described and thought how much more precious it made long summer days like this one. Everywhere she gazed, evidence of industry and hard work had been put to good use, all the while preserving the land's natural beauty.

Her wanderings took her to a stream with a healthy flow of crystalline water. Deep and clear, the water bed flourished with rocks of all shapes and sizes, and she wondered if any fish made their homes amongst the hidden depths. A footbridge spanned a wide area of the water, and though curious about what she might find on the other side, a large boulder with a smooth surface tempted her to sit.

Ainslee had told Colton that she came here in part to see her cousins but mostly for herself. As Amanda said earlier, she needed to find herself again, and it was the same for Ainslee. Careful not to stretch her back and open her wound, she found purchase on the boulder's surface and tucked her feet beneath her skirts with her arms resting on her knees.

She breathed deeply once, twice, and a third time, until every muscle in her body relaxed and her mind cleared. She watched a butterfly dance above the water, and with the quiet of the mountains as her companion, Ainslee wrote a story in her mind.

10

COLTON WIPED SWEAT from his
brow and rubbed an open hand gently
over the neck of the two-year-old mare he
had finished working with in the corral.
He'd been the third hand to try and tame
the spirited animal until they all decided
leaving a bit of temperament was better
for the horse.

The dapple gray would make a fine
workhorse or breeder, Colton thought. A
beautiful creature with alert eyes and a
wild spirit, just as nature intended. He led
the mare to another paddock where she
would be cooled and groomed by Archie
Bligh, the skinny, young man from town

who was apprenticing at the ranch when his father didn't need him at their small farm. Archie beamed his crooked smile, accentuating the freckles—much brighter and larger than Ainslee's—dotted across his face. The kid enjoyed being at the ranch and worked hard.

After Colton left the mare in Archie's care, he glanced back once more at the sleek lines of the animal. When he returned to the ranch with Ainslee and saw the mare in the corral, he immediately had gone to work. The others gave him curious looks, but no one said anything. He needed something to steer his thoughts away from the newest guest at Hawk's Peak. It had worked for a short while.

Colton had seen Ainslee cross the north pasture an hour ago. She was impossible to miss walking through the taller grass, the cattle far enough in the distance not to be a concern. It would be another month before they brought the rest of the cattle down from the higher pastures. She strolled without hat or wrap, and her bright red locks, pulled up and away from her face and neck, shined beneath the sun. He had turned away before lifting himself onto the mare once again and continued working. Now that riding no longer held his attention, his thoughts drifted once more to Ainslee.

"Pete." Colton gained the attention of one of the ranch hands coming from the barn. "How are the fence lines?"

Pete removed his hat and swiped a forearm across his brow. "East and south are good. My horse threw a shoe and I ended up walking back. I'll get him fixed up and head back out."

Colton glanced toward the direction Ainslee had walked. "I'll finish riding the lines. I want to check on Ramsey and

Eliza's place."

"I saw Ethan and Connor head that way after you and Miss McConnell arrived."

It would be easy enough to pull Ethan away from the other ranch hand for a few minutes. "Good. I need to speak with Ethan. Take care of your horse and get some food. You missed the noon meal at the house earlier." So had Colton. The women at the big house prepared the midday meal for the men during the summer months, when food was easily eaten on outdoor tables, the expansive porch, or even an old stump. Colton had worked through the noon meal and decided satisfying one hunger could wait until supper.

He saddled his horse and swung up on the back of the tall chestnut gelding. Brenna, stepping down from the front porch and walking toward him, temporarily delayed his departure. He grabbed his hat from a fence post but left his jacket behind. Colton closed the distance between them.

"Brenna." He and the other ranch hands had tried to remain formal with the Gallagher women, but after everything they had all been through together over the years, the women insisted they be addressed by their given names. After all, they were family.

"Colton." She indicated he should stay on the horse when he would have dismounted. "Have you perhaps seen my cousin? Amanda thought she came upstairs to sit with me and the baby, but she is not in the house."

"I saw her walking earlier and was headed out now to find her." Colton did not talk a lot or share a lot, but when he did speak, he saw no point in avoiding the truth.

"Oh." Brenna glanced beyond him, using

a hand to shield her face from the sun and not sounding the least bit worried. "She always was one for spending time alone." She appeared to Colton as though she wanted to say more. Instead, she smiled up at him. "Thank you. I am sure she is enjoying the fresh air."

The odd interchange with Brenna left him with more questions about Ainslee, who already befuddled him.

It took Colton only ten minutes to locate Ainslee, and when he saw her, lying on the smooth boulder, her hair fallen from its pins and an arm dangling over the side of the rock, he stopped his horse and stared.

Colton recalled a conversation he once had, the night after Ethan first lost Brenna to his own stubbornness. She had returned to Scotland and Colton found Ethan walking through one of the fields, dusted with an early autumn snow. They stood together in the field, watching the moon rise higher above the snow-capped peaks, illuminating the vast ranch. It had been Gabriel who ultimately pushed Ethan out of his brother's misery and back on the right path to Brenna, but Colton never forgot what Ethan said that night.

"There is no greater mistake a man can make than deny his love for the only woman who was meant to have his heart."

Colton never told anyone of that conversation or of the deep pain he had witnessed in Ethan's eyes. Years later, Ethan and Brenna had brought two beautiful children into their family and were happier than Colton had ever seen two people, unless he also considered all the other couples at Hawk's Peak. He thought it might be only the Gallaghers who were destined for great bliss, until he watched Ben and Amanda exchange vows on a cool summer morning at the small church in Briarwood last month.

He did not spend a lot of his thoughts wondering if their joy would one day be his own. Content to track and hunt, work cattle and soothe horses, Colton had everything he ever believed he wanted. Now Ainslee's presence conflicted his simple life, and he found himself without complaint as he watched her shift and heard a soft sigh escape her lips.

Colton's well-trained horse, used to sneaking up on game and men alike, remained silent, swishing only his tail. Less than one minute later, despite the quiet, Ainslee stirred atop her boulder. It was she who shifted and saw him through sleepy eyes. The slow smile she offered him showed no surprise at his presence.

"How long have you been there?" She covered a yawn with her hand and straightened her skirts.

"Not long." Colton dismounted and let his horse graze on the tall grass by the water. "Brenna wondered where you went."

Ainslee's gaze shot upward to look at the sun's placement in the sky. "I was gone longer than I planned. I wanted to stretch my legs and see more of this beautiful place."

"Brenna didn't mind. She said something about you spending a lot of time on your own." Colton watched a bit of color rush into her fair cheeks. "From what you told me, it sounded like you were around a lot of people, at home and at university."

Ainslee shrugged and met his gaze. "Would you mind? Climbing on rocks is always much easier than climbing off while wearing skirts."

Colton didn't mind at all. He slid one arm around the back of her waist and rested the other at her front. Without much effort, he lifted her off the rock and let her slide slowly to the ground. She lingered a few seconds. They did not look at each other, but the connection between them was still as strong as it had been on the trail from Bozeman to Briarwood.

He wanted to remain indifferent, and for a man unaccustomed to great emotion, going against his natural instincts proved to be easier than expected. Colton knew one day, probably soon, Ainslee would return home to Scotland or continue her travels. He did not see her as someone eager to settle down in one place, and he was not a man to leave the only land he ever wanted to call home.

What a fool he'd been to think he could remain uninvolved. Until their paths diverged, Colton would enjoy being close to her, stealing moments like this one, and learning what he could to keep the memories close. He chided himself for having thoughts so foreign to him. Did

Ainslee not mention escaping marriages and introductions to men her mother thought would make good husbands? Colton saw a woman who went where the winds blew, and now that she was free, she could go wherever her heart and adventurous spirit carried her.

Ainslee moved away, her smile brighter like her alert eyes. "I was often surrounded by people, but I found ways to escape the crowds. Brenna and I did not see a lot of each other except when we visited, and not at all after her mother died. Her father, I was told, retreated into himself, and lived only for his daughter. My own mother claimed it was too difficult to return to the place where her cousin had passed away. They had been quite close."

A young buck crossing the empty pasture invited their attention long enough for Colton to think Ainslee did not plan to say anything more. To his pleasure, she did. "I wrote to Brenna, though, a few times when I needed to talk to someone who understood solitude. We made a promise to write often. The difference between Brenna and me is that while I wanted to be far away from people, she wanted to be around them more. Her life had been sheltered and mine had consisted of balls and travels to Edinburgh and London, even Ireland once. She understood me."

Another layer of Ainslee McConnell unveiled, and Colton wondered how much she would share before leaving Montana.

AINSLEE SMOOTHED A hand over the thick mane of Colton's horse to give herself something to do rather than look at the man who at every meeting pushed her senses out of kilter.

Everywhere she looked, she compared

where she now stood to home. The mountains here were certainly grander than anything ever seen in her beloved Scotland, rising so high she wondered if man might ever reach the top. The mountains here were not as green as her Highlands or the woods as mysterious. Here, the air did not hold the rain or fragrance of the sea in its grasp, yet she found the warm dry breeze comfortable against her skin.

Heather did not blanket the landscape—except for Brenna's small touch of it near the house—but the rich grass swaying in the breeze and shrubs of wild berries offered as much beauty. From the minute she had disembarked from the ship that brought her to America, she had gazed upon crowded cities, open prairies, and lush hills, but none compared to these mountains and meadows.

Much like the man who stood nearby,

patient while she stood in quiet contemplation, the landscape rarely changed, yet beneath the surface awaited curiosities to discover. As always, it did not take long for her imagination to overpower sense. Colton was the perfect story hero: unyielding of secrets until the heroine unearths them. Ainslee did not see herself as the heroine of the new adventure she had penned last night before her body begged for sleep. Except, she had been unable to create a woman worthy enough for the hero.

"I should return to the house. After all, I am here to spend time with my cousins."

"Ramsey and Eliza will be back this evening. They will likely come to the main house before going home."

"I look forward to meeting them."

"Do you?"

"Of course!" She realized her voice did not hold excitement, but Colton did not know her lack of enthusiasm had nothing to do with meeting Ramsey. "I truly look forward to meeting Ramsey. I wondered about him often on the journey here. It is still odd to me that Brenna should have a twin brother. Maggie told me of how Ramsey was taken from Scotland by their grandfather. This Nathan Hunter sounds more suited to the ground, where he cannot hurt anyone again."

"It was a long time ago." Colton spoke the words softly.

Ainslee stepped closer to him, unsure if she heard correctly. "No matter how long ago, I cannot imagine Ramsey or Brenna ever forgiving their grandfather."

"He's gone, Ainslee."

When her eyes met his again, she saw the unspoken question in the way he looked at her. "If they have moved on, then there is no reason why I, who never knew the man, should care." But she did care.

She cared deeply because betrayal affected everyone in a family, even those far away when it happened. The treachery and actions of Nathan Hunter would have caused a scandal back home in Scotland, even in the Highlands. Justified or not, Brenna may not have escaped the shame.

Here, people moved on with their lives, never forgetting, but neither allowing another's disgrace to shape their future. She marveled at how two places in the same time could be so different. This raw and beautiful world had spared Brenna and Ramsey. Before she had left, Ainslee's mother told her it might take a place as unpredictable and untamed as the Americas to bridle Ainslee's enthusiasm. Her mother expected her to return one day soon to take up her place in their society.

But is that what she wanted? No place could ever temper her resolve to seek the wonders of life. Not when all around her she saw opportunity for adventure.

Her mother often referred to her as a woman whose spirit roamed free, though Constance McConnell never sounded pleased when saying it. Ainslee believed herself unshackled from a single event that had altered the course of her thinking toward marriage.

Why then did Colton bring the rush of memories to the forefront? "I must return now. Thank you for coming upon me or I might have slept the remainder of the afternoon."

"Ainslee, wait."

She turned around.

Colton stepped forward, shortening the distance between them to less than two feet. "I told Ethan about what happened on the trail."

She remained quiet for several heartbeats. "I see. Was he angry?"

"Of course not. Why would you ask

that?"

"My father would have been angry. Not at me but because of what happened. My mother would have used it as justification to keep me from continuing my adventures on my own."

"You're an adult. What you do is up to you."

Ainslee's lips lifted into a half smile. "Yes, I am, and I had a great deal of freedom growing up, but it did not stop my mother from worrying. She never found a reason for my father to side with her because I never gave her one."

Colton grinned. "These sorts of things happened to you a lot?"

"Not too often."

"You're not in Scotland. Here, your choices are your own. Whom you confide in is up to you. I didn't tell Ethan what happened to go against you. I told him because what happens to anyone on this ranch or in our town, happens to the whole family. While you're here, you are his responsibility—"

"But that—"

"And the responsibility of every adult here."

She appeared to consider. "Like a tribe or clan?"

"Something like that."

Ainslee took one step closer to him. "Will he tell Brenna?"

"No, but he'll tell Ramsey. You should tell Brenna."

"Ethan hasn't said anything to me yet."

"He probably won't. He tends to let people keep their own counsel until they're ready to talk." Colton petted his horse when the animal nudged his shoulder.

"Did you tell him everything?"

Colton did not insult them both by asking what she meant by *everything*. He still saw in his mind the way her skin glowed in firelight, how silky her hair felt between his fingers when he brushed it out of the way. His only regret was he had not kissed her that first night. He wanted to then and still did now.

"I gave him the shortened version."

She accepted him at his word with a single nod. "Thank you for telling me."

"Ainslee."

She half turned and peered at him over her shoulder.

"You make your own choices here."

Bemused, she nodded. "And I will."

"If you were to choose to do anything right now, what would it be? Don't think about anyone's approval, just about what *you* want."

She blinked and faced him. "No one has ever asked me that." Every choice she made, she considered how far she could push herself before someone disapproved.

Considering her mother's constant disapproval, she had pushed too far often. "Anything?"

Colton's smile promised her that whatever she wanted, he would make it happen. "Anything."

She laughed and shook her head. "I want to ride with wild horses." Surely, he could not make that happen, she thought.

"How's your wound?"

"Much better. It's almost closed. Brenna said Elizabeth can take the stitches out as soon as she returns to the ranch, if I don't want to go into town to have Doctor Brody take care of it."

Colton climbed onto his horse and led the animal over to stand next to the boulder. He motioned Ainslee over and held out his hand for her to take. Curious, Ainslee accepted and climbed first onto the rock. His grip did not slacken. She slipped her foot into the empty stirrup, and with Colton's help found a comfortable position behind him.

"Hold on."

They rode away from the ranch, away from the stream and people. They glided together with the horse's movements, all three moving as one over the expanse of meadow that took them farther from the house. Soon they were as alone as two people could possibly ever be. "Where are we?"

"You'll see."

Paradise, Ainslee thought, right before they started down a cliff. "You are not . . . you are!" She gripped his waist tighter. "We'll go over the edge."

His hand covered hers. "Trust me and keep your eyes open. It's worth it."

Ainslee breathed deeply a few times and did as he said. When the ground below stopped moving and her stomach relaxed, she looked beyond the narrow mountain trail. An immense river of crystalline water snaked through the valley below. Peaks jutted up behind swathes of green and a pine forest so thick no light could possibly shine through. The landscape left her speechless.

Colton guided the horse safely to the base of the trail. What she had missed before now lay in front of her.

"My imagination could not have conjured this."

"You put a lot of faith in your imagination."

"'Tis a good one."

Colton chuckled and held out his arm, asked her to grab hold. She did and gasped when he brought her around to sit in front of him. She wanted to know how he managed it. When he settled her in front, her back to his front and one leg hanging over on either side of the saddle, he said, "Do you trust me?"

Ainslee did not know exactly what he had planned nor did she care. "Yes."

"How is your back?"

"It doesna pain me."

"Good. Stay close."

By close, Ainslee realized he meant pressed close to his body, secure in his embrace.

"Watch them. Watch for the one there in the center."

"'Tis a mare."

Colton smiled. "Would it surprise you to learn that more often a female leads the herd?"

The other horses must have heard them or caught their scent, for many looked up. The one Colton spoke of, a beautiful creature of dark brown with flowing black mane, reared up and neighed. When her forelegs touched the ground, she snorted and bounded. In a motion that could only be described as a dance, the small herd moved as one and followed their leader.

Colton joined them, staying far enough back so as not to mingle with the herd but close enough so Ainslee could feel the heat from the horses' bodies as the wind blew across her face. She opened her arms and splayed them wide. The remaining locks of her hair unwound from their pins to be swept over her shoulders.

She loosened her chest and freed the uninhibited joy. Colton had given her wild horses.

11

AN HOUR LATER, they returned to the rock where Colton had found her. She had bound her locks with the few pins still lodged in her hair and smoothed her dress, but no amount of preening would erase the tangles in her hair or remove the red hue in her cheeks brought on by laughter and wind.

Colton dismounted first and lifted her down.

"Why did you bring me back here instead of taking me to the house?"

"Because out here, no one can see me do this." He eased her close, giving her a chance to refuse. She did not. Colton lowered his mouth and she lifted hers in an exquisite melding that enhanced the lingering thrill from their ride. A few minutes later, when he moved carefully away from her, Ainslee touched a finger to her lips.

"I wondered."

Colton cleared his throat. "Now you know."

She opened her mouth to speak and he kissed her again. A quick meeting of lips meant to silence.

"Don't thank me."

She smirked. "How did you know I would?"

Instead of answering her, he kissed her a final time, stepped back, and waited by his horse for her to decide what came next. *Her* choice. The impact of what he was giving her tugged at a primal corner of her heart. She was the mistress of her own life—no master. She liked that. Ainslee said to him, "You let me choose."

"It's always your choice."

"Remember that next time." She smirked. "A walk will do me good." She left him to wonder over her parting words. When Ainslee turned to leave, he did not call her back.

She needed to be alone. Brenna was right, she was more often than not alone, and preferred it; at least, she thought she did. Colton muddled every rational thought in her mind. Ainslee still tasted him on her lips.

She hurried across the grassy pasture, ignoring the friction of her skirts against the grass. Her beautiful leather boots, now scuffed and dusty, carried her from grass to dirt as she passed from the field to the trodden area near the corrals.

Ainslee picked up her pace when she saw Brenna on the front porch with an older woman. Brenna appeared relaxed and both women offered smiles when she approached.

"I am sorry, Brenna, for staying away so long. It is a glorious place you have chosen and I found myself lost in it."

Ainslee noticed how Brenna saw beyond the flowery words, however genuinely meant, but still agreed. "It is beautiful. There is still much to see." One of her fine brows raised a fraction as she studied Ainslee, from her dusty boots to windswept hair. Blessedly, she did not comment. "First, I want to introduce my grandmother, Elizabeth."

Brenna had confided how Elizabeth had given up the Hunter name, much like Ramsey had, and preferred to be called only Elizabeth or Grandmother.

Ainslee stepped forward in what felt like a natural move and embraced Elizabeth, leaving her with a quick kiss on her cheek. "Brenna speaks of you with great affection. I am glad you found each other again."

Elizabeth's eyes grew misty. "We have indeed been blessed. And it was Brenna who found me, with Ethan's help. I thank God every day for her stubbornness and his." The women wrapped their arms around each other. "Brenna mentioned your injury. Does it pain you?"

Ainslee thought of her recent exertions. "I believe it is healing quickly. It was not too deep, but the stitches are becoming a bit bothersome."

Elizabeth nodded. "That's a good sign. If you'll allow me, I can take a look and remove them tonight. We have had a good many injuries on this ranch."

"Brenna said you have tended many of them. I would appreciate your help."

Brenna asked Ainslee, "Do you still ride? We can explore a bit tomorrow if Elizabeth says you are well enough."

Ainslee calmed her breathing, her heartbeat still beating a fast staccato after leaving Colton near the creek. Did she still ride? Ainslee held back a laugh. She rode with wild horses in Montana in the arms of a mountain man. There was nothing she couldn't do. "I do ride, quite often at home." Rather than sit on one of the available chairs, she chose to lean against the railing. "Do you have a favorite place to ride?"

Brenna and Elizabeth took turns talking about what each thought to be the most beautiful places on the ranch. Ainslee listened and enjoyed the companionship of family and new friends, yet part of her mind wandered back to the creek with Colton's arms wrapped around her.

He was the hero in her story *and* in real life. Except she understood the hero made entirely of paper and ink. Colton awakened in her a desperate longing, one unlikely to be fulfilled. The hero in her story would never disappoint or leave her. They eventually moved from the porch to the kitchen, where Ainslee volunteered to help prepare the evening meal. Everyone insisted guests did not work, but she won the argument by slipping on a starched white apron and standing by the stove with a grin until they succumbed.

Catie bounded into the kitchen, dirt clinging to the hem of her dress. She stopped when she saw Ainslee in the apron. "You're cooking. Do you know how?"

"I am and I do. Well, not really, but I am hoping to learn. I can manage the basics and little more. Are you here to help?"

Catie grinned and shrugged. "I walked over with Isy and August. Gabriel is carrying August, who is feeling much better. He's been fussy because he is teething." Catie lifted her apron from one of the hooks and slipped her arms through and tied it around her waist, then back around in front. "Amanda has been teaching me a lot about baking and cooking. I prefer spending time with the horses, but Elizabeth insists I'll need to know a little of everything." She looked up at Ainslee. "Do you like horses?"

Ainslee bent over and kissed Catie's cheek. "The sun certainly shines brighter when you are around, doesn't it?"

Catie tilted her head, considered. "It rains a lot, too. Sometimes when I help in the kitchen, Grandma Elizabeth says a storm is brewing, but I like what you said about the sun."

The women glanced at one another and laughed. Their laughter mellowed when Isabelle walked into the kitchen carrying August. "I daresay that man thinks me incapable of walking from there to here with his son without help."

Brenna lifted August out of her sister-in-law's hands and cuddled him close. "That is because your dear husband is much like his brother. Ethan does not like Rebecca to go beyond the porch steps unless he can see her every minute. They are the most doting of fathers. He was the same when Jacob was born."

Isabelle smiled up at her son, and in that second, Ainslee witnessed the most profound joy in the woman's visage. Isabelle said, "I wondered if the worry mellows when there is another child."

"I fear not. Of course, I do believe Ethan is more concerned because he now has a daughter who will one day gain the attention of men like him and Gabriel."

The women shared another laugh at their husbands' expense. Ainslee watched as a roast that had already been cooked was removed from the stove. Each person moved about the kitchen, selecting a task and working in tandem, as though they had played out the scene many times.

She listened, smiled, and imagined each of them as characters in a book. Not one of them would find their way into a Finn Pickett adventure, for these women and children were too wholesome for the likes of Finn, and yet Ainslee found herself as fascinated by them as by the people of her own making.

"AND, SCALDED BEYOND recovery, she fled up the wilds of Craig-Aulnaic, uttering the most melancholy lamentations, nor has she been ever heard of since."

The eyes of the children remained wide and filled with excitement when Ainslee uttered the words, "The end."

"What do you think happened to Cla . . . Clash . . . ?"

"Clashnichd."

"Yes, her. What do you think happened?"

Ainslee leaned closer to the children. "No one has ever known. She disappeared."

"That's so sad," Catie said.

"We had a ghost at Hawk's Peak!" Andrew said.

"Did ye now?" Ainslee crooked her finger at Andrew and thickened her brogue. "And did ye see this ghost?"

Andrew scooted closer and whispered, "No, but she was here."

"Och, I believe ye, laddie." Ainslee waved her arms slowly around. "Mayhap, there are more ghosts here now."

Catie and Andrew gasped, and young Jacob shared a shrieking laugh and clapped his hands. "Ghost!" Ainslee suspected Catie's overt display of enthusiasm was in part for the younger children's benefit.

"Aye! Do ye like ghosts?"

Catie offered her thoughts. "I've never met one, but Brenna says ghosts can be friendly, like Grandma Victoria."

Momentarily caught off guard, Ainslee left the question of Victoria's ghost for another time. "Och, but ghosts can be very friendly. Brenna and I grew up in a land of wonder and mystery with ghosts in every glen, loch, and castle."

"I'll be."

Ainslee grinned at Andrew's amazement. When she glanced up from her captive audience, she saw Ethan and Brenna standing in the doorway. Ethan opened his arms to Jacob when he pushed up onto his feet and waddled over to his father. Brenna kissed her son's nose and looked to Ainslee. "Ye were telling them the tale of 'The Ghosts of Craig-Aulnaic.'"

Ainslee winked at Catie and Andrew.

"An abridged version."

"Well in that case, there is nothing wrong with a good ghost story. Though I wager Catie and Andrew will not sleep a bit tonight."

"I will!" Andrew said and leaped to his feet.

Catie rose more gently with Ainslee's help and said to Brenna. "Ainslee said Scotland has a lot of ghosts. Can we go there some day?"

Brenna and Ethan shared a look that lasted a few seconds. "It happens that we can and we will." She smoothed a hand over Catie's cheek and kissed Andrew's forehead. "Andrew, Isabelle and Gabriel are waiting for you. Catie, are you still going home with Eliza and Ramsey?"

Catie nodded. "I like helping with the horses in the morning and it's easier if I'm already there. Do you mind?"

"Of course not! We have all come to

think of you as our child, the way you move from house to house. What is most important is that you are happy."

Catie stood on her toes to kiss Brenna's cheek, waved goodbye to everyone, and went in search of Eliza and Ramsey.

Ethan said to Jacob, "Let's leave these women alone to talk and see if we can find more men." He kissed his wife, offered a smile to Ainslee, and carried his son from the room, leaving them alone.

"You are very good with children."

Ainslee straightened her skirts, wrinkled now from sitting on the floor. "I enjoy their company. There were few opportunities to spend time with children at home."

"There is never a shortage of them around here."

"You heard what Catie said about her Grandma Victoria coming to visit. That was Ethan's mother?"

"Yes, and do not ask me to explain it. I believe with all my heart that Victoria Gallagher visited us this past Christmas when Catie was here."

"We were raised to believe. It is not so uncommon, and I suppose I did not expect to hear about ghosts over here." Ainslee had included ghosts in her stories before, but never one at Christmas. Her thoughts shifted again, as they often did. She looked past her cousin to make sure no one else was around. "Where is Catie's father?"

Brenna linked her fingers and let them hang in front of her. "It is a story both sad and filled with hope. He abandoned her. When he tried to take her back, we wouldn't let him. Catie wanted to stay here. We mourned her loss that day and rejoiced knowing she would remain with us. Why do ask?"

"She has a bright mind and mentioned a keen interest in reading. If all she had in her life were horses and books, I daresay she would be content forever."

"Oh, yes, she does have a good mind. Ethan once fought his father about finishing college. He didn't want to leave the ranch, but he now considers education a tremendous gift."

"Will Catie go to college?"

"She will. They all will. Every generation of Gallaghers and Camerons from this moment on will be given every opportunity."

Ainslee looked around at the shelves filled with bound books. She'd noticed more in almost every room of the house. "Do you ever regret not going?"

"To university?" Brenna shrugged. "Sometimes. Knowing what I do now, how limited my time would have been with Papa, I am grateful I stayed home. I had excellent tutors. But how exciting it must have been for you to go away to England."

"It was, and I am grateful. Though I daresay you were the lucky one." Ainslee kissed her cousin's cheek and left her in a state of bemusement.

12

H^E **LOOKED LIKE** Brenna. His coloring was not as vivid and his features more chiseled, but there was no mistaking the resemblance. Ramsey removed his hat when he stepped inside with a woman who was unmistakably Eliza Gallagher. Tall and slim with dark hair and brilliant blue eyes, she, too, looked like her brothers.

Ainslee possessed one or two physical traits from her parents, like her mother's eyes, but not enough to make her stand out as their child. Her mother always said she was the mirror of her father's mother. It was Ainslee's brothers who resembled their parents, each of the three sons receiving equal shares of their handsome features.

She rose from the plush high-backed chair in the parlor where she and Brenna were enjoying an evening cup of tea.

"I hardly believed Colton when he said you were here."

Without hesitation, Ramsey crossed the room and enveloped Ainslee in a warm embrace. He squeezed a laugh out of her and she wrapped her arms around him.

Ramsey leaned back and smiled down at her upturned face. "Welcome to Montana." His wife stood nearby and he made the introductions. "My wife, Eliza."

"I have already had the pleasure of meeting your brothers."

"Pleasure?" Eliza smiled and stepped forward to embrace Ainslee. "You're talking about my brothers, right?"

They shared a laugh. "Oh, I do

understand what it is to have brothers."

Eliza asked, "How many do you have?"

"Three, though we are not as close as you are with yours."

"I did get lucky with them." Ainslee watched as Eliza's eyes held their focus without blinking. She realized she was the subject of this Gallagher's inspection. Neither Brenna nor Ramsey commented. Perhaps Ainslee imagined it, until Eliza said, "And we always have room for more in this family. Welcome to Hawk's Peak."

Ramsey greeted his sister, and when he faced Ainslee again, it was with a smile and curiosity in his raised brow. He said, "Tell me everything."

"What do you want to know first?"

"How did you come to be here?"

"I was returning home from England and stopped at Cameron Manor. Maggie and Iain told me about Brenna coming here and about you."

Ramsey looked between Brenna and Ainslee. "You didn't know?"

Brenna said, "I did not write as I should have. We lost touch and after our father died, Ramsey, my focus—"

"I understand." Ramsey patted his sister's hand. "It doesn't matter. You're here, Ainslee. Brenna mentioned we have plenty of cousins in Scotland and a few in Ireland."

"We do, more than I have ever met. My grandparents had many children, and your father had cousins. A few, I have heard, are in America, in a place called North Carolina."

"I didn't know that," Brenna said.

"Father told me before I left. I would like to see it one day. This country is so vast."

"And growing." Eliza mumbled the words, leaving Ainslee to wonder.

"You do not like progress?" Ainslee asked her.

Ramsey laughed and held his wife close. "You'll find that a lot of people around here don't mind progress, so long as it doesn't change our way of life."

Fascinating, Ainslee thought. She enjoyed her way of life, remote in the Scottish isles, but she wrongly assumed that everyone in America longed for whatever awaited in the future. The unknown thrilled her; yet here, the people were content to live as they had for decades.

They sat and talked for two more hours. Eliza had excused herself to clean up, but Ramsey did not want to leave until he had heard all about Ainslee's family, her home, and her journey from Scotland.

He sat back, amazed. "You and Brenna are so much alike. Your accent is a little stronger sometimes, though. Whenever she spoke of our McConnell cousins from the Islands, it was with a great deal of fondness."

"We did not see each other often enough. After . . ." Ainslee glanced at Brenna.

Brenna squeezed Ainslee's hand. "It's all right to speak of our parents. I try to often with Ramsey. I want him to know them as I did. They would have been so proud."

"After her—your—mother passed away, it was too much for my mother. With as close as they had been, she did not want any reminders." She turned then to look directly at Brenna. "My mother regretted her choice. When I told her I planned to come here, she explained why we did not visit again. My parents invited your father to visit with you when we stayed at the Borders, but you never came."

Brenna shook her head. "I never knew. My father did not enjoy travel after mother's passing. What of your own brothers? They were all at Eton the last time we saw you."

"Maxwell, the eldest, married three years ago. He and his wife have a son and live in Edinburgh. Cormac is engaged to be married to an Englishwoman next spring. I have only met her once but found her quite charming. He spends most of his time in the Cotswolds where her family lives. Gregor—my younger brother who had quite an infatuation with you—is finishing up at Oxford. He left Eton at sixteen to finish there, though I think he wanted to be out of our older brothers' shadows. He plans to join the family businesses in a year or explore Africa. He has not yet decided. In truth, I have not seen much of my brothers over the years. I feel like an only child much of the time. We all became so busy with our lives, and it is too easy to lose touch."

Ainslee realized she had been talking without pause for twenty minutes. "The hour is growing late. I should not have kept you all so long."

"We want to hear all of it," Brenna assured her. The clock behind Ramsey chimed ten times. "But I should look in on the children."

Ramsey was the first to stand and brought Ainslee up with him for another hug. "It's really good to see you. This family keeps growing and with all the best kind of people. We'll have a lot of time to get to know each other."

Ainslee flashed a look to Brenna then back to Ramsey.

"You are staying for a while, aren't you?"

It was said in a question, but with more conviction as a statement. "We'll have plenty of time together." She brushed a kiss over Ramsey's cheek and told Brenna she would clean up the tea service. After a few objections, Brenna finally nodded when a cry sounded from upstairs, and followed her brother out of the room.

Ainslee decided the best time to get her way with Brenna was when exhaustion had grabbed her cousin or one of her children needed her. She admired how beautiful and loving a mother Brenna had become.

She carried the tray into the kitchen, washed and put away the cups, saucers, and teapot, and stared out the window into the darkness. At home, such chores had been relegated to the servants alone. Other than the one week of lessons on caring for a house, lessons her mother had insisted upon, Ainslee had rarely done more than select her own clothing. She enjoyed the simple labors of managing a household.

Her eyes drifted back to the window and the landscape she pictured beyond. Summer meant longer days, and though the others had all gone to bed, a faint blue hue hung gently over the mountain while stars shined in the darker backdrop above.

Ainslee eased the kitchen door open and closed it quietly behind her. This was already her favorite place at the ranch. The view from the back of the house offered meadows, trees, and mountains, making one think he or she were alone on earth. Even the cattle and horses rested in silence somewhere beyond, out of view.

An eerie cry cut through the night. Ainslee grabbed a post and leaned forward over the porch railing. The call sounded again, and it was unmistakably canine. She had never heard a wolf or coyote, for they did not live in Scotland, but she did not think they would sound so different from the Deerhounds her father raised on their estate. At times the howl pierced through the air and silenced everything around.

The cry came once more, this time joined by another. Not merely a dog.

"They're not as close as they sound."

She grappled for the post and hugged it, awkward with the railing at waist height. The yelp that escaped her mouth was followed by a nervous, choked laugh of relief. "Hae a care, laddie." Ainslee pressed a hand to her chest and felt the rapid heartbeat through her layers of clothing. When the shock passed, she saw Colton had moved closer, still atop his horse. "Even your horse moves without sound."

"We didn't mean to startle you."

"I do not believe it is so much you as them." She nodded toward the open land. "Do you ever sleep?"

"Not much after I've been on the trail."

"You are certain they are not close?"

Colton remained on his horse but had moved close enough so it felt as though he stood beside her. "Sometimes wolves get hungry or brave enough to try for a calf, but the game is good this year so they haven't bothered with the cattle so far. When game is scarce or a calf wanders from its mother, a wolf will pick one off."

"'Tis the way of life, I suppose."

"You've hunted."

"Aye, but I would think it is different living with the animals all the time. Seeing them, caring for them, and then to think of them . . . Well, it would be different."

Colton's quiet chuckle might have irritated her had she not heard the foolishness in her own words. Ranchers raised meat for market. They fed thousands of people. It was a necessary cycle of life and someone had to be charged with it. Better people like those at Hawk's Peak who cared.

"You're right." Colton's voice had sobered, though she still made out his smile. "It is different with the animals we raise and fight to keep alive. We lose a few every year to predators or winter, sometimes an injury so great it's a mercy to put them down. Ranching isn't for the squeamish." His gelding rubbed the side of its head against the railing twice before returning to its quiet vigil. "Does it bother you?"

Ainslee reached out to touch the horse, pleased when it nudged her hand, wanting more. "No. When I first learned to hunt, it was difficult for me to see an animal die, but it also taught me to respect them more. I imagine that was part of the lesson my father's gamekeeper wanted to instill. They taught me that the hunting was necessary for the good of the herds, but every kill came with a price to the one who took the life."

She ran her hand up the horse's nose. "Does he have a name?"

"Not yet. He and I get along without one."

"Have you had him long?"

"Five years now. We've been through a lot together."

"He must be a great companion when you're away, out there." Ainslee dared to ask, "Are you going back on the trail?"

"I hope we've seen the last of the rustlers, but until we're sure, we'll all keep watch. I planned to go back out tomorrow."

"Alone?"

Colton recalled his conversation with Ethan in the barn. "I don't know."

"Does rustling happen often?"

Colton shook his head. Ainslee caught the subtle shift of his hand to settle near the pistol at his hip.

"We've seen a few over the years, but most of them stay away from Hawk's Peak. We have more hands than a lot of ranches." He looked her way. "Are you really interested in cattle thieves?"

Ainslee released a deep breath on a sigh. "No." She remembered how easy it was to talk with Colton before they arrived at the ranch. "It's different than I expected. You will think me nonsensical for hoping life here was more like some of the exploits I read about. I do appreciate the serenity and beauty of this land."

"Are you sorry you came?"

"Oh, no, never that." She stared at him, wondering again how he could know her so well. Her reunion with Brenna and meeting Ramsey had been all she imagined and hoped for when she left Scotland. Yet she found herself asking, 'What now?' She wanted to experience everything she planned to write—almost everything. She could do without another gun pointed at her, but otherwise, she wanted to see and do as much as possible.

A surge of renewed enthusiasm bolted through her. "How difficult is it to rope a cow?"

"Rope a cow? Did you read about that in one of your books?"

"Yes. Is it easy enough for a novice to learn?"

"Easier if I tell you how it's done."

"Would you be willing to show me?"

Colton studied her from his perch in the saddle. He would rather stand beside her, feel the heat from her body, and inhale the sweet, clean fragrance he caught when he first rode up to the porch. She managed to always smell like a fresh summer day in the woods. He stayed where he was for both their sakes.

"You have a whole family no doubt eager to spend time with you. A cousin who rides, ropes, and works horses and cattle as well as any man ever to walk this land. Might be Ramsey would like to show you the workings of a ranch now that he's here."

He wanted to keep his gaze averted, to not see her disappointment. Didn't she know it wasn't a good idea to spend more time with him? He already thought of her too much when she wasn't around. Their spontaneous ride earlier with the horses had been so perfect, he could not regret it or the kiss that followed. It was safer to spend time with her with others around, but he found ways to see her, like tonight. The more of her company he enjoyed, the more he wanted. He learned long ago not to enjoy too much of a good thing.

"Of course, I should have asked Ramsey or even Ethan or Gabriel. That is what you meant. For me to ask the family."

The words she spoke were good in themselves, and yet Colton felt he'd been launched onto the ridgepole of the ranch house and told to walk from one end of the other without a single misstep. Except somehow, he'd managed to not only step off but tumble to the ground without realizing it.

"Ainslee."

"I am not angry with you."

"Yes, you are."

"Yes, I am. You would not understand."

"I believe I would."

She glared at him.

Colton rallied his patience. "All right, why not?"

"Because I do not understand." Ainslee gripped the edges of the railing, her knuckles turning white. Colton waited her out while she exhaled deeply. "It is not *you* who makes me angry."

"Then it's all men?"

He anticipated that she would raise her head and look at him again. He was rewarded for his patience when her gray eyes, normally the color of a cloudy sky before a storm, shined bright with . . . he couldn't tell if it was annoyance or regret.

"What you said before, about how I should have asked Ramsey for help, well, you were right. It would be more proper to ask family. It is what my mother would say, to always be proper. And as much as I want to love my cousins and learn all there is to know about them, I want to spend time with you, too."

The words he both longed and dreaded to hear now hovered in the air, a whisper echoing over and over in his head.

"You gave me wild horses, Colton. And I know what I felt in our kiss does not happen with everyone."

His eyes flashed. "And who taught you that?"

"It does not matter. What I feel confuses me. It is thrilling and frightening. I am not certain . . ."

A light appeared in the kitchen window, drawing their attention. Brenna calling out Ainslee's name followed. Colton knew he shouldn't leave her confession without a response but worse still would be to offer her one he'd yet to properly formulate.

He turned and rode into the darkness on the other side of the house before Brenna stepped onto the porch.

"I thought you had gone to bed. Is everything all right?"

He heard Ainslee's voice after a few seconds. "Of course. It is such a beautiful night. I wanted to enjoy a little more of it."

"It often reminds me of home," he heard Brenna say. "When the clouds and sun find balance in the sky and cast shadows over the summer mountains, I think of the Highlands."

Colton heard the smile in Ainslee's voice when she spoke next. He did not know how, but he heard it, and could picture her lips curve upward, her eyes soften.

She said, "I can believe what you say about this place. It is special, is it not?"

Colton also noticed her accent was stronger when she spoke with Brenna.

"It is, but like any place you go, it is what you make it. My heart is here and that makes a difference, helps me to see the beauty of the land as clear as if I were walking the gentle hills of Cameron Manor. I can see there is more to why you are here, more you have not told me about."

He heard nothing for almost a minute and told himself he should leave, yet Brenna's next words stilled him.

"Are you in trouble?"

"No." Ainslee's quick response held a distinct note of hesitation. "My life is positively too dull for me to get into trouble."

"Then what is it? The truth comes and goes in your eyes, even when I sense you are happy to be here."

"I am happy. Oh, Brenna, I am! You

cannot possibly know the depth of the joy I feel to be here, to see you again, to meet Ramsey. I feel a hole in my life has been filled, and I want it to overflow."

"Then—"

"I'm not ready to explain. Can that be all right for now?"

"Of course."

Colton heard footsteps enter the house and recognized them for Brenna's. A full minute later, Ainslee followed and closed the door. The glow from her lantern moved out of the kitchen and deeper into the house. He struggled to ease the tightness around his chest when, with a nudge of his knees, he guided his horse away from their place in the shadows.

13

THE SUN GLISTENED through the open window until it found the exact spot on Ainslee's face where it would annoy her into waking up. She raised one eye, closed it, opened the other, before shutting them both and pulling a feather pillow over her head.

She had written for hours, well into the early morning when the house creaked and all others slept, as she should have done. Ainslee had been unable to stop the natural movement of sitting at the desk and pulled what was left of her ink and paper out of the drawer where she had tucked it away.

The words flowed from her mind to the paper through the swift movements of the pen as she glided her hand over the surface. She filled a dozen sheets—the rest of her paper supply— until the words no longer spoke to her. She wrote because it had been too long since the urge hit with such great ferocity. And she wrote to quiet all of the other thoughts fighting for her attention.

The scenes resting on those precious pages heated her skin even to think of them. Some had been words of love between man and woman. Other pages she filled with a harrowing escape from the very band of rustlers who had plagued the ranch. She knew nothing of them, but she had turned them—Ainslee ended up with three for a pleasant number—into the most loathsome characters she had ever written.

Sleep had not come easily later, and

when she had finally managed to whisk her mind into oblivion, her body was as restless as her dreams. Twice she had awakened to a numb arm, tucked tightly beneath her head, hands grasping edges of the pillow. A third time she had thought the wolves had returned to howl her into the new day, much as her father's Deerhounds had done when they anticipated going on a hunt.

Memories fluttered, each one seeking purchase and a place of prominence in her thoughts. She wanted them all to tumble into the sea and leave her in peace. The strongest of them rose to the surface and caught hold enough to bring her fully awake. Why did it have to be of Colton?

She saw his face as clear as if he lay beside her, and she quickly attempted to brush his image from her mind. Ainslee all but confessed that he was special to her. She groaned, remembering the words: I want to spend time with you, too. Her unladylike grumbling that followed was not due to regret over her choice of words. She believed a woman had the right to speak her mind, but she had always done so under the guise of another name.

When she shared her longings and dreams with the world, it was through the voice of Finn Pickett. She clung to the anonymity like a shield. Why did she now feel the need to brush past obscurity and reveal her true self to Colton? Would he find it so odd for a woman brought up in a proper and wealthy household to desire another way of life?

A gentle rap at the bedroom door brought Ainslee around to face the barrier. She pushed away the covers and fumbled to lower her nightgown that had bunched at her hips during the restless night.

"Ainslee?"

She opened the door and offered her

best half smile to Amanda, who looked cheerful and prim in her apron. A dusting of brown on the white cloth made Ainslee think cocoa. "You are already up."

Amanda blinked a few times and smiled. "It is five after ten o'clock. Brenna has been by to check on you a couple of times but is tending to the baby now."

"Ten o'clock? I have never slept so late in my life."

"Are you feeling ill?"

"No, I am well."

"Perhaps it is being away from home. I know it generally takes me a few days to get accustomed a new place."

"Yes, that must be it." Ainslee offered a wider smile this time. "Thank you, Amanda. I won't be long."

When Ainslee was reasonably certain she did not look as though she had battled demons in her sleep, she made her way downstairs and into the kitchen, where the morning activity had dwindled. Elizabeth and Amanda laughed together while rolling dough. No one else was around.

Elizabeth noticed her first and motioned her closer. "A good night's sleep should wash away all of those traveling cobwebs. I am told it can take weeks to recover from a long journey like yours."

Ainslee sighed, her efforts to not appear exhausted in vain. It was not the journey from which she needed to recover. Between the unexpected excitement and injuries on the trail and her welcome and confusing encounters with Colton, she was surprised to be standing upright. The older woman motioned her to a chair and Ainslee sensed she was being studied. "How about some breakfast and a nice cup of tea to start, or do you prefer coffee?"

"Tea is fine, but I can—"

"No, dear." The words were gentle, but Elizabeth was surprisingly strong for a woman who, Ainslee guessed, was in her late seventies. "You sit and relax. The kettle is on and we have more batter for hotcakes."

It was easy to enjoy the women's company. They asked questions, she answered. They offered up stories about the family and told her more about the ranch. Ainslee sat and listened, but she did not fully relax. She enjoyed their companionship and set it in her mind to ask each of them more about how they came to be at Hawk's Peak—another time, when her under-rested body was not eager to be moving.

Brenna walked into the kitchen holding her daughter. Ainslee immediately forgot about her breakfast and held her arms open for the baby. Brenna obliged with a smile and caution to Ainslee. "Mind your hair. This one has a fondness for pulling it."

A few tendrils hung loose around her shoulders. "I don't mind. Little Rebecca can pull—" Ainslee bit back a yelp. "How is someone so little so strong?"

"She takes after her papa." Brenna grinned and accepted a cup of tea from Amanda. "I was going to go into town today. Isabelle planned to go in and help Sarah Beckert—she's the new teacher, Ainslee—organize the summer benefit concert for the school. August is a little fussy this morning, so she sent Catie around to let me know she's staying home."

"Do they need the doctor?" Elizabeth asked.

"No, I already offered to send one of the men to fetch him. The poor lad is teething and it's keeping him up at night. She said he just needs some rest. Catie won't leave his side, so he's in good hands."

"Catie does have a way with the young

ones." Ainslee gently extricated her hair from the baby's fist. Rebecca gurgled and grinned in response.

"You won't be going then?" Amanda asked.

"Catie was going to look after Jacob and Rebecca for me, but with her gone, I thought to postpone."

"We're here," Elizabeth said.

Brenna smiled at her grandmother. "You both deserve a break from looking after the children."

"Nonsense!" Amanda clucked her tongue like a mother hen, though she was nearly Brenna's age. "Please, leave them with us. I will enjoy it, and Elizabeth is often sneaking in comments about how good it is for me to practice for my own family one day. Where's Jacob?"

"He's playing with Andrew in the nursery. Andrew ventured over with Catie this morning when she came to let us know she'd be at Gabriel and Isabelle's house today. Andrew wanted to stay."

Elizabeth said, "It's a smart thing Gabriel did building his house close enough to this one so the children aren't ever far apart."

Ainslee listened with amusement at the back and forth between the women. She enjoyed a similar banter with the cook and head housekeeper back home. Once they got used to the daughter of the house spending time below stairs, they turned her excursions into games. The cook would sneak her a treat, and they would talk for a few minutes before pushing her out of the kitchens with a wink and a promise not to tell.

Homesickness flashed and burned bright, but she doused the flame and rejoined the conversation. "Brenna, what benefit concert?"

"Sarah had the idea to help raise money

for the school—new primers, books, paint sets, maps, and the like—by hosting a bake sale and small concert put on by the children."

Elizabeth pressed crust into a pie dish and filled it with a spiced apple mixture. "It's a nice idea. The Gallaghers have always provided what the school needed, but Sarah has it right. It's good for the children to feel a part of things. They'll appreciate the books and whatnots more for it."

Brenna nodded. "That is Sarah's thinking. Would you like to go, then?"

Ainslee raised her head. "To the benefit?"

"Yes, of course to the benefit, but today, to town?"

"I rather think I would."

Brenna turned to the other women. "Elizabeth? Amanda?"

Elizabeth said, "I promised Sarah a

dozen pies and a cake for the benefit. Tilly is baking another dozen. This one here is for today's supper. I figure on stopping by to look in on Isabelle a bit later. Fussy babies are hard on a mother. Besides, you look like you're dressed for riding, not driving a wagon."

Amanda lifted the pie when Elizabeth finished crimping the edges and slid it into the waiting stove. "And I promised I would help with the baking, but we do need a few things I forgot to pick up when I was there a few days ago. They will fit in a saddlebag. I will get you a list."

Brenna turned to Ainslee. "Do you mind riding?"

More eager now than before at the prospect of going, Ainslee nodded. "A ride would be nice. I will need to change but won't be long."

Colton volunteered. He told himself all of the reasons why he shouldn't, but when he learned of the outing, he told Brenna he would accompany them. Eliza had a foaling mare in distress—one of their prized animals—and refused to leave her side. The worry was that they might lose the mare, the foal, or both. An unexpected visit from men of the Utah & Northern Railway occupied Ethan and Gabriel and likely would for a few hours. Ramsey did not often ride over to the main house until late afternoon, spending the morning hours with the horses. That left one of the ranch hands to escort the women into town.

It was not uncommon for them to travel the distance from Hawk's Peak to Briarwood without escort, but until the matter of the rustlers was fully resolved to everyone's satisfaction, it was understood that the women and children did not leave the ranch alone.

When Ainslee stepped outside with Brenna and saw him next to the horses, Colton waited to see if she would change her mind about going. He did not believe her a coward and was proven right when after a brief pause, she followed Brenna down the steps. She had dressed to be on the back of a horse, and what she wore could not be described as a typical lady's riding outfit.

They resembled pants more than a skirt, made of a material that managed to flow and mold at the same time. The shirt, in a light fawn color, buttoned up the front and had been shaped to fit her feminine body. The leather vest accented her form rather than covered it. She went without a coat, but the hat she had specially made sat atop her head. Colton wagered with himself that the same seamstress created the rest of the getup.

She did not look directly at him when he held the mare's reins, kindly refusing his assistance. Ainslee swung into the saddle with surprising skill and ease. Colton watched but did not see even a flinch. He wondered if Elizabeth had indeed removed the stitches.

"Colton."

All eyes shifted to the sound of Ben's voice as he rode over. Colton made sure Ainslee had control of the mare before walking the space between where he stood and where Ben stopped. Colton's first thought was Ben wanted privacy. When Ben moved closer, Colton noticed the tightness around the edges of his friend's mouth.

Ben lowered his voice and leaned forward, resting his forearms on the saddle horn. "Jackson and Pete are saddling up for the ride into town. I need your help here."

"Did we lose more cattle?"

Ben shook his head. "Tom is missing."

"Jake told me you sent Tom and Tom Jr. to the high pasture to repair the cow camp roofs before winter hit."

"I know. I sent them up there before we went to Bozeman. They were supposed to return this morning."

"I'll ride up and—"

"Tom Jr. showed up ten minutes ago, and said he hasn't seen his pa since last night."

Colton swore under his breath. He heard the sound of restless horses behind him. "Gabe and Ethan are still in town."

Ben eased to a full sitting position, his voice still quiet. "I sent Connor to find them and let them know what's happened."

Colton nodded once and returned to Brenna and Ainslee as Jackson and Pete were riding from the barn. Ben had chosen two of the better shots among the ranch hands, and Jackson had a good eye for spotting what shouldn't be there. He stopped by Ainslee's horse but turned to speak with Brenna. "I'm needed here this morning. Jackson and Pete will ride into town with you."

Brenna had been among them long enough to know when information was being withheld. When she did not demand an explanation, Colton figured she had just gotten used to it. He wondered if Ethan shared everything with his wife, then called himself a fool for the thought. The slight raise of Brenna's delicate brow led him to believe she did not believe him now and would learn everything when she returned. Her brief glance to Ainslee attracted his attention, though when he looked Ainslee's way, she was staring at him. He saw her curiosity as plainly as if she had vocalized it.

"Jackson and Pete are good company." Brenna looked again to Ainslee. "Are you ready?"

Ainslee nodded, though she darted her eyes once more to Colton. He wished he could tell her more, tell her why it wasn't him going with them, tell her that he wanted to spend time with her, too. Colton said none of those things as the foursome rode toward Briarwood. He waited to see if Ainslee would look back. She did not.

Colton mounted his gelding and turned his horse toward Ben. "Where's Tom Jr.?"

"Waiting for us. He needed a fresh horse."

"Did he say where his father went last night?"

"To get some fresh air. Tom Jr. fell asleep and when he awoke this morning, Tom wasn't around. He spent an hour looking, rode back to the cow camp, then came home."

Tom Jr. rode toward them, sitting anxiously in his saddle. "I'm ready."

Colton did not want to question Ben's idea of having the young man join them because he did not know what they'd find. "Where did you search?"

"I'll show you."

Colton recognized the stubborn set of the young man's chin. "You've ridden hard this morning and—"

"And you don't know what we're gonna find, is that it?" Tom Jr. sat taller in the saddle. "My pa knows what he's doing out there. His horse probably spooked, or maybe it was them wolves. We just gotta find him."

He exchanged a look with Ben, but the foreman shrugged, a likely indication that he'd already had a similar conversation with Tom Jr., and lost. Colton took a few seconds to study Tom's son. He was a young man, nearly nineteen, and worked hard to prove himself to the other ranch hands every day. Colton recalled too clearly what he had already seen and done by age nineteen.

"Let's go."

14

AINSLEE ENGAGED HER thoughts on everything she could except Colton during what turned out to be a surprisingly brief ride to town. Brenna was a remarkable horsewoman, and even now rode Heather, the mare once given to her by her parents when she was a young girl. Ainslee considered again the level of love a man must have for a woman to bring her horse all the way from Scotland, just like the wild heather shrubs that now grew in Montana soil.

How many levels of love could there be? Ainslee listed them silently while Pete regaled them with one of the many adventures of ranching life. This particular one boasted him as the bumbling cowboy roping his first steer in Texas before he decided Texas was too hot and he slowly made his way north, moving from ranch to ranch.

Ainslee's interest rose at the mention of roping, but Pete soon moved onto other tales that while interesting, could not draw her thoughts away from matters of the heart. Brenna and Ethan would make interesting subjects to study. The Finn Pickett books rarely had elements of romance, for Ainslee did not feel herself capable of writing about something she did not know of firsthand.

She managed to tick off three levels of love on her mental checklist before her mind twisted into a tortuous knot of blank paths leading to a big question mark. And that is why I do not pen love stories, Ainslee thought. And yet, the tale that began to spin since she met Colton was a blend of two elements only—adventure and love. As a writer, she had a responsibility to learn all she could.

The power her mind possessed to create allowed her to imagine what it must be like to love, but she did not *know*. Her sources of information were abundant at the ranch: Ethan and Brenna, Gabriel and Isabelle, Ramsey and Eliza, and Ben and Amanda. It must not be too difficult if so many managed to find love and hold true to it.

The men of her acquaintance back home never managed to capture her interest long enough to go beyond a single dance or outing. Yet now, one man consumed her thoughts.

Her thoughts shifted back to the present. They arrived in Briarwood to a bustling main street, the only main road to lead in and out of town. From Brenna, Ainslee learned Briarwood was slowly growing, but most people passed through rather than settling down in their valley.

"The stage comes today, bringing mail. The supply wagon would have arrived yesterday. Both bring more people into town than you will usually see most days."

Curious, Ainslee asked, "Whose idea was the private coach? It seems an extravagance for a small town."

"It might be, but when the stagecoach lines ceased operation in this territory, we needed another option for those traveling without horses and wagons. The men who drive it—brothers—have parents who live in Briarwood. The driving job allows them to work during the week in Bozeman and return home every Friday to see their family."

"It does not sound like a lasting solution. Does the railroad wish to put a line through here? It is out of the way from the main line."

Brenna stopped alongside the others in front of the livery where their horses would be cared for while they attended to their business. "It has worked well for the town thus far, but no, it is not a lasting solution. A few men with interest in the railroad hope to bring a spur line to Briarwood, to open up more of the area to settlers."

"Is that whom Ethan and Gabriel are meeting with today?"

Brenna nodded and absently pointed to the general store as she explained. "Hawk's Peak is the largest ranch in the area, and those with power and financial interests in the territory know that the Gallaghers wield a good deal of influence. A spur line would not succeed if they fight it."

"Do they want to fight a spur line? I should think it would be easier to take their cattle to market rather than drive them all the way to the railroad." Brenna's bemusement brought a smile to Ainslee. "I read a lot. According to Colton, I should not believe everything I have read or heard. I am also told I ask too many questions."

Brenna returned the smile. "You were always curious, and Colton is right. I had my own misconceptions when I first arrived, though my research was more focused on finding my grandfather and not as much on the working ways of the western frontier. In this instance, you are correct. A spur line would simplify ranching in many ways and bring in more people. There are those who welcome the idea, getting supplies quicker and making travel easier. Others prefer to preserve their way of life. They worry a rail line to Briarwood would destroy that."

They stepped into the general store and

Ainslee forgot about her curiosity over the railroad long enough to enjoy the quaint interior of the well-stocked mercantile.

"Well, now. It's right nice to see you, Mrs. Gallagher." An older man with a friendly smile and head of thinning gray hair stepped out from around the counter.

Brenna accepted the man's hand and the gentle kiss he pressed to her cheek. "It is Brenna as always, Loren."

"We've missed seeing you in town. I reckon that little one is keeping you busy."

"Rebecca has been a delight. Between her and Jacob I have no need for exercise any longer. I would like to thank Joanna for the baby gifts she sent last month."

"Now, don't let my beloved wife think those were all her idea." Loren chuckled and turned his attention to Ainslee. "It's always a pleasure to see a new face in our fair town, and a comely one, too."

The storekeeper's jovial spirit charmed

Ainslee as much as his flattery. His compliment was made easier to accept considering he was old enough to be her grandfather.

Brenna made the introductions. "My cousin, Miss Ainslee McConnell. Ainslee, this is Loren Baker. He and his wife Joanna own the store."

In a move that surprised and obviously pleased Loren, Ainslee held out her hand for him to accept. "It is my pleasure, Mr. Baker, to be a guest in Briarwood."

"Ah! A Scottish cousin no less. Your gentle brogue puts me in mind of when Brenna first arrived. I hope you will visit again and tell me a tale of your Highlands. It sounds as though you recently arrived."

Ainslee decided she liked Loren Baker. "Ah hae tales aplenty to share."

"Oh, isn't that lovely."

A woman, close to Loren's age, stepped out from a back room, winding her way around tables to reach them. Loren reached a hand around the woman. "May I present my wife, Joanna. My dear, this young lady is cousin to our Brenna, Miss Ainslee McConnell."

It was, Ainslee decided, the best introduction she had ever received.

"My dear, we always delight in a visit from the fairer side of Hawk's Peak." Joanna turned to Brenna. "Amanda was in here not long ago with Ben. I noticed you ride in with two of the hands from the ranch."

Ainslee waited to hear Brenna's response. She had already discovered the trouble the cattle rustlers could cause. Were they the only reason for the extra precautions at the ranch?

"You know how protective they all are. We have been fortunate not to have run into any problems, but until the rustling stops, they will no doubt continue to be cautious." Brenna handed her small list to Loren.

Loren took a passing glance at the list. "We have all of this in stock. Won't take but a few minutes. We did see those two fellas Colton brought in. Lawmen from Bozeman picked them up this morning since the judge won't be around this way for another month."

Ainslee imagined a town like this had no need for a newspaper. Amanda had mentioned the previous newspaper operator had moved to Salt Lake City, leaving the town without one. All it took was a single person witnessing something for the rest of the townsfolk to hear about the incident. She was surprised her arrival had not been learned of before now, though she did not intend to ask why not. As much as she enjoyed studying others, she disliked being the topic of conversation.

"Do you have ink and fine writing paper?"

Loren nodded. "We have both and even some of those fancy fountain pens they're making in New York City."

"Yes, I have tried them, but I do prefer dipping the pen into the ink and gliding it smoothly across the paper. I feel the process gives one time to properly think before writing."

Loren, Joanna, and Brenna all looked at her with bemused expressions. Loren said, "Well, we have plenty of ink and some paper. If it's not to your liking, we can order anything you want. I'll bring to the counter what we have."

She navigated toward a section of shelves filled with books, drawn to the familiar and welcome spines. Her fingers skimmed over *Common Sense in the Household* and *Cookery for Beginners*, neither of which held any interest. She brushed past other titles bent on teaching domesticity, an honorable practice but not a subject in which Ainslee found herself interested. The selection included works from Dickens, Thoreau, Austen, the Brontës, and others from Europe and America. The dime novels of Edward L. Wheeler caught her attention. She chided herself for believing any of it could be true.

Reality was more profound and simpler than she once imagined. She vaguely heard Brenna and Joanna speaking while Loren helped a gentleman at the counter. She noticed the ink and paper waiting for her inspection and decided they could wait a few minutes longer.

She lowered herself enough to view the books on the lower shelf and held in a gasp when she saw three Finn Pickett adventures. She'd been told by her London publisher that the stories had gained some popularity in America, but

Ainslee never imagined she would see them here, so far from home.

She experienced a slight moment of regret that it was not her real name on the spines. The moment passed and she pulled one of her books from the shelf.

"That's a good one."

Ainslee should have heard the woman approach. She leaned back slightly to see her face and had to step back to put a little distance between them. The back corner of the store did not offer a comfortable amount of space for more than one person, though the woman was slight and did not take up much room.

Ainslee nodded in agreement and slid the book back in its place.

"Do you know, my brother always chided me for enjoying those stories, but I prefer them to romances."

To Ainslee's ear, the woman sounded a little like Isabelle with her soft accent but not as refined as Isabelle's. Ainslee knew Isabelle to be from New Orleans and wondered if everyone from that part of the country sounded similar. The woman wore a long blue shirt over a calico skirt, with the shirt cinched at the waist. A thin, cotton scarf was tied around her neck. Ainslee had not seen such a style before on a woman and found herself wondering how she would look wearing the same.

"My brothers would agree with yours. Are you from here? Forgive my asking, but your accent . . ."

"My family is originally from Charleston." At Ainslee's shrug, she added, "That is in South Carolina. You don't sound from around here, either."

"I am from Scotland."

"You've come a long way." The woman nodded and held out a hand. "Mrs. Davis Jones. Blanche to my friends."

Ainslee took her cue from the other

woman and made an informal introduction for herself. "Miss Ainslee McConnell."

"Welcome to Briarwood, Miss McConnell. My sister and her family live not far from town. My brother and I have been visiting for a few months. I have passed many hours with books from this store."

Ainslee did not look back at the shelf. "I am also a fan of adventure books, although I enjoy a good romance on occasion."

Blanche said, "My mother is a devoted fan of Miss Austen. Will you be here long?"

"Yes, it's my first time in this country, and there are a great many places to see." They both turned at the sound of Loren's approach.

"Mrs. Davis, good to see you again. After another book?"

"I believe I will buy another today." Blanche reached over and pulled the newest of the Finn Pickett books off the shelf. "This one comes recommended." She smiled at Ainslee. "I should finish my shopping. I promised my sister I would pick up one of Tilly's pies so she would not have to bake one of her own. She has been spoiling my brother and me since our arrival."

Ainslee smiled and nodded. "I cannot speak to all of Tilly's food as I have only been here a short time, but I highly recommend the cherry pie."

"Then cherry it will be. It was a pleasure to meet your acquaintance, Miss McConnell. Good day, Loren." Blanche went to the front counter, set money on the glass case, deposited her new book into a basket already laden with goods, and left the store.

Brenna joined Ainslee and Loren. "Who was that?"

"Blanche Davis. She and her brother are

visiting their sister on a farm outside of town."

Loren nodded. "The Bittles. They bought the small Beckert homestead a few months ago. Done well with it, too."

"Sarah did say her farm had sold. I am glad they are doing well here." Brenna removed one of the Finn Pickett books from the shelf, the same one Ainslee had held a few moments ago. "Ethan does not read a lot of fiction these days, but these stories are popular at the ranch."

Ainslee restrained her surprise. "You've heard of the author?"

"Oh yes. Maggie and Iain send crates two or three times a year with items from Scotland. It helps to subdue homesickness. She always includes a few books from Scottish authors. She included the Finn Pickett books a few crates ago, thinking the ranch hands would enjoy them."

Brenna looped her arm through Ainslee's. "Loren has filled my list and he has your ink and paper and a catalog if you have need of something else. We do keep a good paper stock at the ranch in the library that you are welcome to use. I ordered more baby clothes for Rebecca, too. I have a weakness for them. If you would like to see more of the town, we have time. Pete is placing a lumber order for all the extra building they are doing for the new stables."

"I would like to see more of the town."

Brenna left her items with Loren and they stepped outside.

Ainslee pointed to a building across the way. "Is that a saloon?"

"It is. We have only one in Briarwood."

"Are there . . . I mean I have read that some women . . ."

Brenna grinned. "Not here. Not what you are thinking, Ainslee. What would your mother say to such lurid thoughts?"

"'Tis not unreasonable a thought."

"Didn't we already discuss how not everything you read about the West is true? Although, it happens that many such establishments do allow what you—I am not going to say the word."

Ainslee laughed. "Listen to us go on. If it is a respectable place, I would like to see inside. I was never allowed in the pubs at home."

"That is not a surprise. Your father allowed you great freedom, but even that would have been too much for him."

Ainslee nodded. "More freedom than most would have given, but not as much as I would have liked." She did not explain further. "The saloon? It will not take long."

"Millie runs it for her brother who is often not around. She does not tolerate what Elizabeth calls 'shenanigans,' but it is still not a place you should go. Amanda worked there serving for a very brief time before she came to the ranch. If you would like to know more, ask her."

"Amanda worked in a saloon?"

"Yes, she served drinks briefly but I will say no more. It is Amanda's story to tell." They strolled along the boardwalk until they reached the saloon. Ainslee thought her cousin had reconsidered, but Brenna winked and guided her down a couple of steps and onto the road where they walked the remainder of the way to the meadow.

"We will stop in at the school first, and then perhaps the church. When we have finished there, we can go to—"

They heard children shouting before they reached the front steps of the school.

15

COLTON RODE AHEAD of Ben and Tom Jr. once they sighted the cow camp, consisting of four wood-sided buildings that had been a part of the land before Jacob Gallagher had settled here and built what is now Hawk's Peak. Some speculated that the small camp had been erected by the landowners before the Gallaghers arrived, and those who came before simply had not gotten around to expanding.

The sky above was clear and blue, showing no sign of birds of prey, which meant death did not linger nearby. The prospect kept Colton hopeful as he dismounted in front of the larger cabin where Tom Jr. and his father had stayed.

He asked Ben and Tom Jr. to stay close to the cabin in case Tom returned. Ben understood it to mean he should keep the younger man distracted while Colton searched. He studied the footprints, separated them, and followed each path with his eyes until he found the pair he wanted.

Set deeper into the ground than any of the others, Colton concluded the depth could be accounted for by one man carrying another. Tom wasn't so big he couldn't be hauled a short distance, and the boot imprint indicated a tall man, at least six feet. He and his gelding tracked the prints to the edge of the trees where they became less discernable. Two miles later, he reached an opening where drag marks were evident, leading into more trees. He dismounted and followed the signs into the woods.

Near the base of a large pine tree, where the sun managed to filter in enough to keep away permanent darkness, he found Tom. Eyes closed and body limp, Tom did not stir when Colton knelt beside him. Colton removed his pistol from the holster, raised it into the air, and fired a single shot.

AINSLEE AND BRENNA rushed into the schoolhouse to find children huddled in the corner by the door and at the front near the teacher's desk. Sarah Beckert lay in an awkward position on the wood floor, one arm splayed to the right and the other grasped in the hand of Daisy Shaw, the oldest child in the class. Sarah's son, Cord, knelt next to Daisy, urging his mother to wake up.

Daisy looked up when they hurried to

Sarah's side. "I sent Billy to fetch Doc Brody. She's breathing, but I can't wake her. We were all outside. Mrs. Beckert came inside only for a minute. We heard a shout and found her like this."

Ainslee held the back of her hand to the teacher's brow and cheeks and grasped the arm Daisy did not hold to check her pulse. "She is still alive."

Brenna said, "And bleeding."

With her free hand, Ainslee carefully examined the back of the woman's head. When she brought her hand away, blood covered three of her fingers. "It does not feel deep, but it is still seeping blood."

Brenna asked one of the children to bring a clean cloth from the box near the chalkboard. Ainslee pressed the cloth to the injury seconds before the schoolhouse door swung open. Doc Brody, a man of imposing size and gentle nature, strode down the aisle between the two sections of desks.

"What have we here?" He knelt in the place where Daisy once had. Brenna joined her, but Ainslee remained, her hand holding the cloth in place. "You've seen a bit too much excitement for your short time in Montana."

Ainslee knew he spoke to her, though he had not said her name or looked her way. His focus was entirely on Sarah. He did cast a surreptitious glance to Brenna who nodded and turned a still-shocked Daisy toward the door. "Children, we are going to wait outside. Come along." Daisy broke from her stupor long enough to help herd the children out of the schoolhouse.

Cord refused to leave his mother's side.

"I promise she'll be all right, lad."

Cord narrowed his eyes at the doctor. "You're sure?"

"You have my word of honor."

After a few more seconds, Cord gave the

doctor a firm nod and joined the others outside.

When they were alone, Brody's larger hand took the place of Ainslee's. "Let's have a look at that wound, shall we?" Brody removed the cloth and glanced first at the blood. "It's a good color." Ainslee watched him open his brown leather medical bag and remove a small, dark vial. He uncorked it and held it an inch beneath Sarah's nose.

Ainslee caught a whiff herself. "Peppermint?"

"Aye. The ammonia in smelling salts can have ill effects on some people."

"Colton said you have learned to use natural remedies."

"Science does not discount them. I believe when used with modern techniques and methods, they can be as efficacious. Sometimes more."

He was proven right seconds later when

the teacher's eyes fluttered open. A low moan escaped her lips. "That's it, let it out." Brody braced her head with his hand and patted her shoulder. "You'll be all right there." Sarah's eyes closed again and her breathing deepened.

"Will she be all right?"

Brody nodded. "She needs rest. Once the wound is cleaned and the bleeding staunched, she'll be on the mend. Do you know what happened?"

"Not yet. Isabelle and the children found her unconscious. They thought she was alone."

Brody shook his head. "I can't be certain until I examine the wound, but I see no blood on any other surface. This was done to her."

Ainslee agreed. They both turned at the sound of horses.

"I told Billy to bring a wagon from the livery. I'll wager Otis is with him."

"What about her husband?"

Brody raised his eyes. "You've not been here long enough to hear all the gossip. Give it time. Of course, your family doesn't take to talking about others. Neither do I."

Ainslee accepted the rebuke but still pressed. "If she has a husband, he should be told."

"There's no husband, not anymore."

It was not just Otis they saw when the door opened again. Colton and Pete were with him. Communication without words took place, as it often does between men. Ainslee started to rise, only to be assisted by Colton. His hand lingered on her arm while she stepped back. He and the others then turned their attention to lifting Sarah. The teacher was slight, and Brody carried her himself once Otis helped lift her into the doctor's arms.

Ainslee followed them to the door and watched as they laid Sarah on thick blankets in the back of the wagon. Otis climbed onto the seat while Brody sat on the edge of the wagon to brace the teacher.

Colton said to Brody, "We brought an injured man to your clinic, Doc. It's Tom. His boy and Ben are waiting with him now. He's not awake. I'm afraid it looks bad."

Brody shook his head as though trying to understand the sudden surge of violence in their small town. "I'll see to him straightaway."

Ainslee noticed the concern etched around Colton's eyes. "You know Sarah—Mrs. Beckert is what one of the students called her."

Colton nodded as the wagon left the meadow. "As well as anyone else around here. She and her son have been through a lot. The town offered her the teaching position a few months ago."

"Brody said she has no husband."

"Disappeared not long after the family arrived, less than two years ago. I found him this past spring, drowned."

Ainslee filled in the rest of the story and wondered what course of events would lead a man to abandon his family, only to turn up dead long after. "They did not need this to happen to them."

"No, they didn't, but they'll get through it. The strong ones always do."

COLTON STOOD OUTSIDE the door of Doc Brody's clinic when Ethan and Gabriel approached on their horses. They dismounted at the same time, securing their mounts. Neither needed to ask what was already a question.

"Doc thinks Tom will live. The knife damaged one of his lungs, but Brody said it could have been worse. Tom Jr. saved his pa's life by coming back to us for help when he couldn't find him."

Ethan removed his hat and ran his hand through his dark hair. The hat he held in front of him. "Was Tom conscious when you found him?"

Colton shook his head, his gaze darting periodically to the street and businesses within sight. People stopped and looked and spoke among themselves, before moving on to their own affairs. When they'd brought Tom into town, the wagon made enough noise to draw people outside, if they weren't already. "We weren't able to talk with him and may not for a few days. Brody said if Tom does pull through, it may be a day or more before he wakes up. Whoever did this beat him badly."

"Torture?" Ethan asked.

Colton nodded. "Appeared that way to me. I know knives, and some of those wounds weren't meant to kill."

"What the hell is going on around here?" Gabriel asked no one in particular. He also removed his hat to reveal the same dark hair as his brother. "Where's Tom Jr.?"

"He's with Ainslee at the café."

Ethan's brow raised, his body stiffened. "What's Ainslee doing here? Brenna said she was going to spend the day with her."

"Brenna is fine." Colton explained what happened at the school and how Ainslee insisted Pete and Jackson take Brenna back to the ranch. "It wasn't until Ainslee convinced Brenna that she should get home to Rebecca that Brenna relented and returned with the others."

Ethan said, "Rebecca's name is all Ainslee needed to say. Where's Ben?"

"Ben was with me and Tom Jr., but he's at the school looking around to see if he can find any sign as to what happened to Sarah. Cord is upstairs with her and won't leave her side."

Ethan asked, "Tom Jr. went with Ainslee without argument?"

"Ainslee has a way about her." Colton still had difficulty believing the ease with which she had managed to convince Tom Jr. to wait with her at the café. A cup of strong coffee and some of Tilly's pie would help pass the time. "How coffee and pie are going to help, I don't know, but it passes the time. Ainslee's had a day of it, that's for sure."

"Did Tom Jr. see anything?" Gabriel asked.

"Nothing."

"And what did you find?"

"More than Tom and his son had been out there recently." Colton waited for a mother and child to pass the clinic before adding, "Three sets of horse tracks, but only two other sets of boot prints."

Ethan began to ask another question when Brody opened the door.

"He'll live." Doc Brody was never one for a lot of words when a few would do. "I recall telling you lads once that I don't need this much business." He darted a glance to each of them. "You're not the first ranch to need my services recently."

Ethan turned to Brody. "Who?"

"The Hudson homestead west of here. They live a ways out so their son came and got me. Spent most of last night with Fred. He'll live, too, but he's going to be off his feet for a few weeks. Bullet got him in the leg and splintered a bone."

"Did he see anyone?"

"Fred didn't see anything, but his boy, Lewis, said he heard the echo of a gun fire. Thought it came from the ridge north of their property. Lewis won't come down, either, but I'll let him know you're here."

Gabriel said, "We won't disturb them right now."

Colton knew the ridge Lewis mentioned.

"That's more than half a mile from their homestead. They have cattle out there. Maybe seventy-five head or thereabouts."

Ethan turned to Brody. "Did Lewis say anything else?"

"His pa was trying to stop a cattle thief. They've lost a few head and Fred wasn't going to let that happen again."

"All told, it's close to fifty head. Does that sound right?" Colton asked.

Ethan answered, "Closer to sixty. We saw Harry Walters on our way back from meeting with the railroad men. He lost a few more last night."

Colton considered the layout of the Hudson homestead and the pasture where Fred's small herd grazed. Of course, Fred would have been diligent. His family was making a good start of it, but smaller farms and ranches couldn't afford even small losses. "Did Lewis see the rustlers?"

Brody nodded. "At least one. He was

more worried about his pa."

Gabriel said, "Sounds like the same outfit that's been hitting our place and the other ranches."

"Yes, but if a shot came from the ridge, then the rustlers have a lookout ready to shoot if anyone gets too close."

"Hell of a shot," Ethan said.

"It is. Over nine hundred yards."

Gabriel asked, "Do you know of anyone around here who can make that shot, besides you?"

Colton glanced at Gabriel. "I managed it once and it was more luck than skill." Colton remembered the day he first held a rifle in his hands, how right it felt there. Later, he learned to match the beat of his breaths to the beat of heart, counting each thump, and squeezing the trigger. Neither man nor beast had been at the other end of that shot, but he had learned a lesson in caution: if he wasn't careful, the gun could one day control him. He had the mountain man to thank him for hard lessons learned in respect. "No one around these parts, at least no one I've heard of, can shoot accurately from that distance."

Ethan said, "It would be too much of a coincidence if Fred's shooting wasn't by the same rustlers making the rounds."

Brody crossed his arms over his chest and motioned behind him. "At the rate injured and dead are coming into my clinic, the trouble is escalating. I've given my life to healing, but if you need an extra gun, you know where to find me. Tom Jr. can come and see his pa." Brody turned and walked back into the clinic, closing the door quietly behind him.

Gabriel turned to Colton. "You planned to go back out on the trail, but it might be better, for a few days, if you stayed close to the ranch and town."

Ethan nodded his agreement. "Gabe's

right, Colton, but it's up to you. You're a hell of a tracker on your own, but when you do go again, it's not alone."

Colton immediately thought of Ainslee. "You're both right, and I'll stay close for another day or two, see what I can find at the Hudson place, but the only way to stop someone like this is to go to them. They don't have to get close to us to do damage."

He knew of two men with the long-distance skills to make that shot: one a Confederate sniper during the war, and the other a Texas buffalo hunter who had no reason to be up north rustling cattle and shooting homesteaders. Colton experienced a familiar sensation tickling its way up his back, his neck, and lodging between the hollow of his shoulders. He straightened and pivoted toward the street.

"Something wrong, Colton?" asked Gabriel.

"You know the feeling when everything appears to make sense but you know deep down it's all wrong?"

"We've all been there."

Colton listened to the familiar sounds of the townspeople, horses, and doors opening and closing as folks went about their business. "Except this time we can't see who's out there. They shouldn't be able to hide this well."

Ethan said, "We've taken care of five of them, but they keep coming. Whoever is leading this keeps to the shadows."

Colton wondered how much longer it would take to clear those shadows and expose the men hiding within.

16

COLTON FOUND THEM in the meadow by the creek. Ainslee sat beside Tom Jr., her feet tucked under the hem of her dress and her knees against her chest. Tom Jr. stood up twice and sat back down in the time it took Colton to cross the expanse of green, summer grass.

Ainslee turned first, her eyes resting on him as he walked toward her. Her hand went to the shoulder of the young man beside her. Colton did not hear what she said, but her words had Tom Jr. fairly jumping to his feet. As an afterthought, he held out a hand to Ainslee to help her stand.

"My pa?"

Colton tried to form a smile for the boy's benefit, though by the expression of pity Ainslee wore, he had not succeeded. "The doc thinks he'll live. He has a long road of recovery ahead of him."

Relief flushed Tom Jr.'s face. "Thank you, Mr. Dawson. I know it was you that saved him."

"No, when you couldn't find your pa, you came for help. You saved him. Don't ever forget that. What you did takes courage." Colton clamped a hand on Tom Jr.'s shoulder. "Doc said you can go and see your pa now."

"He's awake?"

"Not yet, but I hear resting is good for healing."

"And Sarah?"

Colton diverted all of his focus to Ainslee. "She'll be fine. She woke up before I left the clinic."

"Does she remember anything?"

"Not much. She went inside the schoolhouse to fetch something from her desk. She said a man was in there, searching the room in the back."

"What does a thief think to find in a schoolhouse that is worth anything?"

"Sarah doesn't know. The room isn't used. She and her son live in a cottage on the edge of town."

"She keeps nothing of value in there?"

"Nothing. I'm on my way there to look."

Ainslee shielded her eyes from the sun. "Do you mind if I join you?"

"I'd be glad if you did." He held out a hand to steady her up the slight embankment. He need not have worried for she was surefooted, but it gave him a reason to touch her.

"What is happening around here?" Ainslee walked beside him, their strides in sync. "When Brenna spoke of her grandfather, and the troubles he caused, she made those days sound anomalous."

"They were."

"And yet the events since my arrival suggest the evidence is contrary to your words."

They reached the steps of the school when Colton stopped. "The men who are doing this have their reasons. We may not know them, and those reasons are at their core as evil as the men who devise them, but they are just men. Not all people seek to steal and destroy. The ones who do are exceptions."

Colton let Ainslee consider that while he opened the door, and after checking to make sure the school was empty, he beckoned her inside. The square space looked like a typical one-room, country schoolhouse. Blackboard on the front wall, teacher's desk placed in the right spot to see each of the children as they worked, and two rows of tables that served as desks, two chairs to each table. An aisle separated the desks and opened up to the front of the room.

"I always liked the idea of attending a school like this."

Colton glanced over his shoulder to see Ainslee rolling a pencil between her fingers. "You didn't go to school before university?"

"I had tutors. My father believed in educating his children, but schools for girls were not as prevalent. I was luckier than many young girls. My mother insisted I learn how to run a large household, though I much preferred history and literature and riding."

"You and Brenna have that in common— the riding, I mean."

"Our family on all sides have a fondness for horseflesh." Ainslee smiled and moved to the back of the room where a short hallway and door led to the teacher's private rooms. Colton reached for the handle before she did and pushed the door inward. "Oh my."

He entered first and surveyed the mess. "Whoever hit Sarah obviously thought they would find something."

Ainslee moved to the center of the room. "The pressing question is, what would make him look here? It is obvious no one lives here, yet every piece of furniture was looked under. And look, even some of the floorboards have been torn up."

Colton picked up a fallen chair. Beneath it lay pieces of glass and oil from a lamp. "You're right that there is no indication why someone would search this room."

Colton watched Ainslee pick up a silver picture frame and brush away the broken glass. "Who was this? He looks like a kind man."

Amused, Colton looked over her

shoulder at the image. "You can tell from a picture?"

"Some, in the eyes, but more because of his wife, whoever she was. A woman does not cherish a man's image unless she loves him deeply."

Colton suppressed the impulse to ask Ainslee if she knew about love from personal experience. "That looks like the previous school teacher's husband, Mr. Carver. Mrs. Carver was the last one to live in this room before she moved back to Virginia."

"There hasn't been a teacher here since?"

"There have, but no one permanent, not in a long while. Isabelle did some teaching when she first arrived. It's what brought her to Briarwood. The town had placed an advertisement. Amanda has helped some, and the reverend taught for a couple of years."

"Why has there not been someone more permanent?"

"Depending on whom you ask, some might say the position was waiting for Sarah Beckert."

"You really do take care of your own."

"The Gallaghers always have." Colton crossed the room to the door leading outside. "We'll lock up and I'll get someone over here today to clean up."

He waited for Ainslee to follow him, but she remained near the nightstand, the image of Mr. Carver still in her hands. "Yes, the Gallagher family, but all of you. I see how you all look after one another, even considering each other's feelings before speaking. The ranch hands, the townspeople, everyone."

Colton half-raised his hands and shrugged. "It's a small town, close-knit. Without a rail line, we're somewhat isolated. People get to know each other, and for the most part, everyone gets along."

Ainslee set the heavy frame down and joined him at the threshold. "You are a part of them, of all the good they've done, even if you don't want to admit it."

Colton watched her walk through the schoolroom and open the front door. She stepped outside into the sunshine. She didn't sway like one pictures a woman doing. Ainslee moved with a gentle, yet purposeful walk, not wasting a single step.

When he walked outside and secured the door behind him, Colton found Ainslee waiting on the grass looking to the mountains across the meadow. Much of the land remained as open and free as when the first wood buildings in Briarwood were first built.

He watched her enjoying nature's beauty before his gaze drifted to town. They were far enough away to go unnoticed unless someone sought them out but close enough to see some of the goings-on. Even from a distance, Colton recognized many of the people walking from place to place, loading a wagon, or mounting their horses to ride out of town.

Briarwood was growing. Not with any measured pace, but enough people who found their way here over the past ten years chose to make it their home. He sighted a few cowboys he did not recognize, no doubt searching for work while there was still some to be had. When they realized none of the ranches in the area was hiring, they would move on. Colton noticed a young and pretty woman, wearing a long calico skirt, stepped out of the saloon.

Colton stepped up to stand next to Ainslee. She must have seen what captured his interest because she looked in the same direction.

"You've noticed Mrs. Jones."

He faced Ainslee. "Kin to the Bittles, I heard Loren say last time I was in his store. You know her?"

Ainslee shook her head. "We met only this morning in the mercantile. She's fond of adventure stories. Do many women dress that way? I rather think I like it."

"Some do. It's practical." Colton spared her a glance, foolishly hoping what he heard in her voice was jealousy. "I'm partial to the way Scottish women dress." He sent a brief grin before turning back to the view.

"And a woman like that can visit the saloon."

Colton's brow raised as he stared at Ainslee. "You want to go into the saloon?"

"Brenna said it wouldn't be wise."

Colton chuckled. "Brenna's right." But he would take her into the saloon one day soon, if that's what she wanted. "I need to make arrangements here and then check in with Doc Brody before we meet up with Ethan." He placed his hand on the small of her back, a move that followed no thought but felt as natural as breathing. When she said nothing, he let his hand linger for a minute as they walked.

"Ethan is here?"

Colton moved to walk between her and the road when they left the meadow. "He and Gabriel arrived earlier, after you and Tom Jr. left for the café. Ethan should still be at the clinic. Gabriel had a few telegrams to send."

"Did they mention how the meeting with the railroad went?"

"It didn't come up." He glanced down at her as they approached the clinic. "What is your interest in the spur line?"

"I'm curious about many things."

Colton let the subject pass for now and guided her to the steps of Doc Brody's building. Ethan stepped outside and closed the door behind him.

"Saw you two walk over." Ethan first faced Ainslee, his hand settling in a comfortable grip on her forearm in a gesture not unlike something her brothers would do. "Are you all right?"

"I promise, I am all right. We Scots are a sturdy lot."

"Even Brenna had a difficult time when she first arrived in Montana. Took her a little while to adjust, but you've also seen more than she did in a shorter amount of time."

"I was not quite so sheltered as Brenna. I love you dearly for your worry, and I promise if I feel my legs begin to quake beneath me, I will find a quiet place and cry for days."

Ethan grinned and leaned down to brush a kiss over Ainslee's cheek. "It's good you're here. As far as I'm concerned,

Hawk's Peak can be overrun by Camerons and McConnells, and we'll make room for more."

Colton enjoyed the easy camaraderie she shared with Ethan. One could not stay in her company without catching her good humor and potent attitude of positive thinking.

Ethan's smile faded somewhat when he shifted his focus to Colton. "Tom Jr. doesn't want to leave his father's side. Brody has a recovery room that isn't occupied and offered it for the boy until Tom mends."

"Did Tom ever wake up?"

"Briefly." Ethan's surreptitious glance to Ainslee did not go unnoticed as he might have hoped.

"I will leave if you prefer to speak with Colton in private."

Colton shrugged and said to Ethan, "You may as well say whatever it is in front of her."

"It's about you, Colton." Ethan's eyes darted to the street. "Let's step inside. Brody already heard everything Tom said."

They moved inside the clinic and Colton closed the door behind them. "What about me?"

"Tom said the men who came after him were asking questions about you."

Colton suffered the metaphoric blow to his stomach. He'd been in a few brawls in his time and was familiar with the sensation. "This happened to Tom because of me?" He felt Ainslee's hand on his arm, but it did not stop the tightening of his muscles.

Ethan's voice became softer. "This is not your fault, Colton. They probably would have hurt Tom even if he told them straight off what they wanted to hear. We've all known men like this."

Colton wished he could see the situation from Ethan's perspective, but the blame ran deep and curdled in his belly. "Did he say what they wanted?"

"Tom doesn't remember everything. Brody said he might later, but right now his brain is still foggy—Doc's words, not mine. He said the men wanted to know if Colton Dawson lived at Hawk's Peak and how long you've been there."

"And that's why some of the knife wounds look like he was tortured."

Ethan nodded. "Tom wanted me to tell you he was sorry because in the end, he finally confirmed you lived at the ranch. They left him to die after that."

"I wish to hell they would have come after me instead. They've been watching the ranch long enough to know I was there. It wouldn't have been hard to find me. Why hurt someone else?"

"That might be the answer. Could be

they want you to suffer. Do you have any enemies you can think of?"

Colton studied Ainslee's upturned face and read the concern in her eyes. He had not forgotten she was there, yet her presence remained on the edge of his thoughts while he spoke with Ethan. "I have no idea. I've helped put a lot of men in prison and sent a few to their graves. Any one of them or their families could be behind this. Everything that has happened—the rustling, the attempts to kill Tom and Fred Hudson—they're all connected, and these men are looking for me."

Colton took a step away from Ethan and Ainslee. "I have to find them before they hurt anyone else. Now! I'll leave today."

"Alone?" Ainslee asked.

"No." Ethan brought their attention back to him. Colton knew what his friend was going to say. "These men have eluded us long enough. It's obvious they could have found me without hurting Tom, and they could go after someone else at the ranch or in town next. No one else is going to be hurt, or worse, because of me, Ethan. I'm right here, damn it. If they want me, I'll give them an easier target."

Colton left the clinic and Ainslee made to follow him. It was the gentle tug on her shoulders by Ethan that stopped her. "Let him go."

"He can't go out there alone, Ethan."

Ethan held her close. "He won't be alone."

17

AINSLEE RETURNED TO Hawk's Peak with Ethan and Gabriel. The ride presented them with an opportunity for her to ask more questions, though she finally admitted to herself that research for her story was the furthest thing from her thoughts.

She chided Ethan when she said Brenna's upbringing had been more sheltered than her own, and while true, every moment of her life had been wrapped in privilege and safety. Was it her longing for adventure that grounded her instead of allowing fear to take hold? Had years of telling tales inured her to the true realities of the world?

Even while in England, she resided in a well-appointed home run by a landlady who boarded many of the girls who attended Cheltenham Ladies' College. Ainslee used to believe her daring excursions to London without a chaperone had given her great insight into the world.

She'd been so very wrong.

The history of her own country was riddled with barbaric exploits and fields littered with blood and bodies leftover from battles. She had shed a tear over lives lost she never knew, and yet that is where history rested—in books—where it could be safely read and studied from a library or drawing room. She never once imagined she would witness what could become a part of someone else's tragic history.

"I didn't know."

Ethan and Gabriel flanked her on either

side, keeping a few feet between the horses. She sensed them both looking at her while she kept her eyes forward.

"I didn't know what Brenna's life was like here, not really. I have to confess something to you, to everyone." Ainslee did glance at each of them first, her gaze resting a little longer on Ethan. "I did not come here merely to see Brenna and meet Ramsey." She hurried on with her explanation. "That was my primary reason, but—"

"I know." A faint smile touched his lips. "You don't have to explain. Brenna figured you had other reasons. She said you were one for adventure and it would take more than family to bring you here."

Ainslee had never experienced such guilt, though she did not believe Ethan meant that to be her reaction. "Brenna remembers me well—too well, perhaps."

Ethan shook his head and chuckled.

"She said you would say that, too. Doesn't matter what brought you here, Ainslee, it's only important that you *are* here."

Ainslee wanted to tell them about herself, about Finn Pickett, but she couldn't, not yet. Brenna and Ramsey deserved to know, but even as she thought of how she would tell them, it was Colton whom she needed to tell first.

Her adamancy for Finn Pickett to remain a secret now hinted at childishness. She had always held the persona close, believing that to reveal the truth could lead to catastrophe for herself and her family. For too long it had built up into something of such great importance, to keep her family's good name intact among their social set, she did not consider how insignificant it might look to others. Even now, she recognized the frivolity of her life compared to the real and dangerous situations people here faced every day.

She believed herself free and unsheltered back home, but never did she have to face life or death head-on, not until she came here. Was it wrong that she had never felt more alive?

THE AFTERNOON SUNSHINE presented favorable conditions for gardening. Ainslee needed to do something to keep her hands and mind busy, and writing was not an option with so many distractions.

"Why does Briarwood not have a sheriff?"

Brenna paused in her digging and raised her head enough to look at Ainslee from beneath her wide-brimmed straw hat. "We do not have need of a sheriff full-time."

Ainslee studied her cousin from the sensible leather boots and dirt-covered apron to the hat without adornments. Beneath the practical clothing, Brenna's skin glowed with her usual pale rose complexion. This life suited her, Ainslee decided. No matter how much Brenna spoke of missing Scotland, she had settled well into her Montana home.

She dug her spade into the earth once more. "What about the rustling, and the men Colton has brought into the jail?"

"Those are unusual circumstances." This time Brenna set her spade down and sat back on her heels. "We have done well without a sheriff. When a situation requires someone to enforce the law, Ramsey steps in. He is what one would call an occasional marshal. Ben and Colton and others have been temporarily deputized when necessary, but it rarely is. Talk of hiring a sheriff is mentioned on occasion."

"You have a saloon, and I imagine there

are men who travel through bent on thieving."

Brenna laughed. "You are thinking of novels again. Yes, we have a saloon. Sometimes there are disturbances there, but Milly does not tolerate misbehavior."

Ainslee grew more curious because of what Brenna *wasn't* saying. "Has Briarwood no troubles that would require someone to put on a badge in a more permanent position?"

Brenna unearthed a potato and set it in her basket. "You have an insatiable curiosity that is difficult to satisfy, I imagine. We have troubles, like anywhere else, and not limited to what you have already witnessed. Danger followed Amanda all the way from Dakota. Catie came to be in our family because her father left her to fend for herself in the cold of winter. People die, give birth, lose their homes, and find their fortunes. We do not need a sheriff to manage any of that. We take care of each other."

Ainslee began to understand. "And if the railroad brings a spur line here?"

"They will fight it. Ethan, Gabriel, and Eliza will stand side by side and fight to keep it from coming here."

"Is it not futile to try to stop progress?"

Brenna shook her head. "No. It is about preserving our way of life."

"The railroad connects people and places. If the train came to Briarwood, how much easier it would be for you to start a journey to Scotland."

"Or you?" Brenna smiled. "It may take longer for us to start and end a journey or to receive supplies, but it is not so great a distance to Bozeman, at least not far enough for them to reconsider a spur line."

"And your husband and his siblings will be successful in keeping it away?" Ainslee looked more closely at Brenna and realized she had not looked up to meet her gaze. "What worries you so?"

A fluttering of the air flicked the edge of Brenna's hat back, making it easier for Ainslee to watch as Brenna answered. "To answer your question . . . I worry that the day will come when fighting to preserve what we hold most dear will no longer be an option."

AINSLEE GAVE CAREFUL thought to what Brenna said, and her earlier words about Ainslee not yet understanding their way of life. She struggled to know what deeper meaning still eluded her. She chose the quiet library for an hour of writing, believing the surroundings would bring forth fresh ideas. To anyone passing by, it would appear she was writing letters—if she could write.

The paper in front of her sat blank. The evening before the words would not cease to flow and today her mind lacked inspiration.

"Ainslee?"

She turned away from the large territorial map on the wall to the door. "Ramsey!" They met halfway across the room and embraced. "I was told you and Eliza have a sick mare. Is she well now?"

Ramsey nodded and motioned for Ainslee to sit down in one of the walnut tufted armchairs near the window. "The foal made it through but his mother is still weak. If she survives the next twenty-four hours, she'll have a chance. Eliza is still with her. Gabriel is over there keeping his sister company since she refuses to leave the stable."

"I am so sorry, Ramsey." Her hand automatically grasped for his. "I do hope the mare comes through. The foal is well?"

"He's healthy and strong and has been able to feed. All we can do is wait. The mare would be a great loss. Eliza claimed I was in her way, but I think she wanted time alone with the mare. She's become attached."

Ramsey said the latter with tenderness, and Ainslee imagined his wife noticed the darker smudges under his eyes and the slow, measured speech, as if he had to think twice as hard to form the words he wanted. "You should be sleeping."

"As Eliza has already told me, but the ride over helped. I wanted to see you. We haven't had enough time together since you arrived."

"There is no urgency for my departure. I am becoming rather fond of this land." Ainslee meant every word. "May I bother you with a question?"

"You may ask me anything."

"It is rather personal . . . about how you

came to stay here." When Ramsey smiled and nodded for her to continue, Ainslee did. "When did you know this is where you wanted to be?"

Ramsey answered without hesitation. "When I saw Eliza again."

"It was that easy?"

"How I felt about Eliza and her family, this place, that was easy. Making the decision to stay wasn't. Why do you ask?"

Ainslee prepared to offer her usual "because I am curious" excuse, but she was tired of hiding what she really wanted from the world. She had spent much of her adult life pretending to be someone else, and it had become too automatic. "I have not told anyone else this yet, but there is a part of me that wants to stay."

"And the other part?"

"Yearns to discover what is beyond the mountains and the next great sea. I want to experience all I can, now that I have had a taste of travel beyond familiar shores."

"Why can't you have both?"

Ainslee leaned against the back of the chair and stared at her cousin. "I do not even know how that is possible. Brenna talks of returning to Scotland, to show her children the other part of their heritage, and yet she has not gone back."

"She will."

"You believe that?"

"Without a single doubt in my mind." Ramsey moved closer to the edge of his chair and leaned forward. "You mistake her longing for Scotland with regret that she hasn't returned."

Ainslee did not acknowledge but neither did she disagree. "What if she never returns?"

"You mean, what if you become involved here and don't feel you can leave whenever you want?"

Ainslee gave a slight nod.

"Brenna has chosen a legacy for her children beyond wood and stones and land." Ramsey stood and held Ainslee's eyes for a few seconds. "The next time you go riding or into town or sit with the family for an evening, think of what I've said. All the answers you need will be within the circle of family. There are no fences holding you in one place. The choice is always yours. Perhaps you might consider that Brenna made hers."

Ramsey bent over to kiss the top of her head, and she watched him leave the library.

COLTON STOOD TWENTY feet above the ground on the rocky ledge of the ridge. The Hudson farm stood almost half a mile away, made up of a modest, wood-sided house, a large barn, and a smaller shed behind the house. Two horses stood near each other in the single corral. A few of the thirty acres of fields behind the house had been tilled and a quarter acre appeared to be used as the family vegetable garden. Fred's small herd of cattle grazed on the remaining land.

The Hudson family were relative newcomers to Montana, having left Nebraska the summer before. They had ventured north with money from the sale of their old farm, which gave them enough of a stake to take them through their first two winters and buy the homestead and cattle. Colton knew the land well, and what the Hudsons bought had been rockier than many areas. They bought the land cheap and worked hard to turn rocky dirt into rich soil that would no doubt yield healthy crops.

Fred Hudson knew farming more than ranching, and he was teaching his son well, but with Fred laid up, much of the work would go undone. The herd was small enough for them to handle alone, but without extra hands, it made the Hudsons easy targets for the rustlers. Briarwood needed more people like the Hudsons, who worked hard for everything they had and respected the land.

Colton lowered his body to the ground, much in the same way the shooter would have done, the spot likely chosen because of the burrowed-out log that ran horizontal to the farm in the distance. He rested the front six inches of the barrel on the log, dug his left elbow slightly into the ground, and braced the stock against his shoulder, holding it in place with his hand. His finger hovered over the trigger but never touched it.

He steadied his breathing and focused his gaze over the top of the barrel toward the farm. From this distance, without a scope, it was not a shot Colton could have made. The rustler behind the shooting—and he had no doubt the man was part of the same group—was not a typical rustler. He'd been trained well by someone.

Colton lowered his rifle and raised himself up until he was sitting with his back braced against the log. The short ridge offered the perfect vantage point to see across that section of the valley with a clear view of where the rustlers might have entered and left.

Colton stood and looked back down at the modest house. He'd made some enemies, but none that came to mind who could shoot at long distances. Those skills tended to be noted on wanted posters and in wires or even by reputation. Not a single person he ever helped bring to justice possessed such skills, but people with those talents did exist.

Colton holstered his rifle and mounted his gelding. His was one of the few at

Hawk's Peak without a name. The children at the ranch made a game of naming as many animals as they could, but he always assured them when the horse was ready to tell them his name, he would. Colton called the horse "friend," even if it was a simplistic term for what the animal meant to him. They'd been through a lot together over the years, and he was as true and faithful a horse as any man could hope to have.

Colton didn't know what made him think of it, except his recent ponderings on friendship and relationships, and his limited experience with both. Ainslee's presence made him think of a lot of things he'd rather keep buried, and yet here he was, contemplating names for his horse.

"What say we find this shooter and the rest of his rustlers and put an end to it?"

The horse moved his head up and down twice as though he understood what had been asked. Colton liked to think he did.

Rocks scattered down the slope. Colton's hand moved to the pistol at his hip. When he saw the rider emerge from around a boulder, he relaxed. "Can't sneak up on a man making all that noise."

"I wanted you to hear me coming." Ramsey and his horse, Prince, stopped a few feet away. Ramsey took in the same view Colton had only minutes before. "Ethan thought you might have come here."

"Didn't learn much more than we already figured out. The cattle thieves have a sharpshooter, obviously not one of the men they've already lost because Fred was shot after I brought in the last two."

"We know they've recruited locally, men like Ike, but I can't think of anyone else in these parts who would turn to thieving."

Colton agreed, but added, "Ike has worked a few of the ranches that were hit.

He could have been the outfit's source of information."

Ramsey said, "I sent out telegrams when I was in Bozeman. Gabriel picked up a few replies when he was at the telegraph office. No one has heard of a similar group of rustlers within the surrounding territories."

"Then it's as Tom said. They're here because of me."

"The question is, who would want revenge so much that they're willing to torture you like this?"

Colton stared at Ramsey. "Torture?"

"Tom is like family. Fred Hudson is a part of Briarwood. These are your people—all of ours. Whoever is doing this knows going after others is going to hurt you."

Colton nodded, his gaze on the horizon.

"Not alone, Colton. Not this time."

"I can lead these men away from the

ranch, from town. If I go far enough, they'll have no reason to hurt anyone else."

"And how long will you stay away? Until they get what they want?" Ramsey shook his head and turned his horse around so he and Colton faced the same direction. "You do what you feel you have to do. And we'll do the same."

Dark and angry clouds, colored with varying shades of gray, rolled in over the mountains. Colton estimated they would cover the valley in a few hours, bringing a heavy storm. He had men to find. "Come on then." In tandem, horses and riders turned and rode down the sloped side of the ridge.

AINSLEE PULLED HER horse to a stop when she saw Brenna do the same. They both glanced at the sky. Ainslee had convinced Brenna to go riding so that she could finally reveal her other identity to her cousin. Life as a closeted authoress was not so important a secret when one actually considered the many possible confidences a person might confess.

For Ainslee, it was a monumental confession, and not because she worried what people would think or because others may learn the real identity behind the Finn Pickett adventures. No, it was because this secret had been hers alone for so long, she was too selfish to share it. Ainslee asked herself why she felt the need now to tell someone.

The best way to face a difficult task was to push right through it or so her father used to say. "Brenna, there is something you should know about me."

"Why do you look so frightened?" Brenna's chiding smile faltered. "Ainslee, are you all right? You're positively nervous."

"I know, and it's trivial, but I must get this out."

"If it bothers you to tell me, then do not."

Ainslee blinked a few times, which gave herself a minute to think. "If I cannot bring myself to share this part of who I am, then I fear I will always be too selfish. If I am selfish, I will not be able to . . ."

Brenna's eyes filled with moisture, and Ainslee realized it was a response to her own tears hovering at the edge of her lashes. She swiped them away and cleared her throat.

"What is you want to be able to do?"

Ainslee felt her heart constrict. This confession was not about Finn Pickett. The revelation came as a fierce blow, much like the wind pushing against her back and whipping the mare's mane over the reins. "Brenna, I—"

Brenna said above the wind, "The storm

is moving in too fast. We must return now."

Ainslee heard the concern in Brenna's voice. She had delayed telling her cousin, and now they would—

"Ainslee!"

The first thunderous roar through the sky collided with the atmosphere and shook the air around them. Ainslee's mare pranced and raised her front legs off the ground just enough for Ainslee to lose her grip.

Brenna slid off her horse, her hat captured by the growing wind and carried into the meadow. "Dinna shift. Are ye hurt?"

Ainslee concentrated on her limbs and cringed against the delayed onset of pain. It didn't emanate from the wound in her back, which was more of a twinge now. "Aye." She breathed deeply and focused. "My ankle."

Brenna gingerly lifted Ainslee's right foot and immediately set it down. "I saw that. Yer in pain."

"Aye, a lot. 'Tis nae tae painful if I dinna move." Ainslee examined the options and dismissed all but one. "Brenna, look at me. You need to ride back to the ranch."

"I am not leaving you here! Did you not recognize that sound?"

"It was thunder, and you cannot lift me nor can I stand."

"We cannae ken if we dinna try, and it was the echo of a rifle shot we heard in that thunder, and you well know it."

Ainslee shook her head in exasperation. "The way you and I go back and forth, I suspect it must be maddening to those who listen."

"You thinking such a thing means you are growing accustomed to American ways far more quickly than I did. Now," Brenna made sure the wide legs of her riding skirt were not in the way when she hunched low next to Ainslee, "put your arm around me and I am going to lift."

Ainslee almost laughed. Brenna was shorter and fine-boned. She surprised Ainslee with her strength. When they couldn't get Ainslee on her feet, it was not for lack of Brenna's efforts. The ankle simply would not hold any weight.

"It is no use. It will take longer to get me in the saddle than it will for you to reach the ranch. Perhaps one of the hands are out and you will not have to ride as far for help." Ainslee gave the sky another quick study. "There is still time before the rain comes. Ride now. I promise, Lady and I will be all right."

The mare had not entirely settled down. She did not run when she could have, though, which meant a great deal to Ainslee. She recognized the echo of a rifle shot, too, a sound familiar thanks to the hunts with her father. "If someone fired a rifle, they were not aiming at us or we would be injured or dead."

"You already are injured. Let us try again." Brenna moved once more to Ainslee's side but was brushed away.

"If the rain comes sooner than we expect, it is better for only one of us to be out here drenched. Go now. The sooner you get help, the sooner I will be all right."

It was the last statement that decided Brenna, as Ainslee knew it would. Family first and always, the Gallagher way, and they both knew getting help was more useful than arguing. Brenna led Lady to Ainslee and handed her the reins. She climbed onto the back of her mare and headed in the direction of the house.

Ainslee held fast to the reins and looked up at the horse. "A fine mess you have settled me in, Lady. If you were not such a proper and gentle sort, I might take offense thinking you did not want me on your back." She rubbed the horse's nose when the mare lowered her head. "You *are* a lady and I know you did not mean for it to happen."

She laughed at herself and looked around. The wind had cooled and gained more strength. Not too far in the distance, Ainslee noticed Brenna's hat lift off the tall grass, swirl in the air, and glide back to the ground. It struck Ainslee as ridiculous and she let loose another laugh. "What say we try to get me off the ground before the rain comes?"

Lady remained still except for a slight lift and lower of a hoof. Ainslee managed to scoot and roll herself to a kneeling position, the task made somewhat easier by the special-made riding clothes that allowed her greater movement. She spoke to the mare as she guided the animal forward just enough so she could grasp the stirrup.

Out of breath from the exertion and mounting pain, Ainslee leaned forward, resting her head against her arms. Lady nickered, drawing Ainslee's attention back to the next step in resolving her predicament. If luck found her worthy of its attention, Brenna would have come across one of the ranch hands by now. She imagined soaking her foot in a basin filled with warm water and salts as she relaxed next to the kitchen hearth.

Adventuring came with risks, especially when a young girl had three brothers. Once her brothers were of an age to spend more time at school than at home, she found ways to amuse herself, and one of those outings resulted in the twisting of her ankle. At least this time it wasn't the same foot. However, she decided she had reached her fill of injuries.

"Can we do this, Lady? I think we can."

The first raindrop hit her shoulder, darkening the fabric. Ainslee mustered all of her upper body strength to pull herself up. Lady sidestepped, but Ainslee had managed to grip the saddle horn and hold tight. She balanced her weight on her uninjured leg, but there was no way she could pull herself into the saddle.

When a new blast of noise thundered through the sky, there was no mistaking it carried more than Nature's wrath. The shot sounded closer this time, but still far enough away for Ainslee to not consider herself in immediate danger.

As the rain began to fall in earnest, she almost regretted sending Brenna for help. Almost. She did not want her cousin, a mother and wife, to fall ill because of her. She turned at the sound of more thunder, trying to discern the distance between her and the heart of the storm.

"Ainslee!"

She heard her name carried over the wind but from which direction she could not discern. Over and over, closer and closer, her name echoed. She knew. Before she saw him, she knew it was Colton. How, she did not care. It only mattered that he was there, that he was the one who found her.

He rode up alongside her, dismounted, and pulled her onto his lap. His hat protected his face, allowing her to see the grim set of lips, the hardened lines of his jaw. He helped her onto his horse, lifting most of her weight, and swung back up behind her. Colton grabbed Lady's reins, and pulling the mare behind them, they rode into the rain.

Ainslee buried her face in Colton's chest to ward off the rain. Each drop felt like a sharp pin pinching her skin through her summer-weight clothes. Colton pressed the reins into her hands long enough to slow down the horse and remove his jacket. He covered her, took the reins back, and urged his horse to move faster, away from the ranch.

18

THE LARGER OF the cabins was still drafty but it was in better repair than the others. Tom and Tom Jr. had finished fixing it up before Tom's injuries, which meant it was somewhat stocked. Two cots, a sturdy table, three chairs and a stool, and a long shelf covered in cooking tools, tin plates, and cups. The roof and walls would hold, which satisfied Colton's primary concern.

"We'll be safe here until the storm passes." He laid her down gently on one of the cots.

"Are you angry with me?"

Colton removed his coat and laid it over

the back of a chair to dry. "No." He opened the tinderbox and removed what he needed to start the fire. The flue was clear, and a few dry pieces of wood sat in the stove. He moved them around and added another from the box nearby.

"How did you find me?"

"I was following a trail leading toward the northwest section of the ranch when Brenna saw me. She rode over and told me what happened. She's frantic about you, but I promised I'd bring you back. The rain started by then and so I told her to go ahead home."

"Won't they come looking when we don't return?"

Colton shook his head. "Based on where Brenna said I could find you, they'll figure out I brought you here until the storm lets up."

"You *are* angry."

"Staying behind was a damn fool thing.

What if a wolf or mountain lion found you first? Lady's a good horse, but she would have run if she caught the scent of either." Or whoever fired the rifle. The two shots, along with the fresh trail, had told him he moved in the right direction. He *was* angry but not with her.

"I wasn't thinking, at least not about the other dangers. I thought it best for Brenna to find help and she did. She found you. On our own, it would have taken too long to try and get me on Lady's back."

"No, you weren't thinking." He exhaled and looked at her with a measure of admiration. "But I understand why you did it." He waited until the wood caught and flames began to grow before he closed the stove door and brushed his hands against each other. "Stay here." Colton offered no explanation when he stepped outside. Rain crashed around him, but he didn't care. The storm matched his own fury, and he needed the seconds or minutes to calm down before he returned to her. He looked after the horses, securing them under a lean-to that was in decent repair. It wasn't roomy, but at least the animals would stay dry.

He filled a bucket with water from a larger barrel, giving the horses their fill. He filled a second bucket and hauled it inside. Her long fingers were busy separating her hair and winding it into a braid. Neither said anything while Colton set the water bucket on the edge of the table and removed two cups from a shelf. He placed three candles near the center of the table and lit them. The flickering light combined with the warmth of the stove gave the cabin interior a comfortable glow.

"We don't keep food here but only bring what we need for as long as we'll be here. Draws animals otherwise." When she offered no response, he looked at her.

"What I mean is, we have plenty of water thanks to the rain, but there will be nothing to eat until the storm lets up and we get you back to the house."

"I am not hungry. Besides, they feed a body enough at each meal to last well into the next. I have been storing up."

He felt his lips twitch and almost smiled because that's what she wanted. He couldn't, though, not yet. "The cots are reasonably comfortable and there are plenty of blankets. I suggest you rest." Colton pointed to her feet. "You should dry your boots and stockings by the stove. You'll be more comfortable until we ride back."

"And how long do you think that will be?"

"No telling how long a storm like this will last. We knew it was coming, and all we can do is wait it out."

Colton watched her shift to the edge of

the cot and swore under his breath. He knelt next to her, brushing her hands away. "The foot will swell when the boot comes off."

"I know. I hurt my ankle once before, as a young girl."

"Falling off a horse?"

She shook her head. "Out of a tree."

Colton wondered at a girl who as a child climbed trees and hunted with her father's gamekeeper, and how that girl became the sophisticated woman before him. Except now, with her clothes muddy, her face washed clean from the rain, and her hair in a single, damp braid, she looked more like a woman used to his way of life. He looked away from her face.

With great care, he undid the laces on each slim boot before slipping them off. The boot on her injured foot did not come off as easily. He heard her intake of breath when the leather slid over the ankle.

His fingers itched to continue, to roll one stocking and then the other down her leg, while his hands . . . he silently swore and turned away. His clothes were soaked, but they would warm soon enough if he sat near the stove. "The stockings should dry without removing them."

"It was an accident. I was not paying attention and the thunder spooked Lady."

"The combination of the storm and gunfire would have bothered her."

"You know about the latter?"

Colton nodded. "I heard the first shot before I met up with Brenna. She mentioned it as well."

"Is shooting so uncommon that it bears so much curiosity?"

"It's uncommon during a storm. Only a desperate fool hunts in this weather, and anyone who should be on Hawk's Peak land is neither fool or desperate."

"You are certain they were on the ranch's

land?"

"I am."

Ainslee moaned softly when she rubbed a hand over her ankle. "And now with the rain, you will not be able to find their trail."

"Might get lucky and find something. Besides, you come first. I should have known you were bound to fall into some sort of trouble."

"And why is that?"

Colton ignored the bite he heard in her voice. "You gravitate to trouble."

"I do not."

"You do." He moved both chairs next to the stove, adding another piece of wood. The small cabin filled with a comfortable warmth. "You'll dry faster over here." Without asking permission, he lifted her into his arms and for a few seconds enjoyed holding her close before lowering into the chair.

It seemed to Colton that she spent a few seconds longer than necessary to mull over his words.

"It was an accident. Brenna had just suggested we return when we noticed the clouds."

"I heard you."

"Yet you do not believe me."

"Oh, I believe you. What I don't understand is how you two got so far from the house. Brenna would have seen signs of the storm. She's been here long enough to know how sudden they hit and how dangerous it can be to ride in them."

The rush of color to her face told Colton what he needed to know. "It wasn't Brenna's idea."

"'Twas mine. I had something to tell her and I was thinking of how to do so. The longer we rode, the more time I had to think."

"Must be something important. Did you

get it said?"

She stiffened in the chair. "No, and it turned out not to be as important as I thought."

He enjoyed her prickly side and figured if he could keep her in a constant state of agitation while they were sequestered together, he'd be more likely to keep his hands to himself. "It was still foolish."

"In Scotland—"

"It behooves me—"

"Behooves?"

"Yes, you're not familiar with the word?"

"I am, but I did not expect to hear it from your lips."

Colton checked his smile. "It's a good word. Doesn't matter, though. You talk a lot about what you have done in Scotland, and you need another reminder that you are not in Scotland. You are in the territory of Montana. I lack your acquaintance with your home, but I know this place, and the territories around it. I am familiar with the dangers because I have seen and experienced many of them firsthand."

He shifted so he faced her. Their knees touched, but neither of them moved to put any distance there. "You don't know what this ground will do when it soaks through, or how deep the creek can get, or how much it will overflow when you try to cross it because you aren't thinking about what's coming down from those mountains. You're a skilled rider, there's no denying it, but there are places more prone to holes where a horse can get its leg caught. There'd be no saving the animal from something like that or you if it fell on top of you. Brenna knows the dangers of this land, too, so when she wanted to turn back, it was with your safety in mind. Had Ethan known—"

Ainslee held up a hand as though to ward off further discussion. "I understand."

"Do you?"

"Yes." She met and held his gaze. Firelight flickered from the candles, the effect brightening the darker gray ring around her irises. "I am accustomed to spending a good deal of time alone without considering others. At home—" She held up a finger again to prevent him from commenting. "I knew every acre of our properties. I had my favorite places, and if someone needed to find me, it was not difficult. I am familiar with my home, just as you are with this land. I did not consider the distinction."

"This sounds like the makings of an apology."

She straightened her back a smidgen. "Would you like an apology?"

"Not necessary. Just saying it sounds like the makings of one."

"You're an exasperating man."

"You've said as much."

"I am not sorry for going riding or for asking Brenna along. I am sorry to have caused you or anyone else concern, especially Brenna. Was she truly upset when she found you?"

"Worried enough to want to ride back with me, to assure herself that you were going to be all right."

"It is good she did not. This weather is no place for a woman with her responsibilities as a mother and wife."

Colton latched onto and considered her words. "It's no place for anyone. Brenna knew you would be unhappy if she returned, which is why she went on to the ranch. She knows you well."

"She knew her mother." Ainslee looked out the window when a clash of thunder rolled through the atmosphere. "It sounds closer."

"What does knowing her mother have to

do with you?" Colton wanted her distracted from the tumultuous skies outside. The thunder was close and so was the lightning. A fire or two would not be unexpected, though the heavy rainfall should keep them from spreading.

"My mother used to talk of Rebecca Cameron often, even after her death. She said Brenna's mother was always the more adventurous, wanting to travel and try new things. It was she who often led them into trouble, but my mother willingly followed. My mother once confessed her concern over how much I was like her childhood friend and wondered if it was speaking of Rebecca that led me to become who I am today."

Colton digested the information for a minute. "Your mother isn't happy with who you are?"

Ainslee's shoulders lifted in a dainty shrug. "She loves me, but I am often impressed with the idea that she wishes I grew into someone more like her."

"I like who you are."

Her eyes flashed when she looked to him. "You think I am bothersome."

"You are, at times."

"And stubborn and opinionated, and I believe I once heard you use the term exasperating."

"That's what you call me."

"Was I mistaken?"

He smiled now and meant it. "No, you are all of those things." Colton leaned forward. "Along with courageous and admirable. You're also intelligent, beautiful, strong-spirited—and I say that in a good way—and you care more for the safety of others than you do for yourself."

"Now there you are wrong. I am often more selfish than you realize."

"Nothing wrong with being selfish once in a while."

"You said I was beautiful."

"No, I said you *are* beautiful." Colton slid one hand on either side of her face, cupping it gently and drawing her closer. "Since I first saw you, full of indignation after you threw the knife at—"

"'Twas a dirk."

"A dirk." He inched his face closer, absorbing every ounce of scent and energy emanating from her. As always, she smelled like a summer meadow from whatever soap she used on her skin. He often wondered what it would feel like to run his hands over every inch of her alabaster body. He already knew that beneath her layers of clothing, her skin was as soft as roses and cream. He craved more than the mere glimpses he had caught of her back during his ministrations.

They rose from their chairs in tandem, Colton lifting her, holding her weight.

"This isn't proper."

Ainslee smiled. "And you like to do things properly. You did say I was stubborn."

"You are."

"And I told you I am sometimes selfish."

Colton chuckled and held her closer. "You did."

Ainslee lifted her hands to move up his arms. He felt the heat from her skin through his clothes.

"Ainslee, please listen. I'm still strong enough to let you go, but that strength is fading fast."

Her upturned face and smooth lips beckoned him. "This is one of those improprieties, the kind that makes you afraid to be near me."

He nuzzled her neck, kissed up her smooth cheek, and whispered in her ear, "Tell me to go away."

Ainslee shook her head. "I have never

claimed to be a saint. I am certainly not a hypocrite."

"Ainslee." Her name escaped as a shallow breath.

"I dinna want ye to go away."

He eased back enough to stare into her eyes, searching for uncertainty. Instead, he found liberation. Colton still held her face in his hands. He could, with great ease, guide her to him, but it mattered to him that she meet him halfway. He lowered his head, she raised hers, bringing her mouth closer, and it was all the invitation he needed. They sealed their lips, their bodies pressed together.

19

THE STORM ABATED sometime during the night. Ainslee had slept soundly for a few hours, awakened only by the gentle rise and fall of the strong chest beneath her hand. She could see Colton's face with help from the moon's gentle light drifting through the cabin window and sensed he was awake.

His hand covered hers, surprising Ainslee to tilt her head farther back and look into the warm eyes staring back at her.

"The storm has passed." Colton's voice and eyes were clear, as though he'd been awake for some time.

"It is time to return."

He nodded. Neither one of them moved off the cot. It was a new and wonderful experience for Ainslee, to enjoy the comfort of a man's arms around her while she slept. It was an experience she did not wish to end, and yet dawn would soon be upon them.

They lay in silence a few minutes longer. Colton brushed a kiss on her forehead and rolled to a sitting position before pushing off the cot. He buttoned his shirt and slipped into his boots. "I need to look at your ankle before your boots go on."

Ainslee shifted and sat up, dropping her feet over the edge. His fingers held and gently pressed against the ankle. "There's still some swelling. You're going to have to ride with me again."

He wasn't looking at her. Ainslee cupped the side of his face and turned her toward him. "I have no regrets."

"Neither do I." Colton pressed his face against her hand. "Doesn't make it right. At least it wouldn't, if I didn't plan for us to marry."

Ainslee stared, stupefied. "Colton."

He pressed a finger to her lips. "That wasn't a proposal."

Colton helped her on with one boot and tucked the other under his arm. Ainslee watched him douse the fire in the small stove and put away everything they used. He came and went from outside twice. The third time, without warning, he lifted her into his arms and carried her out the door. He didn't put her down until she was settled on the front of his saddle. Lady had passed the night in relative contentment, her reins now wrapped loosely around Colton's saddle horn.

Colton closed the cabin door, swung up behind Ainslee, and lifted her so she sat on his lap. Only then did he speak. "I owe you a hell of a lot more than whatever explanation I can come up with right now."

"I am the one who told you not to leave me."

He kissed her, hard and fast. "I remember." The memory of her kisses would be forever imprinted on his skin and in his mind. "If I don't get you back soon, Brenna will send every able-bodied man out to look for us."

"Wait." The early sunrise colors escaped the confines of the clouds enough to cast a few ribbons of morning sun on the earth, the light creating a soft halo around them. For a woman who earned a nice living by the power of words, she struggled to find the right ones. He did not rush her but neither did he encourage her. One second to the next, she saw indecision in his eyes, then certainty—two opposite emotions searching for a foothold.

She understood the feeling, for even now Ainslee knew the day would soon come when she must make the decision to stay or to go. "Now is not the time. We should head back."

Colton studied her face for a few seconds. Time seemed an eternity as their breaths mingled and their bodies warmed each other. He broke the spell first when he urged his horse into motion, Lady trailing along.

They reached the house when the sun peeked over the highest mountains. Colton rode directly to the big house and stopped near the porch where Ethan, Brenna, Ramsey, and Eliza waited. Ramsey reached them first, lifting his arms to help her down.

"She can't put weight on her ankle." Colton watched Ramsey shift tactics and lift Ainslee into his arms. He wished it was he carrying her inside. A few brows were raised, and as much as he wanted to ignore them, he couldn't. He dismounted and handed the horses to Pete who had rambled out of the barn.

"Thanks, Pete. They could use a good brushing and some oats, fresh water."

"Sure thing, Colton."

Pete walked off talking with the animals, leaving Colton to face the others. When he turned back to the house, only Ethan and Eliza remained.

"Brenna explained what happened," Ethan said. "You took shelter at the cow camp?"

Colton nodded, unwilling to offer details. "Ainslee won't be able to walk for a few days."

Eliza studied him with her bright, blue eyes. All of the Gallaghers had a knack for looking straight through the outer layers into a person's soul, and Eliza was more skilled than the rest. She took a person's measure, seeing through lies and evasion. She nudged her brother aside and walked down the porch steps. "I could use your help with one of the horses, Colton. Do you mind?"

If he did, Colton knew better than to say so. Had Ethan or Gabriel asked him the same thing, he would have found a way to avoid the inquisition, which is probably why Ethan smirked and walked into the house.

"I consider you family, Eliza, like a sister."

"I feel the same way about you, Colton. I think of you like a brother."

He fell in step with her, her long strides keeping time with his. She wore her usual buttoned-up shirt and vest tucked into riding pants a woman in town made special for her. For as long as Colton had lived at Hawk's Peak, he only recalled seeing Eliza without those special-made pants at evening meals or for visits into town. At the ranch she worked, and she couldn't do that in skirts.

"If I had ever had sisters of my own, I'd tell them what I'm about to tell you."

"That's it's none of my business."

He glanced at her and saw her grin. "Sounds about right."

"We've known each other a long time, and I've never seen you look at a woman the way you do her."

There was a woman once, Colton recalled. He had not wanted her and she punished him for it. He had never loved her, never touched her, and knew she would never have been faithful. "There hasn't been anyone else, not like it is with her."

"She might not stay."

"I know." Colton was the first to stop. With dawn came the start of the workday, though most adults on the ranch, except those who had night watch, rose before the sun. "I'll figure out what to do when the time comes for her to decide."

"I know Ramsey and Brenna would like it if she remained here with the family."

Colton felt the sigh move through his lungs on a deep breath. "It's different for her. She has parents, brothers, all living back in Scotland. She has more reason to go than to stay."

Eliza stepped in front of him. She stood a few inches taller than Ainslee and did not have to lean back too far to look at him in the eyes. "Ethan once believed the same thing about Brenna. Gabriel married Isabelle in part to keep her safe, but more I think to keep her here with him because he couldn't bear the thought of her going back to New Orleans." She inched closer and took his hand in hers. "I was uncertain that Ramsey would stay after the trouble with Nathan Hunter ended." She squeezed his hand. "Are you listening to me, Colton Dawson?"

He nodded, turned her around, and pointed to the muddy dirt near the edge of the barn. "Anyone been out this way since the rain let up?"

"No reason to." Eliza stared at the ground. "Well, hell."

"That's about right." Colton knelt next to the impressions in the mud. "These were made in the last few hours, while it was still raining, but after the worst of the storm had passed."

"Are they from the sharpshooter?"

Colton turned and looked up at her.

She shrugged. "Ethan and Gabriel told me about what happened to Fred Hudson."

Colton moved his eyes over the prints. "I don't know. The ridge near the Hudson farm is mostly rock, so no tracks were at the top. He left signs of his presence, but not enough. He's careful."

"Careful enough to have done this before?"

Colton nodded and stood. "This is an average-sized man without much weight in the boot."

"Could be a woman."

"Not unheard of, but unlikely. A woman cattle thief riding with the likes of the men I've already brought in . . . well, we would have heard of something like that, don't you think?"

Eliza said, "I'll let the others know."

"After I get fresh gear, I'm heading back out."

"Colton."

He shook his head to ward off an argument. "It's not over. We all went through the same hell when Nathan Hunter was alive. You and your brothers took responsibility for everything that happened because you felt you should have been able to stop him. I didn't understand what it really meant, until now."

"Ethan also told me and Ramsey about what the men said to Tom. They asked about you."

"Then you know why I have to find them, before anyone else gets hurt because of me."

Eliza punched him in the arm when he looked away. She had a pretty good swing for a woman and a unique way of getting someone's attention. "I can only do that because I do think of you like a brother. You, Ben, Pete, Tom—everyone. You're all family and that means not doing anything alone." She stood toe to toe with him. "Don't you think we blamed ourselves every day for the things Nathan Hunter did to anyone who wasn't us? The guilt chipped away at us little by little because we knew others would be hurt because of him—because of us."

"This is different."

"How?"

"Because this is somehow about me. I'm the reason these people are here, and now it's going beyond the ranch. What happens when they kill the next person?" Colton left her standing there alone, surprised to see her next to the barn when he walked out with a fresh horse, his own saddle and the rifle he'd left in the scabbard. He swung up on the horse. "I'll return in a few days, unless I find them sooner."

"What do I tell Ainslee?"

Colton turned his head to look at the house. "She'll understand."

"There's a better way, Colton."

He looked down at Eliza from atop his horse. "What way is that?"

She smoothed her hand over the gelding's neck and looked up. "Do you honestly believe my brothers and I could have made it through all those years without help?"

20

"**I AM HEALED**, Brenna." To prove her point, Ainslee stood and walked around the bedroom. Her white, flowing nightgown trailed behind her, and she lifted enough of the edges to reveal her ankle, the swelling gone.

"Mmm. That is what you said two days ago and almost tumbled down the stairs."

"'Twas a minor setback." Ainslee cringed, recalling how Ethan bit his lips from laughing and carried her back up the stairs. "I will not overdo, but I cannot stay confined another day. I would like to go into town and help Sarah with the preparations for the school fundraiser.

Isabelle said Sarah is determined to move forward with it now that she is feeling better."

Brenna raised a finely shaped brow a shade darker than her thick auburn hair. "I cannot stop you."

Exasperated with her cousin, Ainslee opened the wardrobe where her riding clothes hung next to many of the dresses she had brought with her. Other items remained in her trunks. Ainslee had no use for them in this place. She enjoyed dressing without a bustle since her arrival and now wore her corset as loose as her clothing allowed.

"You will not need your riding clothes."

Ainslee glanced over her shoulder at Brenna, her own brow raised in question.

"We will take the wagon."

"A horse would be more comfortable."

"And more dangerous."

"You are sounding like my mother, dear

cousin."

Brenna smiled. "I have fond memories of your mother."

"You did not have to live with her. You were too young last time to remember . . ." Ainslee flinched and walked to Brenna. "I am sorry. I have been truly blessed to have both my parents alive, and here I am speaking with ingratitude."

"I am certain if Mama and Papa still lived, they would think me incorrigible and I would think them dominating." Brenna patted her hand.

"Have you . . ." Ainslee turned away.

"Have I what?"

"It is an unfeeling question." Ainslee sat on the edge of the bed. "Do you ever wonder what path you would have taken had they lived?"

Ainslee saw how the question took Brenna by surprise. Her cousin joined her on the edge of the bed, where they sat side by side for nearly a minute before Brenna responded.

"In the beginning, I often wondered. If they had not died, would I have learned of my brother sooner? If I had learned of him, would I have come here to find him? If I did not journey here, everything I love and cherish . . . Yes, I wondered often in those early months."

"But not later?"

Brenna shook her head and lifted Ainslee's hand into her own. "There was no sense in wondering because I knew the path I had chosen was what they would have wanted for me."

Ainslee wished she could see her own future with such clarity. The choices her mother or father wanted her to make countermanded everything she desired. Her father bequeathed to her a great sense of adventure, though she discerned that as the years passed and she slipped farther away from matrimony, his concern grew. She knew they loved her dearly, and yet they still wanted for her what every respectable and wealthy parents longed for their children—success, normalcy, and families of their own.

Brenna squeezed her hand, drawing her attention. "You have lived with more freedom than I ever could have imagined, yet I see now how confined you must have felt. What truly brought you here? I know you have many reasons, but what, in the moment of your decision, caused you to come here right now?"

It was the question she had prepared for and hoped wouldn't be asked. During her confessions to Colton during the first night on the trail, she did not reveal all for fear of feeling foolish, as well as rash in her decision to leave home. On the sea voyage, she convinced herself that the events leading to her sudden departure had been exaggerated by her vivid imagination. And yet, an occasional shiver still coursed through her when she considered the alternative to leaving.

"My mother arranged a partnership between Drosten Campbell and me. His father is a business associate of my parents, and my mother and Drosten's father thought to create a stronger bond between our families through marriage, to combine properties and wealth."

"Surely your parents did not expect you to marry a man you did not love."

"No, my father put an end to the matter when he learned of it. We both understood my mother believed her actions stemmed from love, and perhaps they did. Father knew why I had to leave. Mother, I think, still believes I will return and marry a man of her choosing."

"Did you know this Drosten well?"

Ainslee rose from the bed, eager now to

be outside beneath the sun. Another storm had passed through after Colton had returned her to the ranch, and she spent four days worrying over him. She needed to occupy her thoughts and time elsewhere. "We had attended the same social functions, though I never intentionally spent time alone with him." Not like she had with Colton. "He made advances, proved he was as eager for the match as his father—perhaps more so— but I believe it was what came with me that interested him more."

"The money."

Ainslee nodded. "I sensed it was the same for any man who tried to court me. Mother insisted my looks played a part, but that excuse was more depressing. It is all nonsense now that I look back."

"Ainslee, you said this man pressed his advances with you."

"Do not worry. Nothing happened I

could not handle. A maid walked into the room and Drosten quickly left. It happened last winter."

"And you did not tell your father?"

"I did not see a favorable outcome in doing so. I do not excuse Drosten's behavior, but I believe he was encouraged in his thinking that he had my mother's support. Again, all nonsense."

"Last winter was—"

"Months ago, yes. Drosten made his intentions known again. I do not believe he would have stopped had I remained. I could have spoken to my father, explained everything, and he would have ended all associations with Drosten's father."

"Why did you not?"

"I have asked the same question many times. Drosten gave me an excuse to leave, and when I learned about your life here, and about Ramsey, I had a reason convincing enough for even my parents."

"Ainslee, dear, I am so sorry. I had so hoped your coming here had been under better circumstances."

"But it has been." Ainslee scooted closer to her cousin. "It has, truly. Drosten may have been part of why I left when I did, but I never considered myself a coward. I did not want to feel I was running away. I considered going to the Continent a few times, but when I stopped at Cameron Manor and spoke with Maggie and Iain . . ." Ainslee sighed and sat back. "I cannot decide if I am selfish or opportunistic. Perhaps both and I do not want to own to either."

Brenna said, "Revenge and hate brought me here, so perhaps we all must begin a journey with the worst of our traits in order to end learning what we needed to discover most about ourselves."

Ainslee kissed Brenna's hand and brought her close for a hug. "You have become a philosopher."

Brenna laughed. "Do not dare say so to Ethan. He already groans when he knows I intend to win a disagreement. If you tell me you do not regret coming here, I will look upon your selfish and opportunistic reasons as blessings, for they are why you are here."

"No, never that." Relief and calm rushed through Ainslee's body.

"Good." Brenna rose and walked to the door. "If you do not mind the company, Catie, Andrew, and Jacob would like to help at the school. Catie is a tremendous help with the younger children. We can make a family outing of it. Amanda and Ben will also be going."

"Where are the others?"

"Isabelle wants to help with the baking for the benefit, so Rebecca and August will stay here with her. Ethan and Gabriel will be with Eliza most of the day. They are finalizing plans for the stable expansion before Ramsey and Eliza travel to Kentucky next month."

Ainslee thought she might enjoy seeing more of the country. "Ramsey told me about their upcoming journey to buy horses."

"According to Eliza, the two mares are a dream and will round out the breeding stock nicely. Ramsey was not sure about leaving so soon after you were injured."

Ainslee remembered the way Ramsey, upon hearing of her injury, had admonished her, even as he made her promise that she was all right. He was both cousin and brother. In truth, Ramsey, Ethan, and Gabriel behaved more as brothers than her own ever had. "Ramsey said as much to me, but I assured him I would soon be out of this wretched bed."

"He also said you promised to be here

when he returned."

Ainslee looked toward the open window where the sun shined brightly and a warm breeze flowed inside. "I did." Grateful that Brenna did not comment, Ainslee asked, "Where is Ramsey now?"

"With Colton."

A smug light in Brenna's eyes appeared. "You did not think he would go out there alone again, did you?"

"In truth, I did."

"You have not yet learned, but you will. Now, be ready so we can breakfast before going into town."

Ainslee laughed at Brenna's antics. "You knew when you first came to check on me this morning that I would want to leave the house today."

Brenna smiled and said, "It has been many years since I last saw you, but you have not changed much at all."

Not changed in more than a decade? Did

Brenna, and others, truly see her still as an impetuous child longing for adventure and rebuking authority? She believed herself beyond the antics of her childhood, and yet . . . she had traveled to America and then on to Montana Territory without companion or escort, all because she did not wish to argue with her mother about marriage.

"I am eager to spend time with everyone, and yet . . ."

Brenna said Ainslee's name to regain her attention. "Your mind wandered for a few seconds. To Scotland, I suppose. It is this place, it can confuse a person into wanting everything, believing we can have it all. Each day here passes like a quiet gift and we do not know where the time has gone."

Ainslee nodded. "This ranch of yours, the land, they remind me so much of home at times. Is that why it is easier for you to stay?"

Brenna smiled, a secretive smile that sent a sparkle to her eyes. "You don't understand yet, but you will." She kissed her cheek and left Ainslee wondering over her words.

One hour later, they rolled into town, stopping the wagon at the school where everyone alighted. Ainslee did not follow them toward the school. "Where might I post a letter?"

Amanda said, "Orin Lloyd runs the telegraph and the post goes through his place, too." Amanda handed a basket of cookies to one of the children to take inside. "I have an order to place at the mercantile, if you don't mind the company."

"I would enjoy it."

Ben also joined them, citing a need to check on Tom at the clinic. He walked close to his wife, placing himself between them and the street. His horse followed at a leisurely pace. They came to the clinic first, and Ainslee would have continued on with Amanda had she not seen Colton through the clinic window speaking with Doc Brody.

Her heartbeat accelerated, even as worry filled her. He had not shaved in days, probably since he left the ranch. Brenna said he expected to return in three days. It had been five since she last saw him. She understood why he had to go, but it did not stop her from missing him.

"Did you know he had returned? Why was he away so long? Brenna said Ramsey went with him, but I do not see him."

Ben shook his head. "We're about to find out the answers to all your questions."

The clinic door opened. Doc Brody and Colton stepped outside, stopping when they saw the trio. Colton's eyes went immediately to Ainslee and hers to him. Brody nodded in greeting to the small group. "You're here to visit with Tom, then?"

At Ben's nod, Brody said, "Colton was just with him. He's mending well enough, but he won't be the same as he was."

Ben asked, "What do you mean by 'not the same'?"

Brody lowered his voice to a whisper and leaned against the open door. "One of the knife wounds hit a bone in his hip. The bone will heal on its own, but it can be months before he'll move around like he used to and years before it doesn't pain him anymore."

"I'd like to see him."

Brody motioned Ben inside. "He's in the same room upstairs. Tom Jr. went to fetch their lunch from Tilly's."

Ainslee saw Colton watching her. She returned the scrutiny with a study of her own. Dark smudges colored the area beneath his eyes, and his skin appeared slightly darker from the sun, which meant he had not worn his hat when the sun finally came out on the other side of the last storm. To her, he looked wonderful and exhausted. They did not sleep long that night in the cabin and he had left the next morning after taking her back to the ranch. They had left too much unspoken.

Discerning the tension in the air, Amanda said to Brody, "Do you happen to have some of the herbs you prepare for Elizabeth's rheumatism? She mentioned it has been bothering her with all the rain."

Brody eyed Ainslee and Colton, then answered Amanda. "In fact, I do. I prepared some yesterday for the Widow Baker. Come along inside and I'll put together a bag of them for you. Elizabeth prefers them as a tea."

Amanda and Brody left Ainslee alone with Colton. When the door closed, Ainslee stepped up onto the low porch that ran the length of the building. "How are you?"

COLTON FOUND IT difficult to breathe. For five days, he had ridden alongside Ramsey in the rain and heat, circling the ranch twice and riding into the mountains, following one trail to the next. When a path led to a dead end, they searched every possible hiding spot within two miles of the ranch and town.

They rode until the horses needed to rest. They slept and ate only enough to get them through the next day. By the morning of the fourth day, Colton had experienced an overwhelming sense of dread when they had yet to come across anyone in the band of cattle thieves or the elusive shooter. By the end of the fourth day, they finally found a reliable sign in the form of a man, half-dead and tied to a tree.

Colton spent six hours waiting for the man to wake up. He gave him water, food, and let him sit by the fire, hands unbound. The man wasn't going anywhere with a broken leg, courtesy of his friends.

After another three hours, the man had revealed little. The only time a flicker of fear had crossed the man's face was when Colton told him his name. The rustler sat now in the jailhouse, which is where Colton was headed before Ainslee arrived. His walk to the clinic was to inform Brody of the patient sitting in jail and to check on Tom. Except now, he wanted to be in Ainslee's presence, to wash away the last five days of dirt, grime, and frustration.

"Your ankle healed."

Ainslee blinked twice. "It did. Did you find what you're were searching for out there?"

"Not yet."

"Are you going out again?"

"Until it's over." And Colton meant it. "Ainslee, I want to talk—"

"Miss McConnell!"

Colton and Ainslee put another foot of space between them. It was Ainslee who addressed the newcomer. "Mrs. Jones. Are you here to see Doc Brody?"

"My nephew has a cough. His mother, my sister, said the doctor makes a special concoction that works wonders."

"He is well skilled. I do hope your nephew is not too sick."

"He will be all right. I suspect he does not want to do his chores."

Colton asked, "You're kin to Ward and Jane Bittle?"

The tall brunette widened her smile for him, revealing straight, white teeth with a narrow space between the two in front. It might have detracted from the beauty of most women, but it suited this one.

"Jane is my sister." She lifted a small, silver watch from a short chain attached to the belt around her shirt. "I should see the doctor now. My sister is expecting me home soon." To Ainslee she said, "It was lovely to see you again. I will think of you when I read another Finn Pickett adventure."

Mrs. Davis Jones knocked on the clinic door and let herself inside. Once again, Colton and Ainslee were left alone, and he almost missed the buffer. With another person present, he did not have to fight as hard to keep his hands to himself.

Colton expected Ben and Amanda to return any minute and he had things to say to Ainslee. "Will you walk with me? I have to return to pick up my horse at the livery and meet Ramsey at the jail. He's with the prisoner right now."

"This town *does* need a sheriff."

"Yes, it does." Colton stepped down first

and held out his hand to help her down the two steps. She did not need assistance, but it offered him an opportunity to touch her. Mindful of his trail-weary state, he did not stand too close as they walked to the livery.

"Have you ever considered the position?"

"Not with any permanency." He glanced at her. "You really want to talk about me becoming sheriff?"

"No, I do not, but since we are in public, I cannot discuss what is really on my mind." Her breath quickened and the words she spoke came out clipped.

Colton looked up and down the street. When they rounded the corner, he led her between two buildings, beneath stairs leading to the second level of the mercantile. "We're private enough now."

"Not nearly private enough." Ainlsee pushed him against the side of the building, more of a gentle nudge, and had Colton not seen it coming, not allowed it, her efforts would have been wasted. "You didn't say goodbye before you left."

"I thought you would understand."

"I did!" In quieter tones she said, "I do. You were gone five days, a little longer if you count the hours of this morning. I expected Ethan to send men out to look for you until Brenna told me this morning that Ramsey had gone with you."

"I should have told you."

"Yes, you should have!" Ainslee stepped into his arms, laid her head against his chest. "No, stay. I do not care if you have a month's worth of trail dirt on your clothes."

Colton circled his arms around her and felt the tension in his shoulders loosen. "You're starting to sound like a local, except for that accent."

Ainslee laughed. "I thought you liked my

accent."

"I do." He lifted her chin so she looked at him. "I like it very much." Colton could not resist brushing his lips softly against hers. It was a quick yet powerful connection. "We can't stay here."

"I know."

Her soft whisper hit him fast and hard. He set her away from him but did not let go.

"I have to go back out."

"I know that, too." Her eyes held a hint of moisture and a well of acceptance. "Will it end?"

"Soon." Colton brushed a stray curl from her forehead. "I promise." It was a promise he intended to keep.

"I am grateful you are not alone out there."

Colton's lips spread into an amused grin. It felt really good. "I've been reminded that *alone* is not how things are done at

Hawk's Peak."

"Then I am glad for whoever enlightened you. Alone is not always better."

"And yet you often go off by yourself, to seek solitude. Is that not the same thing?"

"It is not the same when your life is in danger." She leaned her head back to look at him better. "Ramsey is with you because you feel it would be a betrayal otherwise. You somehow feel you need to find these men and bring them to justice without help."

He let out an exasperated sigh. "I don't know how you see through me so easily, but stop. A man is entitled to his own thoughts."

"And you are more stubborn than any other I have ever met."

Colton kissed her cheek and held her face between his hands. "One day soon I'll tell you all about myself, and when I do, I hope you'll understand. Until then, please trust me."

"I do. And still, I am grateful you have the family."

Ainslee pressed up on her toes, kissed him once more, uncaring who might walk past, and left him leaning against the mercantile. Colton closed his eyes, allowing the taste of her lips to linger. When he pushed away from the wall a few minutes later, his eyes opened. He looked to the street and listened to the sounds of horses, wagons, and people.

"Hell." Colton had finally put the pieces together and they amounted to trouble.

21

"**D**OC?" **COLTON KNOCKED** on the clinic door and entered. Brody stood at a tall, wood table, finely polished with various jars, loose powders, and herbs strewn about.

"Colton, come on in." Brody measured powder, and using a spoon, filled a small bag. "Back so soon. Ben and Amanda wondered where you'd gone."

"Do you know where they went? I need to find Ben."

"I believe they said something about going to Loren's."

Colton left the doctor ruminating while he hurried to find Ben at the general store.

He hoped Ainslee had already met up with him and Amanda, but she was nowhere around.

"She had letters to post," Amanda said.

"Will you find her and stay with her until you get back to the ranch?"

"Of course, but—"

"Wait." He asked them both to follow him outside. When he was reasonably certain of privacy, Colton explained. "I think I know who's behind the rustling or at least part of it. None of what's happened made sense. All of these different pieces— the rustling, the shootings, Tom, and the break-in at the school. I couldn't figure out how they fit together, but they might after all. There was a man five years ago who came up this way from Colorado. The Rocky Mountain Detective Association enlisted my help."

Ben said, "I remember that. The fugitive killed one of their volunteers."

"Yes, and they were given some freedom to work with the territorial marshal, but none of them knew this area."

"And you found him?" Amanda asked.

"We did. Thomas Maxwell."

"How can you be sure it's him?" Ben asked. "That was five years ago."

"And five years ago I put a bullet in Thomas's twin brother, thinking it was him. The brother, Albert, had a hostage. No one knew Thomas had a twin."

"You never said." Ben looked to Amanda. "Find Ainslee and bring her back here. I'll get the others from the school."

Colton paused. "What others?"

Ben said, "Brenna, Elizabeth, and some of the children are at the school. They all came in today to help Sarah with preparations for the benefit, now that Sarah is feeling better."

Colton considered the possible scenarios and decided against the worst case. "If

Maxwell was going to hurt anyone else at the ranch, he would have already. He tortured Tom, but that was for my benefit. They wanted me to figure it out."

"If it's Thomas Maxwell, how will you know where to find him?"

"I won't have to look hard. If I'm right, he's already waiting for me. If he's not, there are only so many places he'll be, now that I know it's him."

"You don't know for certain it's him," Ben said.

"It is. It has to be. I can't think of anyone who would hate me enough to do what he's done."

When Colton stepped off the boardwalk and headed for the livery, Amanda turned to Ben. "Ramsey is at the jail. Should he be told?"

"I'll tell him."

"How will Colton know where to go?"

Ben slid his arm around his wife's waist.

"If I were Thomas, I'd be waiting in the same place where Colton shot my brother."

AINSLEE HANDED HER three letters to Orin Lloyd. Her recent convalescence provided plenty of time for her to pen the letters, giving great thought to each. What she had been unable to do was work on her writing. Her London publishers expected a new Finn Pickett adventure in their offices by the end of September. She usually delivered her manuscripts by hand, under the guise of a shopping excursion.

Her deadline was only one month away, and even if she did finish the book on time, the question remained if she would be back in Scotland in a month's time. The book she plotted and began to write upon her arrival in Montana was not a story

Finn Pickett would write. There was plenty of adventure but too much romance and heart. Her publishers would call it ladies' literature, but it was another Finn Pickett book they anticipated. Those books sold well and as long as the public craved them, they wanted more.

Orin read the addresses while flipping through the sealed envelopes. "These are going mighty far. The one to London and . . . what's that place?"

"Outer Hebrides."

"Uh-huh. Well, those are going to take a few weeks, maybe longer seeing as how I don't know how quick or slow mail travels over there. Telegraph would be faster."

Ainslee had already weighed and discarded that option. "I prefer letters. And the one to New York?"

"Well, now that one will get on the express train out of Bozeman. Takes about a week."

"That's perfect. Thank you." Ainslee set coins on the counter. "When will they go out?"

Orin dropped the letters into the outgoing mail bag. "Supply wagon will take them out tomorrow. If you want them there sooner, there are a couple of young men in town who ride special delivery to Bozeman. Don't get much call for special delivery, what with the telegraph. You sure you don't want to send a cable instead?"

Ainslee smiled at the balding man with kind eyes who wore wire-rimmed spectacles on the tip of his nose. "No sense in letting my carefully penned letters go to waste."

"No ma'am, I suppose you're right."

"Thank you. I will be—"

The door whooshed open behind Ainslee, a bell emitting a soft twinkling sound. Amanda stepped up to the counter beside Ainslee and offered a smile to Orin. "I have a telegram to send, Orin."

"Well, that's what I'm here for. Do you have it all written already?"

Amanda handed him a square sheet of paper. "Ben wrote it out for you."

"All right then." Ainslee watched with curiosity as Orin read the two lines. "This right? What is Ben wanting with the circuit judge?"

"I couldn't say."

Oh, yes you can, Ainslee thought. "Thank you, Mr. Lloyd, for your assistance. I will think on a telegram I can send next time I am in town."

Orin waved them away but had already started to push rapidly down on the black knob, converting Ben's words to dots and dashes. Ainslee dragged Amanda outside. "Why does Ben need a judge?"

"I will explain everything, but right now, we have to go to the mercantile."

Ainslee wanted to run there. Deep inside where instinct dwells and rarely sees reason, she knew it was about Colton. Her ankle pained her some from walking on it too much, but she wasn't going to confess that to Amanda. By the time they walked halfway down the street, Amanda had relayed the conversation she had with Colton and Ben.

It was Ainslee who saw Brenna sitting with the children at one of the outside tables at Tilly's Café. "They cannot be finished at the school already." Ainslee and Amanda walked to the table.

Andrew said, "We're going to have pie!"

"And very good pie it is." Ainslee smiled at the boy before turning to Brenna. "I had hoped to help at the school this afternoon. I am sorry for the delay. We can all go back together after pie."

"Not today." Brenna leaned over to whisper something to Jacob when he wanted to play with his fork. The child quieted but still wore a mischievous grin. "We were putting the final touches on the banner the children were painting when Sarah asked if we could finish up in a few days. She looked rather peaked. I'm not certain she hasn't been overdoing since her previous ordeal at the school."

Amanda asked, "Were there others helping?"

Brenna nodded. "They've all gone home for the day. We made good progress. I assured her we could return in a few days to finish."

Ainslee half-listened, her mind wandering. Images of the ransacked room behind the school, the floorboards . . . . What would Finn Pickett do? If he was writing this story, the hero and villain would have to meet but not where one expected. No, Finn Pickett was too clever to have the obvious conclusion be . . .

"Would you excuse me for a few minutes?"

Amanda reached for Ainslee's arm. "You aren't to be alone. Ben should be here soon. He went to speak with Ramsey."

Brenna looked from her cousin to her friend. "Why can she not be alone, Amanda?"

"Not here."

Brenna glanced around the table. Catie's interest was obvious. Andrew and Jacob were whispering to each other and not paying attention to the adults.

Ainslee removed Amanda's hand from her arm. "Tell Ben I have gone to the school."

"We'll go together," Brenna said as she stood.

"No." Ainslee was channeling that innermost part of herself masquerading as the adventurous and enigmatic Finn. She asked herself what would Finn do, and then, what would Colton want? She knew if the men got away this time, Colton would never forgive himself. Waiting for Ben, explaining her theory, would mean he and every other able-bodied man with a gun he trusted would follow her, and perhaps scare Maxwell away. "No one else." She looked at Brenna. "Trust me."

Brenna did not have to say anything. She let Ainslee go and stopped Amanda when she would have gone along. Brenna said, "Find Ben and Ramsey. We need them now."

22

COLTON SAT ON the mended chair in the back room of the small, red schoolhouse. Two young men from town had repaired what they could and carried the rest away. New floorboards replaced the few that had been torn up.

It had not been easy to convince Sarah Beckert to send everyone home and leave the school. More difficult still to sneak around the back of the school and wait for her to come inside alone. Children had been in and out of the front of the school for fifteen minutes before Sarah entered the back room where she stored extra supplies.

Colton had done his best not to frighten her, a challenge given her recent experience. With all she'd been through since he met her last winter, Sarah had become a strong woman who could take care of herself. Colton knew she trusted him, and he counted on that trust now. She needed no explanation other than Colton's request for her to find a way to get everyone to leave without alarming them.

Whatever she said worked, for ten minutes later the small gathering had dispersed, including Brenna, Catie, Andrew, and Jacob. He released a slow breath when he saw them leave.

If his suspicions were correct, he would not have long to wait.

He heard footsteps on the back step. The door opened and swung inward in time for Colton to witness Ainslee stomp her foot on the toe of Thomas Maxwell's boot.

"Ah wull nae tell ye again, laddie. Dae

nae pull—"

"Shut your mouth. I don't understand a word you're sayin', lady."

"Let her go."

Ainslee and Maxwell shifted their attention to Colton, who now stood, gun pointed at Maxwell.

"Colton, it is not what you think. This . . . gentleman . . . has sworn—"

"I said shut up!" He ground out the words close to her ear.

"Let me go and you can go about your business."

"*Now* you talk English?"

"I spoke English before, you simply did not—"

Maxwell yanked on her arm. "Will you keep your trap shut!"

Colton didn't have a clear shot, not without risking Ainslee. He dared a glance at her face, surprised to see her expression controlled and without fear. It occurred to him then that she had come looking for him, and the only reason she would have done that is if she had put the same pieces together that he had. But how? He planned to ask her as soon as he got them out of this mess and she was no longer in danger.

"If you want the gold your brother buried here, Maxwell, you'll have to let her go."

Maxwell stared at Colton, his surprise evident.

"Don't know what you're talkin' about."

Colton raised a brow and said to Maxwell, "We couldn't understand why someone would go to the trouble of destroying this room. There'd never been anything worth stealing. Then I remembered the bank robbery in Butte a week before I found your brother hiding outside of Briarwood. If that robbery in Butte had been done by the Maxwell Gang, as the sheriff and territorial marshal suspected, you would have known exactly where you buried the box."

Colton stepped one foot closer, his eyes focused on Maxwell. "It was never you, none of it. It was your brother, Albert, who killed the volunteer in Colorado, him who robbed the bank. Albert ran, but he wasn't a coward like you are. He was a killer."

"You're the killer, Dawson. You shot my brother in cold blood."

"There was nothing cold about it." He took another step closer, this time moving toward the doorway into the front of the school. "Your brother had a hostage and nearly shot the man. You'll end up in the ground next to your brother if you don't release her."

"I'm taking that box *and* her. Payment for what you did to my brother."

"You can have the box. You can't have her."

MK MCCLINTOCK

"Might I suggest another solution?"

"No!" both men said in unison. Colton wished he could figure out what was going on through her head.

She said, "I will fetch your box, you will leave, and no one has to die."

"He'll shoot me before I get ten feet, lady."

"Not if I am standing between you and his gun."

Now Colton dared another glance at her, tried to tell her without words that it was time to be quiet. She ignored him.

Ainslee continued. "You will have time to leave, and if you have any sense you will ride out of the territory without looking back. I have heard that Mexico is warm."

Maxwell looked like he wanted to strike her. If Colton had been in his position, he might have been tempted, too. Ainslee had a plan of her own, only Colton hadn't figured it out yet. He had only one choice.

Colton drew Maxwell's attention back to him. "I'll do what she says."

"What's that?"

Maxwell definitely had not been the thinker in his family, which left Colton to wonder who led the gang now.

"Well, hell."

"What are you sayin', Dawson?"

Colton spared another glance at Ainslee. This time she wore a hint of a smile. He didn't smile back because he was about to alter her scheme. "Let her go and take me."

Ainslee's smile faltered. "Colton."

He shook his head at her but his attention remained on Maxwell. "She'll bring you the box, I give her my gun, and you take me and the box. I promise she won't shoot."

"Dae nae be certain."

Colton offered her no response. "Do we have a deal, Maxwell?"

"She has to find the box first."

"I already did," Colton said. "Front room, under the teacher's desk. The board is already removed."

Maxwell indicated with his gun. "Drop that pistol."

Colton did. Maxwell smiled. He pushed Ainslee toward the doorway. "Get the box."

Five minutes later, after some muttering and clanging, Ainslee dragged a small, rectangular metal box into the back room. "Ah canna carry this."

"You won't have to." Maxwell jerked the gun toward Ainslee. "Get the box, Dawson."

Colton did not hesitate. He walked over, lifted the box, and hefted it so he could carry it like he would a calf.

"Colton."

Her whisper almost stopped him. "It's all right. Trust me."

They mounted, and with Maxwell pointing his gun at Colton, Ainslee watched them ride away.

IT WAS THE place he had wanted to avoid. The spot where Albert Maxwell died was just ahead. Three others stood around a fire. They stopped their horses and dismounted. Two of the men in the group came forward when instructed by Thomas and lifted the box away from Colton.

"Now you have me here, Maxwell. You plan to kill me? If so, it might have been easier by the river where you could have thrown my body into the water. Now you have to bother with burying me."

"You tryin' to die faster?"

"No point in delaying the inevitable."

"You talk too much, just like that lady of yours."

Colton prodded a little more. It wasn't

only Thomas he wanted. "Whatever you plan to do with me, just get it done."

"Time for that later." He said to one of the men, "Tie him up to that tree there."

"You're not in charge, are you, Maxwell?"

Thomas lunged. "Shut up!"

"I have told you to watch your temper, Thomas."

Mrs. Davis Jones walked out from behind a cropping of rocks dressed in shapeless men's clothing. The only thing that appeared to fit her properly were the boots and the gloves he'd seen her wear in town. She wore a man's shirt tucked into pants held up by suspenders.

"You look surprised, Mr. Dawson."

"You're unexpected. You don't look like your brothers."

She peered over her shoulder at her brother. "And yet you've figured out who I am."

"Standing there next to him, you have the same eyes."

"Our mother always said the same thing. I never saw it."

"Is there a Mr. Davis Jones somewhere or did you kill him?"

The back of her hand swung out and across Colton's cheek. "A man just like you killed him."

"He should have thought better than to marry into a family of thieves."

"I don't like you, Mr. Dawson."

"Then we are of the same mind because I do not like you either, Mrs. Jones."

"You are going to die, when I decide, of course."

"I figured that was your plan."

She knelt by the fire, the men nearby and quiet. "What did your Miss McConnell say about me?"

"That you like to read."

"Ah yes, well, that was true. I liked her,

your Miss McConnell. There was something else about her that reminded her of me. Do you control her like most men control their women? She could be spirited beneath her genteel exterior. Yes, I liked her very much."

"She's nothing like you."

"And you would be wrong. Men never want to see the truth."

"What about your sister, Jane, right? Your kid sister, if I'm not mistaken. Is she a part of this?"

Blanche stood. "She has nothing to do with any of it, and neither does her family. Jane is like your Miss McConnell. Naïve. She doesn't understand how the world works. She believes all the happily-ever-after endings in novels really do come true."

"How did the three of you end up with a sister as sweet as Jane?"

Maxwell swung a fist into Colton's

stomach. "Our family ain't none of your concern."

Colton felt the punch deep in his gut. It took a few seconds for him to remember how to breathe. He choked out, "Maybe you're not completely gutless, Maxwell."

He took a step toward Colton again.

"Enough of this." Blanche told one of the men to open the strong box. He shot off the lock and raised the lid. Blanche stared into the box and said to her brother, "Where is the gold, Thomas?"

"It's there. That box was heavy."

"Sand and rocks."

Thomas brushed past his sister and knelt by the box. "No! Albert told me where to look. He told . . ." Maxwell turned on Colton. "You did this."

"Your sister's hired man over there shot off the lock, a rusted lock. The box hasn't been opened since it was buried and the school built over it." Colton had suspected as much. "Rumor was, another fellow rode with your brother, or who we believed was you, Thomas, but turned out to be Albert."

Blanche said, "Talking will not extend your life."

"Didn't think it would. As I was saying, we heard of someone else riding with your brother. Never could prove it because he disappeared. We never did find the gold and money from the bank robbery in Butte. You want the money? Think who might have ridden with Albert back then."

Blanche circled the camp twice before stopping in front of Colton. "I have no more need for you."

"Revenge for Albert."

She raised a brow and put her back to him.

"I wasn't the only one shooting that day."

Blanche slowly faced him again. "No one else was there who could have done it.

Word was that it was you."

"People talk, doesn't make what they say true, unless you were there. I wanted him alive long enough for the detectives to take him back to Colorado. He forced my hand when he wouldn't release the hostage, but you knew that. The shot that almost hit me came from you, didn't it? I have to wonder now why you didn't kill me that day."

Blanche sighed and told her brother to be quiet when he wanted to speak. "My husband was a sharpshooter on the Confederate side and a very good teacher. If I wanted you dead, you—"

"I would be dead. You let your brother die."

"A pact. Better dead than life in prison."

"And Tom?"

She took a few seconds to think. "The ranch hand? That was Thomas, not me. After all, he did think you killed our brother. I convinced Thomas not to kill him."

"You nearly did."

"I saved him! No one ever tried to save my husband. Davis was worth a dozen of you. I took mercy on those men by not killing them."

Thomas ignored everyone else and stepped up to stand an inch from his sister. He towered over, and she did not flinch. "You watched Albert die and did nothing?"

"He would have done the same for me, Thomas, or for you. It was better for him. He didn't want to go back to prison." She patted her brother's cheek. "We'll talk of this more later, just as family, but for now, we must get rid of him."

Thomas lacked his earlier conviction, his gaze darting back and forth between Colton and Blanche. Colton had bought as much time as he could.

"You're not going anywhere, any of you."

Blanche laughed, a deep, throaty sound that might have been seductive had she not been a murderess. "You are partly correct." She drew with surprising speed and raised her gun to her brother's gut, finger on the trigger.

"You'll put the gun down, Mrs. Jones. Now!" Ramsey appeared from the trees, a Winchester at his shoulder, aimed at Blanche's back.

Gabriel stepped into the small clearing from the north and pointed the barrel of his rifle at the two hired men.

Colton asked Ramsey, "You hear everything?"

"We did." He stepped forward with the marshal's badge he sometimes pinned to his chest visible for everyone to see. "You have a choice between prison and a pine box." He nodded toward the two men. "I don't know who you are, but if you're dumb enough to be riding with them, then you likely have papers on you somewhere."

The men put down their guns.

Gabriel stayed back, but circled around and said to the group, "If you're thinking you'll manage to pull the trigger and kill one of us before we shoot you, Mrs. Jones, rest assured we did not come alone."

Blanche looked at Colton. "You planned this."

Colton shook his head. "Someone a lot smarter than me thought this one out."

Maxwell dropped his gun and stepped away from his sister. Blanche still held hers in her right hand, and Colton had already seen how fast she could raise it. He recognized the defeat in her eyes. Her mouth curved into a cold, calculating smile . . . no warmth and a lot of regret. She raised her gun to Colton's chest. A single shot from behind and to the left of Colton brought her tumbling to the ground.

Ethan walked out from behind the same rock Blanche had walked out of earlier. He stopped when he reached Colton, pulled a knife from his boot, and cut through the ropes. Colton stood while Ramsey and Gabriel secured Thomas and the two nameless men.

"She didn't leave you a choice."

Ethan said, "I know. She wanted one of us to do it."

Colton placed his hand on Ethan's shoulder. "In that moment, yes, she wanted someone else to pull the trigger. Hanging or prison weren't options in her mind. But I think a part of her died a long time ago." When the others were rounded up and Blanche's body covered and laid over the back of her horse, Colton asked, "Where's Ainslee."

Gabriel lifted himself with ease onto the back of his horse. "At home."

Ramsey said, "It only took her a minute to find me. I was already at the school when Maxwell forced you to ride away with him. Ainslee, though, was under the impression you'd done it all on purpose."

For once, Colton did not mind how easily Ainslee understood him. "I hadn't thought that far ahead. Her involvement at the school was unplanned."

"She's like Brenna, with a stubborn mind of her own." Ethan sat atop his mount, a steed of glossy black and eager to move. "I swear she was going to follow us. It took Eliza threatening to tie her up to keep her there."

"Did it come to that?"

Gabriel secured the reins of the horse carrying Thomas. "We'll find out soon enough."

Ramsey led one of the men, Ethan the other. Colton insisted on leading Blanche's horse. Colton could not forget the look in her eyes seconds before her death, when she raised her gun knowing her final breath was near. He'd seen sorrow and love in equal measure, but never at the same time in the same person, and never with such finality. He hoped never to see it again.

Colton followed behind the others. No matter the wrongs Thomas Maxwell had committed, he did not deserve the punishment of watching his sister's dead body sway on the back of a horse.

23

COLTON DISMOUNTED, NEVER so happy in all his life to have two feet on the ground rather than to be on the back of a horse. It was over, as he promised Ainslee it would be, and just as she had predicted, he did not have to finish it alone.

Doc Brody saw to the body of Blanche Jones while her brother and the two hired men, cousins by the name of Wilkes, they learned, who had never before done anything as foolish as to take up with Blanche and her brother. Thomas Maxwell decided to confess everything in exchange for not going to prison. They had no evidence that would send him to the gallows.

Ramsey and Ethan remained in town to handle the prisoners while Gabriel and Colton returned to the ranch. He looked for Ainslee, expecting, or at least hoping, she would be waiting for his return. Dusk settled comfortably over the valley, and he hesitated to go to sleep without seeing her.

When she did not appear beside Isabelle, who came to greet her husband, or Brenna, Amanda, and Elizabeth who wanted to hear what had happened, Colton looked to Brenna with the question clearly written over his face.

Brenna walked with him to the edge of the house and pointed to the meadow where Ethan had planted the heather for his wife. "She has been out there all afternoon, since we returned from town. Thankfully, Ben already guessed where you might end up. He was already saddled and prepared to go for help when Ainslee saw Ramsey outside of the school. You did not think any of them would let you do this alone, did you?"

"When I saw Ainslee enter the school with Maxwell, I realized quickly that she had a plan of her own. Then again, no one here does anything alone if they don't have to." Colton moved his eyes over the landscape before him, Ainslee at the center. "Or so I've been reminded more than once."

"She will struggle with that truth in her own heart. Ainslee will not be easily tamed from your mountain man way of life. When you are here with us, a part of you is still up there in those mountains, as wild and free as the day you first entered them. But no, it will not be you who has to be tamed."

"I don't intend to tame her, Brenna. Her life, as well as the path she chooses, are her own."

Brenna looped an arm around Colton's waist, a sisterly gesture and something she had not done before. He remained still, touched by the support she offered. "When I first noticed the way you looked at each other, I thought it was you who would have to be tamed. But you knew from the start that your heart belonged to her."

There is no greater mistake a man can make than deny his love for the only woman who was meant to have his heart. Ethan's words floated once more to the surface of Colton's memory.

Leaving Brenna's side and taking with him her counsel, he crossed the meadow to Ainslee. She held a sprig of heather in one hand and brushed a curl from her face with the other. A mellow wind blew around them. Another storm would follow, perhaps that night or the next morning, this one milder than before. The clouds did not appear as dark and angry.

"You saved my life." He walked around her so he stood facing her and she him.

"Ben had already figured out what would happen. He told Ramsey. It was those two and the others who saved you." She brushed the heather over her cheek. "You weren't going to be alone."

Colton nodded. "I figured that out as soon as you walked in with Maxwell. You could have warned me."

"Then it would not have worked out so well."

"Why was it so important to you to be the one to catch them? Why did it have to be you? Alone against the world."

"It wasn't like that, Ainslee." He wanted to reach for her hands and pull her close. Instead, he remained where he stood with too much space between them. "I've never been the reason anyone was hurt before.

Tom is family, and so is everyone else here, but I've kept just enough distance between them and me to protect them. At least I thought I had."

"I know."

Colton shook his head. "You don't. When I saw what they'd done to Tom, the torture they put him through, and the pain on Tom Jr.'s face when he thought his pa might not make it . . . that was because of me." He stepped forward and pressed a finger to her lips to keep her from disagreeing. "It may not make sense to you, but the blame rested on me. I had to make things right. Ethan, Ben, Gabriel, Ramsey . . . they all understood that."

"Yet they never intended for you to finish the fight on your own."

Colton dropped his hands to her arms. "No, and until I saw them step from the trees, and I realized my life wasn't over, I didn't know how grateful I was they were there. You made sure they would be there."

"I am used to being alone, too. It is not a terrible way to live."

Colton blew out a breath and brought her into his arms. "Not terrible, until a person realizes what they've been missing all along."

"TELL ME SOMETHING about yourself."

"You already know more than most."

Ainslee rested her head on his shoulder. They shared a bench on the back porch of the house. Twilight replaced sunset and stars appeared in the multitude. A faint light diffused the sky casting a faint glow over the silhouette of the mountains. Ainslee had been unwilling to be apart from him longer than it took for him to bathe and for them to share in the evening meal with those who were at the house.

Ethan returned to say Ramsey planned to remain in town for the night, to keep watch over the prisoners.

"Briarwood needs a sheriff."

She felt Colton's chuckle against the palm of her hand where it rested on his chest. "Yes, we do."

"I understand now why the family does not want the spur line. A train would make it easier for people like Blanche Davis and Thomas Maxwell to come to Briarwood and bring their evil with them. This beautiful place should not have to suffer people like them."

Colton murmured his agreement.

"Brenna worried that one day Ethan and his siblings would not be able to stop progress. How can they stop it? They cannot stop the railroad if the men who control it truly want to come to Briarwood."

"No, they can't control the railroad, but they can refuse the right of way."

Colton peered down at her. "The Gallaghers own the land the railroad needs to build the spur line."

"But that is on the other side of town, far from the ranch."

Colton shrugged and rested an arm over her shoulders. "Jacob Gallagher, their father, bought up more land than what the ranch rests on. Whether or not he predicted what future generations might face, no one knows, but he'd been wise. I remember once Ethan telling me that his mother had worried buying so much land from the start would bankrupt the family, but Jacob knew what he was doing."

Night settled around them like a warm blanket, but they had no need for extra heat between them.

"Who is Moses Bent?"

They shared an uncomfortable silence

for a minute before he responded. "Where did you hear that name?"

"You said it."

"I've never spoken of him to anyone."

Ainslee's head came up. "Is this one of those times when you sound angry, but when I ask, you'll tell me you're not?"

"Could be." Colton eased his torso to the right, enough so he was facing her. "When did—"

"While you slept in the cabin. You sounded in pain, like you were struggling with someone. You mumbled the name."

Colton blew out a breath. "This was at the cow camp."

"Yes."

"I'd guess it hasn't been easy for you to keep that to yourself."

"No, it hasn't been. Is he someone important to you?"

"You could say that."

Colton reached for her hand. Whether

he needed it or sought to keep her still while he explained, Ainslee neither knew nor cared. She covered their joined hands.

"I met Moses Bent when I was thirteen years old. He taught me everything I needed to know about living in the mountains and off the land."

"How did you meet him?"

"That's a longer story."

Ainslee used her free hand to turn his face toward her. "We have time. Brenna has promised no one will disturb us."

Thank God for Brenna, Colton thought.

"You do not have to tell me if the memories are painful."

"They're not, at least not in the way you think." He stood first and raised her from the bench. "And I do need to tell you. Do you mind a walk?"

Ainslee held his hand and followed him down the porch steps into the damp grass below. The ground was still coated in dew from the afternoon storm. It had come early and lasted only an hour. Cloudy skies had prevented the sun from drying the earth, but Ainslee did not mind. She enjoyed the misty air and the earthy fragrance carried in the gentle evening breeze.

When he spoke, Colton's voice softened with his attention on where they stepped. "I never knew my father. My mother once told me about him but would not tell me his name. According to her, he owned a bank in Denver and came from a prominent family. They weren't married when they met, and she was too young to know better than to get involved."

The ground muffled the sounds of their footsteps as Colton veered them toward the creek. "My mother did right by me for as long as she could. She fell ill with pneumonia and the doctor told her it wouldn't be long. There was an old widow,

Effie Guthrie. My mother was her companion. They met in church and Effie took it upon herself to take me in when my mother passed. I had a roof over my head, three meals a day, and Effie was like a grandmother to me, always kind."

Ainslee could see in her mind the young boy, uncertain of his future, staying strong because it's what his mother would have wanted.

"The education you keep mentioning, well, Effie was a retired schoolteacher. She and her husband left Chicago for Denver when she was thirty, and he died one year later after breaking his neck falling from his horse."

"What happened to her?"

"I lived with her for the last six years of her life. They were good years, all of them. She was kind to me and taught me all she could. She had a nice library of books and I read most of them." He found them a log and with their hands still joined, guided her to sit down. "She died a month after my thirteenth birthday."

Rather than try to tell him she understood the loss—because she did not—Ainslee eased closer. She liked that he wrapped an arm around her.

"She left me some money, but I was still young enough to be sent to a boys' home in the city. Instead, I took the money and everything else I could carry in a single bag and made my way north. Moses Bent found me north of Salt Lake."

"How long were you with Moses?"

"I was eighteen. Moses died of a heart attack. The best I could guess, he was well beyond eighty years. He enjoyed a good life."

Three people raised him and he had lost all three. It was no mystery now why he considered the Gallaghers family, or why he was so loyal to them and to the people of Briarwood. And no wonder, before coming to Briarwood, he thought of himself as a man all alone in the world.

"And then you found Hawk's Peak."

He exhaled and Ainslee thought she felt some of the tension leave his body. "Took me a few years to get this far north. I didn't need to work for money, but I needed to feel useful, to feel like I was a part of something."

Ainslee could understand that need.

"I heard about Hawk's Peak. Ethan and Gabriel weren't much older than me when I showed up and offered my services."

Ainslee shifted to get a better look at him. "You mean you asked for work."

"No, I told them I *wanted* to work for the family but to hire me on a trial basis, no wages required."

She whispered, "Because you wanted to be a part of something."

Colton nodded. "It's the only place I've

ever called home."

Every question Ainslee ever had about him was answered. Honor, duty, and sacrifice were not merely traits he possessed, but the way he lived—the *only* way he knew *how* to live.

"If you sought work today, would you be able to do so without compensation?"

He chuckled. "That's a fancy way to ask if I'm rich."

"Yes, it is."

"I might suspect you were after my money if I didn't already know better." He brushed a hand down her back. "Not rich compared to you. Mrs. Guthrie left me well off enough. Most of it sat in a Denver bank until last year. Ben and I have small shares in the ranch."

"You might be wondering why I asked."

He pulled her up, catching Ainslee by surprise. She grasped his arms and stayed there while she steadied her legs. They'd fallen asleep from sitting in one place too long.

Colton said, "I suspect you asked to be sure I wasn't after your money." He leaned close, moved his lips along her jawline until he reached her ear. "Rest assured, Miss McConnell, when I declare my intentions, you'll know it's for you—and only you."

Ainslee's heart clenched inside her chest. "And what are your intentions, Mr. Dawson?"

"That depends on you."

"You are wondering if I plan to return to Scotland."

"I expect you'll want to someday, maybe travel more. You won't let grass grow under your feet, not with the way you talk of adventure."

"No, I don't suppose I would." Ainslee wanted to continue living in the joyful moment, to keep reality at bay. She made her living on fiction, and though she realized fiction was not life, she had hoped what she wrote on the page would come true. "I have something to show you."

"You can tell me."

"I am not sure I can explain."

"Is this your secret, the one that brought you to Montana?"

She nodded. "Part of it." She would tell him about Drosten Campbell one day, but to her, this was far more important. "Have you heard of the author, Finn Pickett?"

"I've read a few of the stories. Brenna has them in the library." He shrugged. "We all borrow books now and then."

Ainslee put a little distance between them and took a deep breath. "I am Finn Pickett."

Colton stared at her. She waited for any kind of indication that he disapproved.

"You have nothing to say?"

"I had already figured that out."

"How could you possibly? I have spent years cultivating his persona. I do not tell anyone. My father and my publisher know, that is all. I have not even told Brenna yet."

"That's what you planned to tell her, the day the storm hit." He grinned and pulled her to him so she could feel his breath in her hair. "I told you I've read a few of the books. You may not have remembered everything you said the night we met and camped on the trail. Something triggered a memory. When it came back to me, I remembered where I had heard it before."

Ainslee thought back to the many conversations with Colton, and no, she did not recall everything from their first night under the stars. "I quoted Finn, or rather I quoted myself?"

"Some, but it was the salt. You wanted to know if I had any. I had to wonder about a father who puts his daughter in a position to know about cleaning wounds or hearing the sounds a man makes when his skin is cauterized."

Ainslee's mouth moved a few times without sound. She managed to say, "'Twas research. My father never knew. You figured it out from salt?"

"The way you talk helped some, too. Finn Pickett talks the same way."

"I never realized." She sought out Colton's eyes, held them, and looked deep. "It does not bother you." It was not said as a question.

"Why should it?"

Because it bothered her father and mother, as much as they loved her. It would have bothered the likes of Drosten Campbell. Her publisher still thought it odd that a woman was capable of writing such stories.

"I have a question for you."

"Anything."

"Who is Finn Pickett to you?"

Ainslee realized he genuinely wanted to know. "He is a part of me I cannot explain. I have tried to think of how to define him—the part of me that is him—but all I ever have figured out was how I feel." She fisted her hand and held it against her chest. "I have existed through him for so long, I cannot separate us. When I first wanted to publish my stories, the publisher did not believe a woman's name on an adventure novel would ever work. Fionn mac Cumhaill or Finn McCool is a mythological hunter-warrior of great legend to the Irish and to my people. Finn means many things, among them fair, just, and true. If I was going to move forward with my work, writing what I wanted, I needed the strength of a warrior to give me courage."

"And Pickett?"

Ainslee smiled. "The surname of a friend

from university. It is not a Scottish name as might have made more sense, but my friend inspired me to reach for whatever dream might await."

"But she didn't know?"

"No, she did not. Margaret Pickett wanted to be like Florence Nightingale, a crusader, a pioneer of greatness. Had it not been for her influence, I might not have searched inside myself for the strength I needed to pursue my own dream. Writing is not noble work like healing the sick, but it is who I am."

A few tears breached the hold Ainslee had on them and fell down her cheeks. She wiped them away. "And he will remain a secret, except to family. I thought I wanted to reveal to the world who he really is—who I am—but I realize now how much I rely on Finn Pickett. To rid myself of him would be to tear away a piece of my soul."

"Finn Pickett." Colton said the name

softly on his lips. "A crusading warrior who stands for fairness and justice. He *is* you."

"I hoped you would understand."

"You will never have to wonder if I understand you, or worry that I won't accept some part of you." He rubbed one of her silky, red locks between his fingers. "And you'll never run out of material for your stories. There's more than enough adventure in Montana to fill a dozen books."

"In Montana." Ainslee mumbled the words. She needed to think and needed time. "I have discovered there is adventure everywhere. We should get back to the house. If I know my cousin, she will eventually look in on me, or send Ethan to do it."

They walked together, hands clasped, neither speaking. When they reached the house, Colton ran his hands up her arms and brought her close. He pressed his body and lips to hers, a branding seared into her memory for all time.

24

HAWK'S PEAK WAS home. Every rock, speck of dirt, and the blood, sweat, and tears soaked into the earth belonged a little to each of them. It never occurred to Colton to go anywhere else, until he gave his heart to a spirited, charming, beautiful, and independent woman from the Scottish Highlands.

He pounded another nail into the new addition on the stables. Two days had passed since his talk with Ainslee. She needed time. As much as she might have tried to mask it, pretend it wasn't there, he recognized panic in her voice. Why she felt the need to keep her writing a secret, he didn't know, but it was important to her.

Colton worked until his body ached. He worked to keep himself from thinking she would decide to leave. He worried about his own decision if she did leave. Would he go with her?

He found a home and planned to spend the rest of his life in Montana, at Hawk's Peak. Now he was uncertain. He wanted to die on this land one day, but to die here, he had to live here.

"You've made a lot of progress today." Ramsey approached from around the south side of the new addition.

"I had the time."

"Heard you haven't taken the noon meal at the house with the others the past two days. I can see now where you're putting your energy."

Colton pounded in one more nail, dropped the hammer on the makeshift bench, and drank deeply from his canteen.

"Good a place as any."

"Maybe. Ethan mentioned your idea to make Tom the new sheriff."

"Makes sense." Colton took another drink of water, savoring the cool liquid wetting his parched throat. "We don't need a sheriff all the time. He'd be someone everyone can trust when we do. Doc said Tom will mend, but never quite the way he used to be. Not enough to work cattle day in and day out in the saddle."

"That's not on you."

Colton disagreed. "Tom is smart. He'll learn what he needs to do right by the job."

"He will. I also heard last night that Fred Hudson will be going home soon. He still has some recovery ahead of him, but Doc Brody expects he'll be back working the fields and cattle soon enough."

Colton glanced at Ramsey. "Fred has what it takes to survive here. Not everyone does."

"Is that why you're sawing wood and hammering nails?"

"You're not here to talk about the stables, Ramsey."

"No, I'm not." All pretense gone, Ramsey got to the point of his visit. "Normally I would let a man work through his own issues, but since your problems have everything to do with my cousin, here I am." Ramsey's brow arched when he smiled. "Well, it was me or Brenna, and my sister does think there is reason for concern."

"Brenna is eternally optimistic where I'm concerned. I cannot tell you why." Colton wiped his forearm across his face. "I won't put Ainslee in a position to choose me over anything else she might want. Her choices, her decision."

"She said as much."

"You talked with her?"

Ramsey nodded. "Let me offer you some

advice, from a man who has already been through what you're suffering now."

"Suffering?"

"Women have that effect on us. Eliza and I put ourselves through hell before we accepted that we were meant to be together and figured how to make it work."

Colton's lips twitched. "And you want to save me the suffering? Too late."

"Tell her how you feel."

Colton capped the canteen. "She already knows."

Ramsey whistled on an exhale. "That explains your condition. You do know she isn't keeping you at a distance to be cruel."

Colton nodded. "She needs time. I'm giving it to her."

"And if she decides to go back to Scotland?"

His chest tightened. "Then I'll be going with her, if she wants me."

"Is that what you want?"

Colton gazed over the land. He loved it here. "I want her to be happy. If Scotland makes her happy, so be it."

"You both deserve contentment, and that will mean a united decision to leave or stay. Making her happy isn't the same as you being happy."

"It can be. We can be."

"She's my family, Colton, and I love her."

Colton leaned against the bench, his eyes moving over the valley. "I love her, too."

Ramsey pushed away from the side of the stable. "That's all I needed to hear."

When Colton returned to the bunkhouse an hour later, he found a flat package, half an inch thick, sitting on his bed. No one else was around. He untied the twine holding the paper in place and smoothed the edges down. He recognized Ainslee's writing. In her neat lettering, across the center of the first page, she'd written: *The*

Mountain Man Takes a Bride by Finn Pickett.

AINSLEE PACED THE same five feet next to the shallow embankment. Three hours had passed since she handed the pages, wrapped tightly, to Pete outside of the bunkhouse, and asked him to leave it for Colton.

Three hours was surely enough time for a man to read a few pages.

"It's customary," Colton began, "to let the man ask the woman."

Ainslee stopped at the first sound of his voice. He wore a clean shirt and a smile.

"Unless the man hasn't asked."

Colton closed the distance between them one slow step at a time. "Maybe I didn't want to be the reason you made a choice you might regret. I've learned a lot since you showed up, mostly about myself, and if anything I ever did made you unhappy, I couldn't forgive myself."

"You read it all?"

He nodded and stepped closer. "That's what you've been doing for two days?" He had gone without a hat and rolled up the sleeves of his shirt. "I thought you were thinking."

"A good deal of thinking goes into writing."

"Your mountain man is a little rough on the edges, though. Might be he doesn't deserve the bride."

"Oh, he deserves her." Ainslee held up a hand when he inched forward. "Wait. There's something more I need to say."

"You said a lot in that story. Are you going to have it published?"

She smiled, thinking of what her publishers would say. "Perhaps. It is not a tale Finn Pickett would normally write, but it is appropriate. What I did not put in that story is this: I have learned a lot about myself as well. Brenna told me I did not understand this land or the people. When I asked her the reasons why she stayed here instead of returning home, her explanation eluded me. It was not the words I did not grasp but their deeper meaning.

"My family owns vast lands and grand houses. When we speak of legacy, it is in terms of what holds monetary value. It is different here. While I wrote that story—*our* story—the truth finally penetrated. The legacy of Hawk's Peak is not land. It is not the impressive house, cattle, or horses. It is not even the people—at least not on their own. The legacy Brenna wanted me to see was inside of me all along."

Ainslee ignored the tears welling at the edges of her eyes. "It is love and family. It is hope for a future and promises kept. I love my family dearly." Ainslee fisted her hand against her heart. "And yet before now, I had never truly allowed anyone to be *a part of me.* It has always been me and Finn Pickett, but I know now there is room in my heart for more." When he reached for her hands, she welcomed his strength. "The legacy we leave behind is love. It is honor, tradition, and family."

Colton's thumb brushed away the first fallen tears and kissed away the rest. "You stole my lines."

Ainslee choked on what she was going to say next. She leaned back and saw his wide grin. Loud and giddy laughter escaped her mouth. It came from a place so far deep inside, she wondered where it had been all along. "Your lines? There is only room for one writer in this relationship."

"There isn't a relationship yet."

Ainslee sobered. "You said you read the story. All of it. I am not leaving, Colton. This is where I want to be. I want to go home again, to visit, and I want to show you Scotland, and someday I may convince you to see more of the world, but this is where—"

He silenced her with a quick kiss. "Being a writer, you're not so good with reading between the lines."

"Excuse me."

"You got one thing wrong in that story." Colton lowered himself to one knee. The tall grass swayed and the sun shined high above them. "I told you. It's customary for the man to ask the woman."

She smiled. "And if he hasn't asked?"

"Maybe he just needed a little more time to do it right."

"It only takes a few pages for people to find love, even the stubborn ones."

"We're more stubborn than most."

"Have you had enough time, then?"

Colton growled low in his throat, stood, and lifted her into his arms. "Proper hasn't worked for us yet." He carried her to his horse a short distance away. She had not noticed the animal before now. He lifted her into the saddle and found a place behind her.

"Where are we going?"

"You'll see."

They rode away from the ranch and into the forest. They emerged on the other side at the base of a mountain, and up they went. Ainslee gripped his legs, and his arm around her middle secured her in place. The land flattened slightly after a steep ridge. The horse knew where it was going for it continued with little direction from Colton.

"Close your eyes."

She shook her head.

He chuckled near her ear. "You forgot to make the bride a headstrong and independent woman who throws knives. You need a rewrite."

"'Twas a dirk."

He whispered, "Close your eyes."

Ainslee sighed and leaned back against his chest. "They are closed."

The horse stopped and Colton dismounted first. Ainslee kept her eyes shut to please him, even when he lifted her down. She slid against his body. Instead of moving away from her, he turned her so her back was pressed against his front. He said, "Trust me." He guided her forward a few yards and wrapped both arms around her so his hands overlapped. "Open your eyes."

Mountains rose high, so tall and close Ainslee wanted to reach out and touch them. Forests blanketed the land and opened to valleys so boundless she marveled how she ever crossed them. The splendor of what she beheld overwhelmed her senses. She thought before he had showed her the most beautiful place, her valley of wild horses, yet here was a scene more glorious than the first.

They stood above the world. She closed her eyes once more and breathed deeply.

Colton's lips brushed against her neck. He pulled aside the thick curls that fell during their ride and kissed her ear before he asked, "Will you?"

She opened her eyes to the landscape once more, and turned in his arms. "Aye, but ye must give me something in return."

His lips curled into a smile against hers. "Anything."

"I would like tae sleep under the stars again."

Colton lifted her and carried her to a grassy area not far from where his horse decided to graze and lowered her. The bed he laid her on was not as soft as the cot they had shared in the cabin, but the outcome would be as infinitely pleasurable for them both.

She looked above. "There are no stars in the sky yet."

"Just because you can't see them, doesn't mean they aren't there. Besides, we can wait. We have time." He lay down beside her. "Tell me a story."

Ainslee found a comfortable space tucked under his arm, her face resting against his chest. "'Tis a known fact that warriors of old roam the Highlands. Their spirits fade into the mists. Their cries are carried in the winds. No one escapes their wrath, should someone be unfortunate enough to wrong a great warrior spirit. One warrior—"

"What story is this?"

"*The Ghost of Ben Nevis* by Finn Pickett. Now, where was I? Yes. One warrior . . ."

Colton listened to the lulling sound of her words, her accent a hot caress to every sense in his body, and he planned for their tomorrows. They would go to Scotland

and walk the land of her heart and ancestors. They would walk the trails of her Highland ghosts and find adventure in life's everyday moments. Both stubborn and flawed, no doubt they would argue. Laughter and love would be there to get them through challenges. Below in the valley, Hawk's Peak stood against time and elements, housed within it the truest of legacies. He wanted to build her a house on the ranch, close to her family. A place to raise children and create a future built on hope, for together any dream of their choosing was possible.

Colton once thought a life of hard work was enough. She showed him that mere contentment had no place in a full life worth living.

He planted his roots in Hawk's Peak soil, but it was Ainslee who gave him a home in her heart. Colton lay beside Ainslee in his mountains, the place where he'd once been lost and was now reborn. For with her, he had found the promise of a future more rewarding than he ever could have imagined.

As her lilting words filled his mind, he pictured her in front of him, her hair unbound and her arms wide open, as they rode with abandon behind the untamed herd, deep in the mountain valley. He looked forward to whatever adventures awaited them on the wild Montana winds and wherever those winds might take them.

Thank you for reading
Wild Montana Winds

Don't miss *The Healer of Briarwood*, the next book in the Montana Gallagher series.

Visit mkmcclintock.com/extras for more on the Gallagher family, Hawk's Peak, and Briarwood.

If you enjoyed this story, please consider sharing your thoughts with fellow readers by leaving an online review.

Never miss a new book!
www.mkmcclintock.com/subscribe

THE MONTANA GALLAGHERS

*Three siblings. One legacy.
An unforgettable western romantic
adventure series.*

Set in 1880s Briarwood, Montana Territory, The Montana Gallagher series is about a frontier family's legacy, healing old wounds, and fighting for the land they love. Joined by spouses, extended family, friends, and townspeople, the Gallaghers strive to fulfill the legacy their parents began and protect the next generation's birthright.

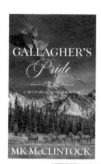

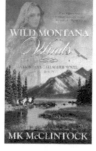

THE WOMEN OF CROOKED CREEK

Four courageous women, an untamed land, and the daring to embark on an unforgettable adventure.

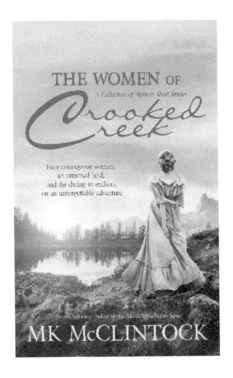

If you love stories of bravery and courage with unforgettable women and the men they love, you'll enjoy the *Women of Crooked Creek*.

Available in e-book, paperback, and large print.

Whitcomb Springs Series

Meet a delightful group of settlers whose stories and adventures celebrate the rich life of the American West.

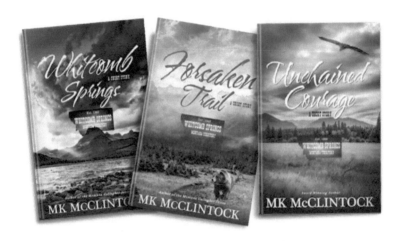

Set in post-Civil War Montana Territory, in the mountain valley town of Whitcomb Springs, is a community of strong men and women who have worked to overcome individual struggles faced during and after the war. Escape to Whitcomb Springs with tales of adventure, danger, romance, and hope in this special collection of short stories and novelettes. Each story is written to stand alone.

Available in e-book and paperback.

McKenzie Sisters Series

*Historical Western Mysteries with a
Touch of Romance*

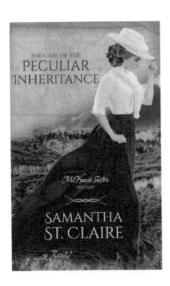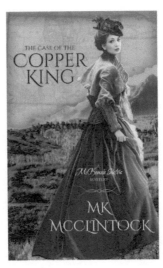

Cassandra and Rose McKenzie are no ordinary sisters. One is scientifically inclined, lives in Denver, and rides a bicycle like her life—or a case—depends on it. The other rides trains, wields a blade, and keeps her identity as a Pinkerton "under wraps."

Immerse yourself in the delightfully entertaining McKenzie Sisters Mystery series set in Colorado at the turn of the twentieth-century.

Available in e-book, paperback, and large print.

MEET THE AUTHOR

Award-winning author MK McClintock writes historical romantic fiction about chivalrous men and strong women who appreciate chivalry. Her stories of adventure, romance, and mystery sweep across the American West to the Victorian British Isles, with places and times between and beyond. With her heart deeply rooted in the past, she enjoys a quiet life in the northern Rocky Mountains.

MK invites you to join her on her writing journey at **www.mkmcclintock.com**, where you can read the blog, explore reader extras, and sign up to receive new release updates.

Made in United States
Troutdale, OR
08/17/2023

12144487R00311